One Boy Missing

Stephen Orr is the author of several published works of fiction and non-fiction. His novel *Time's Long Ruin* was shortlisted for the Commonwealth Writers' Prize and longlisted for the Miles Franklin Award in 2011. He lives in Adelaide.

One Boy Missing

STEPHEN ORR

WITHDRAWN

TEXT PUBLISHING MELBOURNE AUSTRALIA

textpublishing.com.au

The Text Publishing Company
Swann House
22 William Street
Melbourne Victoria 3000
Australia

First published in 2014 by The Text Publishing Company

A different form of the *memento mori* story was published as 'The Photographer's Son' in *Quadrant*, November 2013.

Cover design by WH Chong
Page design by Text
Typeset in Adobe Garamond Pro 12/16.5 by J & M Typesetting

Printed and bound in Australia by Griffin Press, an Accredited ISO AS/NZS 14001:2004 Environmental Management System printer

National Library of Australia Cataloguing-in-Publication entry
Author: Orr, Stephen, 1967- author.
Title: One boy missing / by Stephen Orr.
ISBN: 9781922147271 (paperback)
            9781921961663 (ebook)
Subjects: Detective and mystery stories.
            Kidnapping—Fiction.
Dewey Number: A823.4

This book is printed on paper certified against the Forest Stewardship Council® Standards. Griffin Press holds FSC chain-of-custody certification SGS-COC-005088. FSC promotes environmentally responsible, socially beneficial and economically viable management of the world's forests.

Prologue

THE BOY WAS nine or ten years old. He was still in his pyjamas, baggy track pants full of holes with a frayed cuff where he let them drag. Now he pulled them up, but they slipped; he only bothered when they were down past his hips. He wore a plain white T-shirt, covered with food, and an adult's pyjama top—buttons missing, sleeves down past his fingertips.

Stopping, he closed his eyes. His lips moved. He might have been saying, '...where?' He clenched his hands and started to cry, briefly. Punched himself on the thigh, then turned and ran down a laneway that provided rear access to most of the shops on Ayr Street, the main drag through the centre of town. There were bins, piles of flattened cardboard boxes and empty milk crates. On the other side, a fence, and hard up against this, a pair of industrial waste bins branded with hippo heads.

The boy ducked into the gap between the bins. There was a strong smell of Chinese food. He felt something soft between his toes and looked down at a pile of rotten fruit that had turned black. He was out of the wind but it was still cold and he started shivering.

There was the screech and grind of a rubbish truck. Sounds

from the main street: bags of grain being dragged out of the fodder store; wind-chimes being hung out in front of Elder's Hardware.

Random voices called out across Ayr Street, Guilderton.

Minutes passed before a tall man opened the back door to his shop, jumped down the few steps to the laneway, took out a cigarette and lit it. The boy could see he was wearing a vest with the words 'Mango Meats' above a pocket full of pens. The man inhaled a quarter of the cigarette in one go, held the smoke and blew it out.

The boy moved a little towards him, tempted. Then sank back.

A voice called from inside the shop. 'Where are yer?'

The man shook his head. 'What?'

'Larry's here.'

He flicked the cigarette to the ground, stepped it out and went inside.

Silence.

A crow landed near the boy's feet and started working on the remains of a ham roll. A cyclist turned into the laneway, sped up and was gone. The boy leaned on the fence and allowed his body to slide down. Then he heard the car. He breathed sharply and squeezed himself deeper into a corner wet with black syrup. The car moved slowly, and stopped. There was a heavy chug from the motor and the smell of poorly burnt petrol; the handbrake; a door opening; the click as the boot released.

He took the boy quickly. His big hands wrapped around the child's arms and he yanked him out of the gap then grabbed him around the chest so he was pinned.

'*Don't move.*'

The boy struggled, but could only move his legs. The man's hand was across his mouth and he bit down into a ring, and bone, and the taste of salt. The man released his hand and jagged him to the side to shut him up.

The boy started screaming. In a single movement the man threw him into the boot. The boy's ribs landed against a spare tyre and jack. He screamed again. The man reached for the boot lid and as he did a small, bony fist struck him in the ribs. He grabbed the boy's hair and forced him down. 'Y'little cunt.' He spat and slammed the boot.

The boy started kicking at the boot lid.

'Stop it,' the man said, close to the metal. 'Or else.' He opened the door of his car and in one movement, slipped into the driver's seat, released the handbrake and planted his foot as he closed the door. He wrestled the wheel; collected the side of the hippo bin anyway as he tore off.

The butcher stepped out of the back door of his shop and saw a man in a car turn and shout. Then he saw the boot fly open, the car stop and the man get out and shout at a figure in the boot, a small boy, perhaps. The man shut the boot, glanced up at the butcher and slammed his hand against the rear window. He got back in the car and took off.

The butcher went back inside. The laneway was still, the cold metal of the bins and fence warming in the early morning light. The crow returned to the ham roll. Seconds passed. The butcher emerged from the back door with another man. '...not sure, maybe someone in the back,' he was saying. 'Anyway, not too many dads put their kids in the boot.'

Both men stood in the middle of the laneway. 'What was he doing?' the second man asked. 'The kid?'

'Mate.' The butcher shook his head. 'Scared fuckin' shitless.'

They looked up and down the laneway, as if this might help them decide what to do.

'Well, I reckon we call the cops,' the second man said.

The butcher stared at him. 'Y'reckon?'

'We don't know who he was, eh?'

'Yeah.'

The butcher went in and a moment later the other man followed. Minutes passed. The butcher emerged with a woman, pointed to where the car had been, and they both went back inside.

A delivery van pulled up in front of the hippo bins. A man got out, pulled back a tarp and produced a pile of newspapers. He threw them up against the back door of the newsagent. Then he returned to his truck and drove off down the laneway.

1

BART MOY'S HEADACHE extended from his temple to his shoulder. He'd tried a warm shower, a series of stretches and a few tablets he'd found in the pocket of his jeans. He knew it was all a waste of time—what he needed was sleep.

He waited at Guilderton's only set of traffic lights. They always seemed to be red, no matter what direction you were going. He noticed the screwed-up piece of paper on the seat beside him. Picked it up, flattened it on his knee. 'Application for Professional Development'. He hadn't filled it in. What could you do in Guilderton? DNA sequencing? Still, he wondered if it was symptomatic of something greater. Why apply if you didn't want to be developed? *Why can't I just do my job? Or is that the problem? Just a shithouse copper, going through the motions?* Like the old man who walked past his house every day. Socks and sandals. Returning with a litre of milk.

He stopped and got out of his unmarked Commodore. Straightening his back, he remembered he hadn't brushed his teeth. He ducked back in to search for mints. Nothing. Then he stood looking down the laneway behind Ayr Street.

Moy glimpsed his face in the wing mirror. He was getting fat, he knew; he'd lost his chin, gained a blush on his cheeks. He didn't care anymore. He'd passed into his forties with little or no fuss: the stomach had arrived, the trainer-bra boobs along with a sort of giblet effect under his arms, but his legs were still strong, his buttocks tight, his mind sharp. Growing old didn't bother him; the glib childhood promises of career and wealth had long since given way to gas bills and self-pollution. Now life was just movement—a slow progress through the world in the dawning realisation that you were stuck with your own company for the rest of eternity.

A tall figure appeared behind him and asked, 'Detective Sergeant?'

Moy turned. 'Bryce.'

'Down the laneway,' the younger man said, indicating with a nod.

Moy looked at him. There were still traces of enthusiasm in his eyes, in the way he kept his shirt ironed and his shoes polished. Since arriving in Guilderton, Constable Bryce King had done all the right things: joined the Guilderton Maulers, Mallee League '91 Premiers, where every Friday night pig farmers and diesel mechanics got to tell him to fuck off; continued a tradition of Stranger Danger talks at Guilderton Primary; helped replace a urinal at a Civic Park working bee and, to the delight of most, started dating the girl from the forestry office who walked with an audible limp.

'You meant to have knocked off?' Moy asked.

'I can wait,' King replied, and Moy remembered what pissed him off most about the young and ambitious.

'Where's this butcher?'

The constable took a moment, wondering. Moy studied his eyes and guessed what he was thinking. His lips almost formed words, but he stopped short: *It's because I haven't shaved for three days, isn't it? Give it twenty years and see if anyone thanks you for your sixty-hour week.*

'There he is,' King said, pointing to the butcher, emerging from the back door of his shop.

Moy locked the car and walked down the laneway, under tape that had been stretched between fence posts, past the hippo bins and broken crates left, he guessed, by the old wog baker he'd arrested for laying into his wife.

He attempted to tuck his shirt into his pants where it kept coming loose around his hips. Walking around a mud-splattered patrol car, he shook hands with the butcher. 'Detective Sergeant…' he began, but stopped short.

The butcher smiled. 'Moysie,' he said.

'Justin Davids, isn't it?'

'Yeah, good to see you. Where you been all these years?'

Moy shrugged. 'Working in town.'

'What brings you back?'

'You know…Dad's ill.'

The butcher studied his old friend's face and made up his mind about this new, middle-aged Moy. 'Well, welcome home.'

Moy could guess what he was thinking: Wife shot through? Couldn't get ahead, couldn't get a promotion, couldn't afford the nice house, the car, the trips? Had to come home and slum it with all the farm boys and bush pigs?

Moy had one strong memory of Justin Davids. It was primary school—grade six or seven. There was a little Lebo and Justin and his tribe of followers had given him hell. They'd called him Castro which, Moy realised at the time, just proved how completely stupid they were. They'd spoken to him like they were clearing phlegm from their throats: 'Hey…*cchk*…Mohammed.' Justin had inspected Castro's sandwiches and confiscated the mettwurst to flick at his mates.

Standing at the back door to Mango Meats he found himself wanting to mention Castro but stopping himself.

Moy could remember the day Justin and his mates chased

Castro into a cubicle in the boys' toilets and proceeded to throw fruit, missiles of wet paper and a floater from an adjacent toilet over the concrete wall at him. He could remember laughing as the olive-skinned boy with the black curls flung open the door, threw a punch at Davids, ran out and wasn't seen at school for another two weeks.

He could remember the talk about the evils of bullying, and he could still see Davids looking at the ground and smirking.

He took out a notepad and a pencil that was mostly blunt. 'So, what did you see?'

'Dark colour, blue I think,' the butcher began. 'Falcon. Early eighties...you know, the boxy ones.'

'We've got a book. Can you come and look?'

'When I knock off.' He closed his eyes, took a moment. 'Sticker on the back window. Red and black, mighta been a car-yard sticker. And the back mud flap was loose, dragging.'

Moy wrote it down. 'And what about this kid?'

Davids described a boy, maybe ten, in a pyjama top and baggy track pants. Middling hair: between long and short, blonde and dark. The man throwing him in the boot, kicking and screaming. 'Didn't want to go with him, that's for sure.'

'See the boy's face?'

'Just quickly...we were in the shop getting the meat out and I heard screaming. I thought it was kids playing, so I ignored it. By the time I realised and went out...'

Then he described the man. Thirty, a few years older; dark hair; tight T-shirt; goatee. 'Big bastard, you know, muscly. No taller than you or me, shorter perhaps.' He told Moy about the slammed boot, the wheels skidding on small rocks.

'This kid, he was still in his pyjamas?'

'It looked like it.'

'In the boot? Strange, eh?'

Davids paused, maybe wondering if there was some suspicion attached to the comment. 'Why?'

'Outside, playing, in pyjamas?'

'He wasn't playing.'

'And you've never seen this kid?'

'Never.'

'Or the fella?'

'No. I would've recognised him. He looked up.'

Moy was struggling with his pencil, and the picture of the boy. 'So, was this fella an Aussie?'

Davids shrugged. 'Yeah.'

'Nothing distinctive? Big nose, scars?'

'I can see him but…'

'Okay. We got someone can help you with that too.'

Then they looked at the hippo bin, the scar of paint left by the car. 'Looks like he got spooked,' Moy said.

'He gave it a fair whack.'

Finally, Moy looked at him and said, 'You remember Karim?'

Davids remembered, and smiled. 'Yeah.'

'He still around?'

The butcher wiped his cold hands on his apron and laughed. 'He's running Cummins these days.'

'Cummins?'

'The concrete people.'

And Moy smiled. 'Castro…concrete?'

'Yeah. He coaches my son's footy team.'

2

THE MORNINGS WERE best. Wheatbelt mornings, enough damp in the air for the smell of wet grass. Moy would often go for a walk in his thongs and shorts and singlet—no one saw him, stranded on the edge of town—running his hand through waist-high barley in one of Paschke's paddocks that ran along Wauchope Road.

Bart Moy loved piggeries. Rex Paschke had one of these too, packed with three hundred sows, emptying their bowels into concrete gutters that drained into tanks the size of swimming pools, filling the early morning with a smell the locals on the west of town had been going on about for decades.

Moy guessed the boy was somewhere close. He might have been kidnapped or taken by a dirty. Then again, crime in Guilderton was usually about stolen timber, some horny kid who couldn't wait for his girlfriend's fifteenth birthday, graffiti on a new Toyota in Olsen's car yard. Not enough to justify a full-time detective. But there were other issues that had brought him home.

Later, he drove down the same streets he walked, aware of the morning, damp clothes on heavy lines, bikes left on frosty lawns, tractors and grain trucks starting and revving in farm sheds on the edge of town. He moved slowly, his window down, his hand drumming on the car roof. Occasionally he'd stop and ask some old fella, 'You seen a kid…a boy? In pyjamas?'

'How old?'

Thinking, *what the fuck's it matter if you haven't seen him?*

'You see him, you call the police, okay?'

'What's yer number?'

'It's in the book.'

He arrived at a big bike park where town met paddock. It was full of pine trees that kept the few hectares dark all day. Usually it was crowded with kids building jumps with their dads' spades, flattening the mounds with their little feet in farm boots, spending Saturdays jumping into a sky that promised twisted ankles, and fun. Other times, especially early on a Sunday morning, it was the place to bring your girlfriend.

He parked, got out and walked along the bike track, dragging his feet, thinking he should call out and having no name to call.

'Who you looking for?' A kid's voice.

He turned to the nine- or ten-year-old standing with his hands in his pockets. Not a missing child, this one. 'Kid your age.'

'You his dad?'

'I'm a policeman. He's lost.'

The boy didn't seem concerned. 'No one here,' he said, almost defiantly, and Moy could smell the cigarette smoke on his clothes.

'You gettin' ready for school?' he asked, but the boy almost laughed.

'Dad got me harvest leave. No one goes to school this time of year.'

He turned and ran off and Moy took a few moments to survey the rest of the park. He could remember coming here himself, in the days before the track. Back then it was all about climbing the pine trees.

He looked up, as if the boy might be hiding in the limbs. He saw himself with a slingshot, waiting for an old woman to go past with her shopping. Remembered just sitting there, unable to do it, the rock heavy in his hand.

He cruised the length of Gawler Street, a succession of cream-brick government houses full of teachers, nurses and coppers who'd come from other places, marooned in the wheatbelt, biding their time, planting vegetable gardens to soak up weekends with absolutely nothing to do. The smart ones loaded their cars on Friday night and drove to town, returning in a semi-depressed state every Sunday night, deadening the rest of the week with overwork and alcohol. But mostly it was just the hum of harvesters, conversations about reflux and milk teeth, the taste of microwave meals and snowdrift *CSI*, no matter how big your antenna.

Most people with a guvvie house had given up on caring for it. For one, they were inspected annually and if the agent decided the place was in good condition they'd put the rent up. Secondly, the government didn't do routine maintenance. Paintwork, cracked windows, nothing. The message was clear: just do your time. Survive, marry a local girl and buy something decent, or piss off.

Moy passed his own house, slightly shabbier than the rest, the broken blinds drawn, the window shades blowing in the breeze. He could see down the drive, into the backyard, where his undies and T-shirts hung on the line.

There had been problems with truants—harvest kids, or other ferals—bored shitless during the holidays, stealing washing from clothes lines. Making their way to Civic Park and dressing the busts of old mayors in bras and singlets. Mayor Humphris (1878–1883) in a summer frock with a lace collar.

Moy pulled out just as a grain truck flew past raising a shower of dust and fine gravel. He listened to it pepper his car and noticed a chip appear in the middle of the windscreen. He reached for his lights and planted his foot; overtook the truck and slowed it to a stop in front of the Guilderton Rotary. He got out, fuming, and the driver climbed down to meet him.

'Well?' Moy said.

'I got me tarp on.'

It was one of Paschke's sons, a farm boy who spent his days driving between his father's place and the silos. 'How fast were you going?'

'Wasn't much over fifty.'

'How much?'

'Fifty then,' the driver changed tack.

Moy took a deep breath and wondered whether it was the chip, his headache or other things. 'You chipped my windscreen,' he said.

'Council needs to sweep these roads. Dad's been on at them.'

'If you go slow enough it's not a problem.'

The Paschke boy shrugged. 'I stick to the limit but there's two headers, full up, waiting in the paddock. Twenty minutes each way and a line at the silo. Maybe you should tell 'em to build some new receiving bays.'

'What's that got to do with speeding?'

Here, Moy guessed, was why he was becoming a second-rate copper; one of the reasons. If he were any good he'd find his infringement book and start writing, but he just didn't care enough anymore. Paschke's boy would be back along this road in his truck, ten times a day, raising a cloud of dust and gravel that no one gave a shit about. A few neighbours, perhaps, but they never complained. It was just the way it was if you lived on the western edge of Guilderton. Gawler Street was the only road the trucks could take to get to the silos.

He looked at the boy. 'Slow down,' he said, and walked back to his car. The truck pulled out around him, raising another shower of dust and double-tooting its horn: See you later, *mate*.

Moy switched off his lights and let his head drop onto his steering wheel. He noticed a sticky mess where he'd spilled something on the console and thought, *things could be a lot worse.*

Which reminded him of the boy.

He drove along Murchland Drive, over a railway line that was only ever used by a tourist train, and along Creek Street, the waterway dry two months early. He slowed to look in the crevices along the creek, the roots of ghost gums covered in leaf trash where the soil had been washed away. He pictured a small, pyjama-clad body trapped in dead branches. A grazed shin, a lick of wet hair across the mouth and a twisted limb. For a moment he wasn't sure if he actually hoped to see it.

There was nothing in the creek. He stopped his car and went into a toilet block. Nothing. Except paper shoved down the head and a cracked sink. Cracked, as it had been when he was a boy, and probably always would be.

He walked another thirty or so metres into Civic Park. There was an old steam train that kids still climbed over, pretending to be drivers and firemen, burning their legs on iron plates in summer. In the cab all the knobs had been removed and the firebox welded shut. Even as a kid he'd known there wasn't enough train left for a decent imagining. Surely it was just an easy way to get rid of industrial junk? Shit. Give it to the kids, they won't know.

Nothing under the train.

Then he searched a set of concrete pipes laid out for the kids to crawl through. He found a used franger and a dead bird but no boy in pyjamas. Started to wonder if there really was any boy. A kidnap? In Guilderton? Who was this butcher, this turd-thrower turned meat-trimmer, and why had no one else seen anything?

He checked the rose garden, the wisteria arbour and even the little bit of space under the electric barbecues.

Nothing.

He gazed up and, across the road, noticed the Wesfarmers man dragging rolls of wire out in front of his shop. Then there were packs of droppers on a wheelbarrow, bags of starter rations on a trolley

14

and a few water pumps. He returned to his car and drove down Ayr Street, the shops open now, or opening. The word had got around and a few shopkeepers stood about chatting. They looked at him and he raised a finger from the steering wheel. A pair of mechanics stood at the gate to Boston's Motor Repairs, looking at something in a newspaper and laughing.

Moy turned the corner and stopped in front of the butcher's laneway. Bryce King was still standing with his hands behind his back, scanning the road and laneway as if something might happen.

'Bryce, let me know when Crime Scene arrives,' Moy called from his car.

'When are they due?' King asked, approaching.

'It'll be mid-morning. Everyone in Ayr Street—' He wound up the window. He hoped King hadn't noticed the rubbish in his foot wells. 'Don't care when they arrived. Ask 'em if they've seen a lost kid hanging around.'

Moy started to drive off. 'Oh, by the way,' he called back, 'remind that butcher to get down to the station.'

He followed a tractor with a raised plough. Each of the tines was tangled with roots, weeds, pieces of paper, and one with what looked like a flannelette shirt. He studied it, but wasn't sure. Then, it fell to the ground, and the tractor turned the corner. He stopped, got out, examined it, even smelled it. But it was too big for a boy.

And how would it have got there?

3

IT WAS MID-MORNING before Moy arrived at the station. Up the
road a small group had gathered outside the courthouse. He recognised a man with a goatee done up in a white shirt and loud tie.
It'd been three weeks since he'd arrested him. Stealing from his
employer, a shed company. Coming in on the weekend to help
himself to sheets of stainless steel and aluminium that he sold to a
cousin who made kitchens. Simple case, no one believed he intended
to replace the stuff. And here he was, looking up at Moy, mumbling
something to his wife and parents. They turned and glared at him.

He passed through the glass doors, already trapping heat,
announcing: *Guilderton Police Station: If Unmanned Seek Assistance
at 13 Gawler Road.*

He greeted the desk sergeant, a forty-something Gary with
sideburns and a strange semi-afro, and said, 'Tell me they've found
him.'

'Not a word.'

An old man sitting in the waiting area said, 'You'd think
someone would've missed him by now.'

Moy turned and noticed the handcuffs on his wrists. 'What do you know?'

The old man replied through a beard full of crumbs. 'Maybe Mum mighta slept in. But it's a school day, eh?'

'You keep quiet,' the sergeant said.

'You wanna find him quick. It's the first few hours that matter.'

'You wanna stop your mouth flappin'.'

The old man shrugged, leaned forward on his knees and snorted back into his adenoids. 'That's what happens, eh? *CS* fuckin' *I*.'

Moy stopped himself from smiling. 'What you been up to?'

Sergeant Gary Wright tasted and spat back the dregs of a cold coffee. 'Our Mr Venables was seen emptying his bladder on the front window of Norrie Carmichael's shop.'

Moy shook his head, and the old man looked up at him. 'I'd say you got bigger problems, Detective.'

'I dunno. You gotta take care of the little things first.'

'Whoever's got 'im, he could be halfway to Melbourne by now…or have 'im tied up in a room somewhere. Like I said, Detective. First few hours.'

Moy turned and took a few steps towards him. 'And you don't know anything?'

'They brought him in at five,' Gary said.

'What were you doin' out at that time?' Moy asked, but the old man just looked at him.

Moy pulled off his tie, worked it into a ball, put it in his pocket and stepped towards the desk. 'Axford's out?' he asked.

'And Jason Laing.' Gary Wright moved a map of the town centre between them and used a nicotine-yellow finger to point out streets. 'Ayr Street,' he said, 'between Dunlop and Irvine. Side streets—Clyde, Bute, all the way along. Bryce and Ossie agreed to stay on, so I've got them searching the showgrounds.'

Moy looked at the old man. 'So, what more do you think we could be doing to find this kid?' he asked.

The old man smiled. 'What kid? You can't have no kidnapping if no one's missed him.'

'Maybe they haven't noticed yet.'

'Would you notice if yer kid wasn't in his bed?'

Moy turned to the sergeant. 'Why's he in cuffs?'

'Took a swing at Constable King.'

Moy looked back at him. 'Well, that changes everything doesn't it?'

He approached a door, tapped his code into the pad and passed through into a haze of disinfectant. Benches lined the hallway; he could see where the Filipino lady had wiped between the files that littered them. He walked down the hallway into an office which, surprisingly, was also clean. The black and gold letters on the door said *Detectives*, although he was the only one they'd had in thirteen years. The cleaner had organised his desk, leaving papers in piles held down by parts from an old copying machine. She'd dusted a vase that hadn't held flowers for years and cleaned the fried chicken smears off his keyboard. The window was open. Moy could hear the distant voices of children playing in the yard of the primary school.

He leaned out of the window, into the car park of Ritchie's Bakery, closed his eyes and thought. Then he sat down and flicked through his phone book.

After a brief tussle to explain himself to a receptionist, he was speaking to the principal. 'A boy, nine or ten. Mousy hair, medium length.'

'That narrows it down to forty, forty-five kids,' the principal said.

He waited, listening to the children's voices. 'Could you check today's absentees?'

'I could, if you think it would help. There are always plenty away—especially this time of year. But if you want me to.'

'Yes, I think that would be best,' he said. 'Brown hair, medium height...wearing some sort of pyjamas. What grade do you think?'

'Four or five,' she suggested.

'That must narrow it down.'

She didn't sound happy; couldn't, perhaps, see the point of all this mucking around. Didn't like to be told what to do.

'Give me ten minutes,' she said.

4

MOY RECLINED, STARING out of his window, listening to the blinds rattling in the wind. He tried to imagine the boy but could only see his own son, Charlie. The small boy with his few freckles, lip indented where he always bit into it, was playing on the floor of his old office in the city. He could remember Charlie handcuffing himself to the desk and recalled cursing, having to get up to unlock him. Charlie was singing a Wiggles song—no lyrics, just bum notes and nonsense words—occasionally getting a line right.

Moy opened a folder on his desk. Photos of a body: the stretched neck and the rope mark, the tongue still jammed between the teeth and the cheek. Upper torso hairless, covered in freckles and a scar where subject B73/2013 had been sliced by fencing wire. He was a forty-seven-year-old farmer, and he'd tied a decent knot first. He'd allowed seven or eight inches for the rope to stretch and he'd written a letter which he pinned to the front door: *Carol, firstly, don't let the kids in the tractor shed…*

Moy looked down and his son was still there, staring up at him. He closed his eyes and he was walking out of the hospital, into the night. There was a bench, and he sat down beside a woman sucking the last gasp out of a cigarette.

'Good news?' the woman asked.

Moy looked at her. 'What?'

'Good news…you just had one?'

'Had what?'

'A kid. You look like you've been in there for days.'

He stood up and walked down the ramp where the ambulances arrived. The smell of paint from a handrail made him feel sick. Sicker. He stopped, turned and looked over the ramp, down three levels to the asphalt below. There was another ambulance unloading. Parents, and relatives, trying to console each other.

Before he reached the street he saw Megan coming up the ramp. She was shouting at him, standing screaming a few inches from his face. He stepped back and lifted a hand but she just kept going.

'Where is he?' she was saying, and he pointed.

He remembered footsteps and watching his wife storm off. He remembered her stilettos, the sound they made on the concrete.

And then the phone rang, and the principal was back in his ear. 'We've got a couple missing, but we've rung home and they're accounted for,' she said.

'No one that age?'

'No.'

He took a moment to think. 'A kid doesn't just appear from nowhere. Not in Guilderton anyway.'

'Maybe he's not local.'

'Yeah.' He waited, annoyed that she didn't want to be more helpful. 'Well, if you hear anything, my name's Bart Moy.'

'Moy? Didn't they farm out near Cambrai?'

'Many years ago,' he said, looking at a photo he kept propped up on his desk.

It was old. 1915. Black-and-white, blistered. It showed a man in his late forties or early fifties with a bushy moustache extending from his nostrils to his ears, a flat forehead, and wisps of fine brown hair. Daniel Moy, Bart's great-grandfather, was dressed in a suit, and he'd forgotten to do up a button on his vest. He stared at the camera with a sort of quick, get-it-right expression. His wife was looking down into the mid-distance, her face devoid of any emotion. Helen was wearing her best dress, finished with a brooch and a lace collar, her hair tied back (clumsily, as though done in a rush).

Between Daniel and Helen lay their twenty-three-year-old daughter, Elizabeth, in a black velvet dress and pearls. She, or her mother, had taken time with her hair—braided into a long ponytail that had been posed over Helen's arm. Elizabeth's head was tilted, supported on her father's chest. Her fingers were interlocked, resting in her lap, which was covered with an old rug.

The room was plain: a raw, board wall; a mirror covered with a sheet and what looked like a harmonium framing their heads. Moy could almost smell the grease, the wood, the fire.

It was a standard Edwardian portrait, normal in every respect except that Elizabeth was dead. Her eyes were open; she seemed to be looking up at the ceiling. But she was four days dead. Daniel and Helen had posed her, as though they might be trying to fool future generations, but they weren't. It was a *memento mori*, a photo taken to remember a loved one lost early. Moy knew it was a way for parents, twenty or thirty years later, to remember what their child had actually looked like. When the body was gone, this would be all that remained.

According to family history, Daniel had walked two days to find a photographer. Sore with grief, he'd trudged wheatbelt roads, ignoring the blisters on his feet and the dust in his mouth. Meanwhile, Helen, exhausted by tears, had tried to keep her daughter's body cool, at one point, in the heat of the afternoon, placing her in a bath full of cold water. At night, while Daniel was still walking, she lay next to her daughter in bed, stroking her hair and talking to her.

All that was a long time ago, Moy thought. All of them gone and nearly forgotten.

He walked from his office down the hallway and arrived behind Gary. 'No one missing from the school,' he said.

The desk sergeant shrugged. 'I think your butcher might be full of shit.'

'Why's that?'

'Kidnapped?' Gary looked at him. 'In Guilderton? That'd be the first time in…ever.'

'Y'reckon?' Moy hoped he was right.

'Guilderton, seriously? Most parents would've lost count of the kids they've got. Why would they want to kidnap another one?'

'Gary, how long have you lived here?'

'Long enough to know. Tell you what it was, some dad about to give his kid a whack and he does a runner. Wife says, let him go, but do you think he's gonna let him? Right now there is a little kid with a very sore arse.'

'No kidnap?'

Gary just shook his head.

Moy noticed the empty seat where the old man had been sitting. 'You lock him up?' he asked.

'No, he's gone to buy us some lunch.'

5

AFTER LUNCH MOY took his clipboard and set off to get to the bottom of this non-case. He went into the deli and stood waiting, mesmerised by a pair of flies fucking on a finger bun. The assistant, a *yeah-but* child-woman in leggings, was talking to an older friend who kept checking to see that her baby hadn't escaped from its pram.

'It's so predictable, every morning, right at the start of the twenty-five zone,' the shop girl said. 'Standing there with his little zap gun. As soon as he's got one, there's another.' She stopped for breath. 'I mean it's not like anyone's actually speeding, is it? A few k's, so what?'

Moy looked at the burnt pies in the warmer and wondered exactly what it took to become a local. The Moys had farmed Cambrai for years before the soil had given up on wheat. But they'd never really become townies. Locals. Although his dad, George, had become a Guilderton fixture, a bolt rusting in place on the fringes of what passed as wheatbelt civilisation, he himself no longer had any claim to citizen status. He'd forfeited that years before when he'd left for the police academy. You never got it back.

Now he was a curiosity, a 'boomerang', although they'd never say that to his face. An in-between person who'd severed his roots, who had no chance of returning to the soil from which the Moys, and Guilderton itself, had sprung.

He looked at the assistant, trying to catch her eye.

'Well,' she said, 'he only ever makes it home two or three times a week.' She turned to Moy. 'Can I help?'

'A plain pie with sauce.'

She smiled at her friend and asked, 'What time's netball tomorrow?'

'Five forty-five.'

'Who we playing?'

'Fortescue. The inbreds.' The friend laughed then studied Moy as if to say, *you don't come from Fortescue, do you?* Or more likely, *I couldn't give a fuck if you do come from Fortescue.*

The girl looked at her baby again, darted a final stare at Moy and left the deli. The shop girl was stabbing his pie with the sauce bottle, apparently injecting it with litres of White Crow as she wiped sweat from her cheeks with her forearm.

Moy knew exactly who they'd been talking about. Jason Laing with his little zap gun, getting his leg over as Guilderton watched, gossiped and passed judgment on a man who should have known better. A not-so-young constable who had a wife, a kid and one on the way; straying towards the backblocks of Guilderton East, shamelessly parking his patrol car outside a government semi-detached rented by the new kindy teacher six months out of uni.

The girl handed him his pie. 'That all?'

'Thanks.' He could feel the sauce pooling in the bottom of the bag. It was only a matter of time before it split open. Still, she hadn't done it on purpose…couldn't have, surely? There was the rattle of the till, and sweaty change thrown across the counter.

'You didn't see a kid on his own, early this morning?' he asked.

She looked at him as if he was stupid. 'Pardon?'

'A kid was abducted from the back lane, four shops down—behind Mango Meats.'

'You're the police?'

'Detective Sergeant Bart Moy.' He waved the pie that prevented him getting to his ID.

'I got in around seven.' She shrugged. 'No one in the back lane when I opened.'

'No car?'

'No.'

'Didn't hear any noises? Screaming, arguing?'

'No.'

Moy hoisted the pie. 'Could I have a new bag?'

She sighed, and her lips came together. As she transferred the pie to another bag she asked, 'What, he was actually kidnapped?'

But he didn't see the point of telling her. 'Perhaps.'

As he ate his pie in front of Turner's Shop he watched the mums with their well-worn prams, strolling in T-shirts and tight pants. He studied every roll of cellulite, every bulge, and thought, fuck. He remembered a local telling him you only became 'one of us' when you died in Guilderton, or at least an adjacent paddock. And he wondered what that meant—about going, or staying?

Christ, what have I done? he thought. Watching some old fella with one foot in a thong, one in a slipper.

He lifted the pie to his mouth but it was so bloated it split open, lukewarm meat and cold sauce running over his hands and wrist. He dropped the carcass into a bin, found a tap and rinsed the offal from his hands.

The whole staff of Walker and Sons was standing in a line in front of their shop. Fire drill? Maybe they were posed for some sort of promotional photograph. Heads followed him like a row of side-show clowns.

He could remember his first summer back, nine months ago. He'd talked over the back fence with a neighbour, a fourth generation local by the name of Stuart who claimed his great-grandfather had built some sheds for a Moy, but didn't think it was out as far as Cambrai. They'd talked two or three times and during their most recent conversation Moy had invited him over for a beer, but he'd never come.

Weeks later there was a heatwave. Moy had sat inside, huddled in front of his one horsepower air-conditioner, listening to Mr Stuart entertaining his friends in his swimming pool. Every day he'd go to work, to keep Guilderton safe, and come home to listen to the perpetual pool party. Couple of dozen children, he guessed, and fat old bastards dive-bombing their way through an endless Guilderton summer, as he sat and sweated. Thinking, *why don't you scrape your own fucking relatives off the road?*

He went into the newsagent. The owner, a fat, stubble-headed man with a decent paunch and man-tits like Moy's, stood behind the counter on a raised platform and asked, 'What'll it be, darls?'

Moy was still taken aback. He'd come across him before, parading around his shop in track pants that outlined a package the size of a Christmas pudding. A Scottish crypto-queen restocking his shelves with the *Legume Journal* as he stopped to chat with retired farmers in search of stud almanacs and soft porn. 'What can I do for you, darls?' Or *love*, like he was trapped in some sort of fly-blown *Coronation Street*. He was a local, apparently, but mainly just a curiosity. A sort of Ayr Street freak-show in pink shirts, even though everyone knew he wasn't a poof. There was a wife, Betty, inscrutably manning the till, dispensing rolls of Lotto tickets like fencing wire from a cradle.

'You don't know anything about a young boy picked up in the back lane?' Moy asked.

The newsagent leaned forward. 'I heard,' he said, lifting his eyebrows. 'You're a policeman?'

Moy said his piece, and showed him his card.

'Listen, darls, I've already spoken to one of your little friends, and I told him I don't get here until after eight. So that's no good, is it?'

'You've never seen a kid hanging around?' Moy asked. 'Nine, ten...brown hair?'

The newsagent shrugged. 'They come in lookin' for a few titties, but when they realise they're all covered...'

'That young?'

'What else is there to do in this god-forsaken dump?'

And then Betty appeared. 'Gentleman here's looking for *Scientific American*,' she said.

The newsagent looked over at the customer and said, 'Oh, no, we don't stock that one. We've never stocked that one.'

Moy continued along Ayr Street, past Goldsworthy's Homemaker store, rifles and shotguns on display behind mesh in the window. The guns still had Christmas tinsel draped across their stocks. At *Mango Meats: Country Killed Daily* there was a trickle of blue water running down the inside of the front window. It gathered in a little trough surrounding a patch of synthetic grass. On the grass were melamine trays, and on the trays were miniature acres of red meat: rib-eye and loin, corned, porterhouse and rump.

He stepped inside, fronting up to a counter of chipped veneer. 'Justin?'

The butcher shrugged, lifting his hands in mock surprise. 'Hadn't forgotten you, Detective...Bart. I was gonna pop over after it got quiet.'

'I just wanted a quick word.'

Justin Davids turned to the sink and started washing his hands. 'No luck?' he asked.

'No, nothing...which sorta makes you wonder.'

Davids dried his hands and forearms with an almost surgical concern. 'Wonder?'

'What's actually going on?'

There was a long pause.

'No one's reported anyone missing. All of the kids are accounted for at school.'

Davids looked up at him. 'So?'

'It's hard to say it's a crime if you don't know who's done what to who. Whom.'

The butcher leaned forward, his head over a chopping board. 'I know what I saw.'

'No one's doubting that,' Moy replied.

'I mean, the way you say it.' He lowered his head, but looked up at Moy.

'Justin, I'm guessing you're a hundred percent correct. Something happened. But what?'

'Well, you're the copper.'

'Was there anything that suggested this fella knew the kid? Anything the kid called him?'

'No, just screaming and kicking.'

Moy paused, listening to the trickle of water. 'Nothing in the body language?'

'Like what?' But he didn't know himself. His phone rang; he answered it, lifting a finger and stepping outside.

'Yes, sir,' he muttered, to the distant officer.

Superintendent Graves was a spectre in his life. Moy had only met him a few times but he rang at all hours. Hassling him about reports, mainly. Avenues of investigations not followed, meetings not attended. Moy knew the type well: all procedure, no originality; strangled by a black-and-white view of the world that placed paedophiles a few rungs above Aborigines.

'There's no sign of him?' Graves asked, and Moy heard, almost as clearly: *Can't even find a lost fuckin' kiddy.*

'Not since this morning. He's not enrolled at the school, but he could've come in—'

'Just hurry up and find him. Can'ta gone far.'

Moy explained how busy he'd been that morning; how many places he'd visited; how many locals he'd talked to. 'I can't see it's anything sinister,' he said.

Graves wasn't convinced. 'So, you want me to send some fellas up to help you?'

'No, I don't think so. I mean, where are we going to look?'

Graves took a moment. 'Yes…just get the word out, okay?'

Moy felt the old man backing off. 'The consensus is some sort of domestic. If he was local he would've been missed…but we'll see, after school, if someone's kid doesn't come home.'

Moy could hear Graves working on a nostril.

'Funny one,' the superintendent concluded. 'Custody issue, I'd say. Still, write it up, let me know.'

'Yes, sir.'

And then he was gone, and Moy felt himself relaxing.

6

THAT EVENING MOY drove home with his head full of possibilities: some sort of goat-lady, refusing to send her boy to school; a family holiday, camped out somewhere, kid runs away from dad. Or perhaps something more sinister. He drove past a Mr Whippy van. Maybe he's in there, he thought. Classic way to catch kiddies. He looked at the young girl behind the wheel.

Not Mr Whippy, then.

He parked his car and made his way up the drive with his arms full of groceries. There was a flower garden, half-weeded where he'd tried to do the right thing but lost interest. Not that he'd planted anything. The stocks had just come up, fighting against wild oats, truck dust and a year-round lack of water.

He surveyed the casserole dish on his porch; knelt down and lifted the lid. The contents were brown, involving carrots, peas and maybe a pack of two-minute noodles. There was a holy card beside the dish: St Francis holding a staff, lifting two fingers: *Where there is hatred, let me sow love...*

Mrs Flamsteed again, her Catholic mission to his little house at the end of Gawler Street. Since she'd heard what had happened to Mr Moy, his wife, and his poor kiddy Mrs Flamsteed was a regular visitor. Coffee, her hand covering his as she asked about the little fella, the *tch* of her lips and the sorrowful tilt of her head. She was the wife of the deputy principal at the high school. Here for over twenty years but no more local than him. Mr Flamsteed had joined the bowls and his wife umpired netball but even they weren't accepted.

He dropped the dish and rolls on the kitchen bench. Emptied his pockets and slipped St Francis under a magnet on his fridge beside Saints Patrick and Anselm and the others who kept watch over his Kelvinator. He adjusted them, so they weren't covered by bills, just in case. And just in case Mrs F noticed.

…Where there is greed…

He surveyed the catalogue of his failings: impatience, intolerance, inability to forgive…Mind you, St Francis probably didn't know what sort of shit humans were made of. He hadn't attended a multiple fatality or seen what a drunken dad could do to a crying six-week-old.

There were dishes in the sink, floating in grey water. That's the way it was these days, the beginnings of something—a bed-sheet straightened, the vacuum taken out—but then a strange feeling of *why bother?* How will a made bed or clean carpet improve anything? Then he'd force himself to keep going for a few more minutes before ending up lying on the bed, staring at the ceiling.

He took one of the plates, dried it and covered it with Mrs Flamsteed's casserole. When the microwave pinged he poured himself a glass of milk and went into the lounge room to watch the regional news, read by a woman with bobbed hair framed by images of Ayr Street on an (almost) busy Thursday night. Impending Civic Park development, controversial council decision to limit parking on Dawes Road, three boys from the Harvest Christian School selected to play in the state under-sixteen hockey team.

Finally, the small, pale face concluded, there's been another death on our roads. Familiar footage of a crushed car and a mostly intact grain truck. A driver in a blue singlet weeping as an ambulance closed its doors.

Moy was lost, his eyes full of the red and blue light. He could feel the small body in his arms, could still sense its weight and see how his son, unconscious for ten or fifteen minutes now, had lost the flesh colour from his face. He could feel the looseness of his body and the way the boy's legs bounced as he ran towards the door of the emergency department.

Moy talking to him. 'Hold on, we're there now,' and he could feel his own heart racing, his arms sore but strong.

'Could someone help, please?' as a room full of faces turned towards him.

'This way.' A nurse's professional calm.

When she took him, Moy dropped his arms, shook them and turned to the sea of faces. He remembered stopping to look at a few of the children, and to see what was on the television. To this day he had no idea why he'd done this.

Moy was staring at the carpet on the lounge room floor of his government house. Outside the persistent *thwack* of a soccer ball against a brick wall. A voice saying, 'See, that was nine in a row.'

He looked up at the television and there was more about local sport: the Guilderton Thunder ladies' netball team into the district finals. He turned to his casserole, loading his fork.

Then he heard the ball again. He was standing at his front door, watching Charlie kick a ball against the wall, stop it with his foot and kick it again. 'One, two...' he was counting, as Moy forked noodles around his plate.

'...three, four, five, six...'

And then there was shitty home-made organ music and a chorus of locals singing, *wheatbelt quality home improvements*. A shot of ten or twelve men standing in front of a brand new pergola.

He felt sick.

33

'…seven, eight, nine…'

He could feel himself falling, again. There was no way to stop it. The ground opened, and he dissolved. Tears began, and he surrendered to them as he slipped from his seat. The casserole tumbled from his lap and spilled onto the carpet, then he was on his arse on the floor, his diaphragm squeezing and sucking air from his lungs as he wept. All he could think was *stop, stop*. He caught his breath and looked up, wiped the tears from his cheeks and took a deep breath; fumbled at the casserole on the carpet, depositing some of the mess back on his plate.

'…ten, eleven…'

As Charlie's face lit up.

He was off again, this time settling on his knees, burying his head in the dog-smelling cushion of his couch.

'The weather,' the newsreader continued, explaining how there was no rush to get the grain in this year, how there wasn't even a sniff of rain across the district.

A morse-like tap on the door. Moy knew it was Mrs Flamsteed, wanting but not wanting to disturb him; Mrs Flamsteed, in search of used casserole dishes. He could imagine how she was standing, arms crossed, leaning forward to peer through the bubble-glass.

She would've heard the television. He wiped his face and took another deep breath.

'Just getting changed,' he called, noticing the remains of the stew on the carpet.

Moments later he was in the bathroom washing his face and drying it with a stale towel. He checked his eyes and took another deep breath. 'Coming.'

When the door opened Mrs Flamsteed squinted to see him through the flyscreen. 'Hello, Bart. How are you, dear?'

'Fine, thanks, Lou.'

'You got my casserole?'

He remembered he couldn't let her in.

'Yes, looks lovely, ta. I might have a bit tonight.' He had no choice, he had to open the door. She looked at him, studying his eyes.

She knows, he thought.

'Everything okay?'

'Yes, fine.'

There was a pause—quiet, except for a distant tractor.

'Get my card?'

'Thanks. I've got them all on the fridge. It all helps.'

'Yes,' she said, slowly. 'Yes it does.' She lit up with a thought. 'I hear you're looking for a lost kiddy?'

And he explained, concluding, 'That might be the end of it, unless someone comes forward.'

'There was a story in the *Argus* last week. Seems the father kidnapped his own son, from the mother, cos he couldn't get custody. Couldn't even visit his boy, imagine that? Still, probably was more to it. Maybe he was a druggie.'

He wondered whether he should risk it, take her straight to the kitchen—but then she'd see he'd already warmed the casserole.

'From what I hear,' Louise Flamsteed continued, 'the courts favour the mother. Is that true?'

'Mostly.'

'So it's no wonder. The police talked to this fella, but he said he didn't know anything about it. Said he hadn't seen his son for weeks.'

'Maybe he hadn't.'

'Wife reckoned he took the kid interstate, to the rellies.'

Another long pause.

'Maybe that's what you got, Detective Moy,' she said. 'A custody battle gone bad?'

'Perhaps.'

'Well, if you could just leave the dish on my doorstep.'

'Of course. I do appreciate the food, you know.'

She squeezed the meaty bit of his hand.

7

THE FOLLOWING MORNING was cool, a slight breeze rustling the stubble. Moy pulled up in front of an old stone cottage on the south side of town, close to the city road. The original porch had gone, replaced by tube metal that supported a functional verandah. He got out of his car and approached a fence with a proud little wooden gate.

The path to the front door of his childhood home was littered with paper and envelopes. As he came into the yard he picked up a gas bill addressed to his father, George Moy. Then he cleared up the whole mess. There was a letter from Centrelink and brochures for some of the Ayr Street shops.

George and Bart had moved to this house in Clyde Street when Bart was twelve. His mother Anne dead already, claimed by breast cancer when he was nine. Their thirty thousand acres of low-yielding country at Cambrai sold three years later to a neighbour, their debts cleared with enough money left over to buy a place in town. Then came the moving truck, the furniture gone (from the very same room of Elizabeth's *memento mori*), their sheep trucked off to the abattoir and George left to cry, secretly, in the empty tractor shed.

'Dad,' Moy called out, mounting the front steps. He noticed three coffee mugs on a table on the front porch. Most of them were half full and there was a small swarm of flies gorging themselves on the separated milk. He put the letters and junk mail in his pocket, balanced Mrs Flamsteed's casserole in one hand, gathered the mugs by their handles and went inside. 'Dad?'

'Over here,' a voice replied.

'You dropped your mail,' Moy said, searching for his dad in the dark lounge room.

'Help us up will yer?'

George Moy was sitting on the floor, gazing into a television that glowed with a kids' animation about a happy rabbit.

'What are you doing down there?'

'Just help us up, will yer?'

Moy dropped the mugs in the kitchen sink, took his father under the arms and lifted him. 'Come and sit at the table.' He walked him to a small table where he ate his meals, picked his horses and worked on his crosswords.

After George was settled, Moy asked, 'You didn't have another fall, did you?'

'No.'

He sat opposite him. 'Why were you on the floor?'

George's face was set hard.

'Dad?'

'I don't have to answer to you.'.

'You couldn't even get up.'

'Yes, I could.' He glared at his son.

Moy looked around the combined lounge, dining and kitchen area. He could see what looked like dried tomato soup on the floor, and where his dad had walked through the mess and carried the stains onto the carpet. 'You been okay?' he asked.

'Fine.'

'They bring your lunch?'

George pointed to the empty Meals on Wheels plates.

'I've got your tea,' Moy said.

'Yeah?'

'It's a stew.'

'Mrs Flamsteed's?'

'That okay?'

His dad took a moment to think. 'Guess it'll have to be. Why's she always makin' you food?'

'Suppose she feels sorry for me.'

'She still prayin' for you?'

'Probably.' He stood up, approached the fridge, opened it and looked inside. The smell of mouldy cheese wafted out at him. 'Dad,' he said.

'I's getting to it.'

Moy smelled the milk. 'It's off.'

'I wasn't going all that way for a bit of milk.'

'You put this in your tea?'

'Boiling water will kill anything.'

Moy looked at the four casserole dishes lined up in the fridge. Each had its own square of masking tape with a date, name and contents carefully recorded. Butter chicken, lasagna, sweet and sour pork. A shepherd's pie with the mince scraped out and eaten leaving a collapsed crust of burnt potato.

'Have you finished with these?' he asked. 'I think she wants her dishes back.'

'Get rid of 'em,' George said, waving his hand.

Moy spent the next ten minutes cleaning out the fridge, scraping the casserole dishes and washing the cups and crockery. Most of the food was so old he had to fetch a paint scraper from the tool box to get it off.

George was a tall man and he'd grown lanky in his old age. He had freckled skin and sunken cheeks with high bones. There were a few wrinkles on his forehead, only noticeable when he frowned or lifted his eyes to let the Meals on Wheels lady know he wasn't happy with the menu. His arms were all bone, joint, long fingers and careful hands.

Moy sat down opposite his dad. He dried his hands on a tea-towel and looked at a pill box on the table, a plastic container with holes for each of George's pills: before and after breakfast, lunch and tea, Sunday to Saturday. He restocked it every Sunday morning when he visited; following his Saturday morning trip to the chemist with his father's scripts; following his semi-regular Friday afternoon visit to the doctor with George.

The pills for the previous evening were still in their little plastic slot. 'What's this?'

George looked at the pills. 'I thought I'd had 'em all.'

'Dad, you can't afford to miss any.'

'I didn't mean to.'

Moy knew it was time for his usual speech: how he had to be more careful about his pills; how it wouldn't be an issue if only he'd agree to move to a nursing home; how he, DS Moy, couldn't be here all the time (although George always countered with the fact that Bart had told him he'd only returned from town to help look after him); how the house was run down and needed tens of thousands of dollars spent on it; how George couldn't look after himself anymore; how he needed specialised help, especially considering what was just over the horizon.

'Should I take them now?' George asked.

Moy paused to think. 'No, I don't think you should.'

'Why not?'

'It'd be too much, I think. I should ask Dr Smith.'

George crossed his arms. 'What would he know?'

'He's a doctor.'

'Didn't stop me from getting sick.'

Moy raised his hands in desperation. 'So you *are* sick?'

'You tell me.'

'Dr Smith told you.'

'Doctor? Ha! He's been doin' it fifty years. Lot of things change in fifty years.'

'People still get sick…people die.'

George tried to change the subject. 'Haven't seen Megan for a while.'

Moy tried to work out what he meant. Eventually he said, 'Neither have I.'

George looked confused. 'Why's that, she busy?'

Moy stood up and went into the laundry. He filled a bucket with hot water and found the mop. 'Don't you remember?' he called to his dad.

'What?'

'We separated—eighteen months ago.'

George struggled to remember. 'Right…you were together… then you moved here. She didn't come, did she?'

'No.'

'Cos you separated?'

'Yes.' Moy returned to the kitchen and started mopping the floor. His father glanced down at his unfinished crossword. He picked up the newspaper and a pen and read the clue. 'Pulsing star? Seven letters, third letter u.'

8

THE PRINCIPAL'S NAME was Rebecca Downey and Moy thought she looked far too young to be in charge of three hundred little people. She'd gathered her hair in a bun, he thought, to counter that impression. 'Nice bunch of kids?' he asked as they walked down the hallway towards the assembly.

'Mostly,' she replied, fixing an earring. 'The farmers' kids are just…content.'

'Content?'

'You know, passing time until their legs are long enough to reach the brake on the header.'

They passed an older woman emerging from a room that smelled of fresh bread.

'This is Mrs Maxwell,' the principal said, stopping. 'Mrs Maxwell has been here for…how many years?'

'Thirty-four,' the older woman replied. Mrs Maxwell was wearing an apron. She took a tea-towel from a pocket and wiped her hands. 'I think I might have taught you.'

'Yes. 1981?'

'Very likely.'

'This is Detective Sergeant Bart Moy,' the principal explained.

'Very impressive,' the teacher said.

'Yes, I was the only boy in the class,' Moy recalled. 'All the boys chose plastics and metalwork, but I liked cooking. So, they all assumed I'd turn out gay.'

'And did you?' She laughed, squeezing his arm.

'I remember it came to sewing,' he said, 'and all the girls had some frock they were working on and you…I think perhaps it was you, or that other lady, the Chinese one, Mrs…?'

'Lee, she passed, four years ago.'

'Oh, sorry to hear…One of you said, so, Bart, what are you going to make? And I said, well, perhaps it's time to go back and make a spice rack.'

Mrs Maxwell smiled. 'You were quite a pioneer.'

Rebecca Downey was growing impatient. 'We must go, the assembly's started.'

'Nice to see you again,' Moy said, as Mrs Maxwell waddled along.

Moy said to the principal, 'Nothing much has changed.'

'Well, she's way past retirement, but it's hard to find a good home ec teacher…Any home ec teacher, really.'

'I mean, nothing much has changed physically. Same lockers, same chairs, same desks.'

She looked at him strangely. 'We have a master plan. Most of the rooms have been renovated and recarpeted.'

'Really? Well…' He looked in one of the grade five classrooms. 'Looks just the same.'

'Interactive whiteboard,' she pointed out. 'Data projector.'

'Yes, but look at those macaroni murals. What's that one?'

'I think it's meant to be a face.'

They arrived in the gym. All three hundred children were waiting for them, sitting on the ground in year level lines: the youngest, their hands in the little valley of flesh created by their legs; the grade ones and twos, more alert, staring at the strange man beside Miss Downey; the threes and fours, laughing and holding their nose because someone had farted; the older kids, their lines snaking across the floor at the back of the gym, their legs stretched out, whispered threats and promises passing up and down the line.

Principal Downey waited at the front of the hall with her arms crossed. Eventually, over a minute or so, the students fell quiet.

'Well, that was quite a wait,' she said. 'I don't understand why I should have to wait here for so long when it's obvious what I want you to do.'

Silence; as the teachers thought the same thing as the kids.

'I've explained,' she continued, 'how it should be so quiet that I can hear the air-conditioning.'

And they all listened, realising no one had turned it on.

There was a boy staring at Moy with a scowl on his face. Moy glared at him, opening his eyes wide and clenching his jaw. The boy mouthed a word. Moy couldn't make it out. Was it *please*? Was he pleading for something? Perhaps he was saying his name: Peter, Paul? Pavlich? He said it again.

Poof.

Jesus, nothing changes.

'Howard!' the principal growled, and the boy looked forward. 'The Student Council is meeting this Thursday. They'll be voting on four proposals put forward by you, the students.' And she indicated, in case they'd forgotten who they were. Then she read from a clipboard. 'One: soft drinks for the canteen.' She looked up. 'Well, I don't know how that one got through.' She smiled at an efficient-looking woman to her left. 'That wouldn't fit our healthy eating policy,' and Moy wondered, if that were the case, why there were so many fat kids.

He noticed a wall covered with sporting pennants dating back to the 1960s, boasting first, second and thirds for football, cricket, hockey and athletics. No pennants for netball. There were clubs for that.

On his first day at high school Rodney Elvis had given him the best advice of his life. 'In your first sport lesson,' the older boy had said, 'make sure you put in zero effort.'

'Why?'

'They're watching you. In your second lesson they'll put you into groups and they make the advanced group run, play footy, do weights.'

And so it came to pass that by March the advanced group was running circuits, jogging around the school and battling each other for the title of longest kick and quickest sprint. Meanwhile, the remedials were escorted to Judell's Pool Room for an hour of snooker.

'And now, Detective Sergeant Moy, from the Guilderton CIB—is that right?' the principal asked.

'We don't really have a CIB, as such.'

But she didn't care. 'Mr Moy wishes to speak to you. So, best manners, no talking or you might end up in handcuffs.'

He came forward. 'I would like to ask for your help,' he began, and there were murmurs at the back of the hall.

'Perhaps if you could speak up,' the principal said.

'Fine. Is that better? Can you hear me?' he asked, and one of the grade sevens said, 'Loud and clear, Detective.'

The whole group laughed. Downey stood glaring at them with her hands on her hips. A few of the other teachers stood up and started walking in the spaces between the rows.

'Yesterday we had a report of an abduction from a laneway behind the shops on Ayr Street.' And he explained. When he stopped he noticed the poofter boy mouthing something different: Gary, gate, get off…gay…Gay, yes it was gay. The boy repeated it.

'Sorry, what was that, son?' he asked, but the boy just looked down.

'We think, perhaps, this boy didn't come to this school,' Moy continued, 'but we're wondering if anyone knows of a new boy that's been in town?'

Silence.

'Someone new. Maybe someone's relative…a cousin?'

More silence; a distant truck.

'Maybe if you mention this to your parents. You don't have to say anything now, you probably don't want to, but if you stay behind…or speak to a teacher, or Miss Downey.'

He let his eyes settle on the group and felt in control.

'Alternatively,' he said, 'this boy may be sitting in front of me today. It may be that he was not taken but has things going on at home, with Dad, or another relative…something Mum doesn't know about.'

Why was it his job, he wondered, to say these things? There was no point saying any more; they either knew what he meant or they didn't.

'So, maybe it's not you…maybe it's a friend. And if you were a good mate…' He let it hang, then looked up. 'Miss Downey?'

'Thank you, Mr Moy.' She returned to the front and started telling the kids what an exciting life a detective leads.

9

IT WAS MID-MORNING, cloud threatening a blue sky, when Moy received a phone call from Justin Davids asking him to return to the laneway. He drove past a row of empty shops and slowed past the old cemetery. He'd sometimes spend an hour on a Sunday morning walking around the graves. The marble headstones, their names and dates and *Asleep with God* all faded.

He arrived in the laneway behind the Ayr Street shops and the butcher and two girls from the two-dollar shop were waiting for him. He got out of his car and shook hands. 'What's up?'

Davids indicated the tape that had been strung out around the crime scene. 'All my deliveries,' he said. 'The guy has to park on Boucaut Street and carry everything in.'

'We're trying to bring stuff in the front,' said one of the shop assistants, 'but it's in the way, and we've got people tripping over.'

Moy looked up and down the length of the laneway. 'Haven't seen that car again?'

'No, nothing. Is anyone official actually coming?'

Fuck it, Moy thought. He pulled the plastic tape from the wall and started gathering it in a ball. 'That's probably the end of it,' he said.

Davids started on the other end and soon the cordon was down, the tape dumped in the hippo bins.

Moy moved on, driving a few blocks, stopping beside Civic Park where three teenagers were sitting on the bottom rung of the monkey-bars, white school shirts hidden under windcheaters. A tall boy lit a cigarette, inhaled deeply and passed it to a girl. She took a quick puff and passed it to another girl who kept inhaling and refusing to hand it back to the boy.

Moy stared at the teenagers. Fuck it, he thought again. Who made me the truant officer? There'd just be excuses and arguments and then they'd walk off. What would I be taking them back to anyway? Surface area of a sphere? Quotes from *Macbeth*? Stuff that couldn't possibly mean anything to anyone in the wheatbelt.

His mobile phone rang and he checked the display.

'How are you, Gary?' he said, recognising the voice.

'You're never gonna believe this.'

'What?'

'A house fire.'

Moy watched the teenagers stand up and walk back towards the high school.

'I didn't hear any sirens,' he said.

'Fire's out…but they want you there.'

Cigarette in bed, Moy thought. Someone falling asleep in front of the telly. Faulty wiring. There were a few people in town who claimed to be electricians. Generally they were also builders, tilers, plumbers and carpet-layers.

'What is it?' he asked.

'A woman, what's left of her.'

Gary gave him directions and he scribbled down the address. He drove out of town in a north-east direction. A few minutes later he turned onto Creek Street, a faded stretch of bitumen with grass

47

eating away at its edges. The street followed what was left of Belalie Creek as it narrowed and became overgrown with weeds. A kilometre out of town there was still enough of it to warrant a small bridge but another hundred metres on it flattened out into a rocky patch of scrub.

As Moy left the town behind the road turned to gravel. The houses along Creek Street started spreading out. Dead orchards and wrecking yards; chooks, and a few sheep. These were the backblocks: fences overgrown with prickly pear, goats that hadn't been shorn in years, whole yards full of door-less fridges and lid-less washers, children that ran mostly naked through forests of salvaged fence posts.

Moy had visited a family on Creek Street a couple of months back. There was no father and the mother would tie a rope around the three-year-old boy's leg and tether him to the front porch when she went out. A neighbour, sick of the crying, had eventually called the police. Inside the house Moy had found an old box with a rug, a bottle for the boy to piss in and a scattering of shit left by the family of rodents that helped him eat the food left for him every second night.

Another two hundred metres along the houses stopped altogether. Then there was just scrub along the road that led to the one-pub town of Cambridge, another thirty minutes on.

There were farms behind the scrub: wheat and barley stretching back to the horizon. Distant homesteads with grain bins and tractor sheds. Every few hundred metres along Creek Street gates led to access roads that cut through the wheat.

In the middle of the scrub that lined Creek Street there was the smoking ruin of a house. Moy looked at what was left of the collapsed structure: the floorboards, mostly; two of the four outer walls, a few internal walls and the roof trusses. The roof iron had fallen into the rooms. In the lounge room, which was now completely open to the bush, there was a blackened couch and a charred table without legs.

Strange, he thought, looking at the bush around the house. How the fire hadn't ignited the scrub or nearby wheat crop; how the rising embers hadn't caught in the overhanging trees.

There were two CFS units. A few men in orange overalls were hosing down smoking walls and furniture as others lifted wet bedding and carpets. Other men, and a few women with smoke-black faces, stood about with their arms crossed.

Constable Jason Laing approached Moy. 'Busy couple of days, eh?'

'Too much drama for Guilderton,' he replied.

Laing led him towards the house. 'We don't know who she is,' he said. 'No purse, bag, nothing. No letters—unless they got burnt.'

They climbed three concrete steps. There was a stripped-down engine on the porch with a box full of parts beside it.

Moy stopped to look. He bit his bottom lip and felt the stubble that had grown since yesterday morning. 'Kids?'

'Just her,' Laing replied.

They went inside, following floorboards that were unburnt, protected by a runner that had been dragged out front. 'Have you rung the council?' Moy asked.

'My brother-in-law.'

'He still there?'

'All this verge is council land,' Laing said, 'but according to their records no one's lived in this house for forty years.'

'She was a squatter.' One of the CFS volunteers had overheard. 'Years ago they tried to get the council to demolish it but in the end they never bothered.' He wiped his nose with his sooty hand.

'Ever seen anyone around here?' Moy asked.

'No. I live on Doon Terrace. No one ever comes out here. Could be running a meth lab, no one'd ever know.'

The volunteer walked out of what was left of the house. Moy noticed a few pieces of Lego on the floor, bent down and picked them up. One piece had melted but he clicked the others together.

'There's nothing in the other rooms,' Laing said.

'No toys? Kids' clothes?'

Laing shook his head. 'There are two other beds in the front room. It looks like someone was sleeping in them.'

He led Moy to the bedroom at the front of the house. There was bedding smouldering on the floor. A wardrobe and chest of drawers were empty.

Moy sniffed the air. 'Petrol.'

'Diesel.'

'How do you know?'

'I've got a good nose. And I worked at a servo for four years.' Laing led him back to the lounge room and there, partly covered by roofing iron, was the woman's body, stretched out on a piece of singed carpet. Her legs were twisted together and her charred left arm was bent up under her body. Most of the corpse was burnt and swollen.

Despite his line of work, death wasn't something Moy had ever quite got his head around. There it was, this thing of flesh, blood and bone. Human as anyone, minus a heartbeat. Out of the game, and because of what? A poorly installed downlight; a kid trying to light a match. He always experienced a moment of black-and-white fascination—like watching news footage of twins joined at the head, or the *memento mori* on his desk—before the enforced separation. The distance, which came before the technical concerns.

Still, she was dead. He couldn't help but stare for a few seconds to try and comprehend how a living thing had stopped working.

'What do you reckon?' Laing was watching Moy study the body.

'It was a hot fire.' He knelt down. 'Funny, isn't it, the way she's fallen?'

'How's that?'

'You'd think she'd be near a window or door if she was trying to get out.'

50

'What, you reckon someone's walloped her?'

'Don't reckon anything. Not till someone's looked her over.' Moy stood up. 'Maybe this time they'll send someone.'

10

MOY LEFT LAING and King with the body and headed home, stopping at the Taj Masala to buy a chicken vindaloo. He opened his musty house and sat on the back verandah in shorts and thongs. Admiring the view of his dead lawn, contemplating his curry. There were big blocks of hard potato which he pushed aside. Then he tried the chicken, enormous lumps joined by skin and sinew, trailing watery sauce that had started life in a packet.

Undercooked.

Now, he supposed, he'd get sick.

Guilderton had nothing resembling a health inspector. Apparently teams were sent from town to spend their days trawling the pubs and takeaways. Ineffectually, since he always got sick.

He binned the debris, locked up and headed to the Guilderton public links. A ten-minute walk, passing front yards full of home-made Coke-can windmills and lacework outdoor settings. Murchland Drive was alive with galahs celebrating the last minutes of sun. He noticed one of the Paschkes out on a header, its lights cutting through the wheat dust and its giant wheels compacting the earth. He could feel the rumble through his feet.

Checking to make sure the club house was locked, he jumped a waist-high fence and took a plastic bag out of his pocket. Started walking through the bush and leaf litter beside the first three holes. Within five minutes he'd found half-a-dozen balls.

He checked the sand-trap on the fourth hole and moved on to the small lagoon beside the fifth green. It was getting dark so he produced a small torch from his pocket and searched the murky water: six, seven, maybe more. He took off his socks and sandals and waded in.

The lagoon was his best bet, always had been. After he and George moved to town he'd come here of a night with his mates and collect half a wheat bag full of balls. On Saturday they'd fill a big tub with water and bleach and wash them. Then they'd leave them out in the sun to dry, package them in bags of a dozen and sell them to the local sports store.

He crawled out of the water and wiped his feet clean on the grass. Dropped his socks and sandals in the bag with the two dozen balls and continued on.

The scrub beside the sixth and seventh holes ran beside Murchland Drive. There were homes on the other side of the road so he had to move quietly. Three, four months before, an old woman out working in her garden in the twilight had noticed him in the bushes. Minutes later there'd been a patrol car cruising down Murchland Drive, moving its spotlight in and out of the bushes and trees. He'd waited as the light got closer, wondering how it would look on the front page of the *Argus*: 'Rogue Cop Stalks Locals'. Just as he'd been about to step forward, the woman had flagged the car down and pointed in the opposite direction. Seeing his chance he'd walked out of the scrub, across the ninth, and sprinted over the fairways towards the back fence. When he was well clear he ran through the sprinklers like a ten-year-old, jumping in the air and calling out at the top of his voice, 'Who's been naughty tonight?'

There were no dusk gardeners or patrolling cars now, though. Moy climbed a hill towards a grove of pine trees that always hid balls in a bed of pine needles. He used a stick to search through the litter that sat on the edge of the grove and looked out across Guilderton, squatting grey and solid in the moonlight. Ayr Street was deserted and he could see lights flashing from the Commercial Hotel's bottle-o. Music was still thumping from the converted cellar that passed as their night club. The back door of the bakery was open and he could feel its lavender light and the heat from its ovens.

His phone rang. Gary. 'The fire investigator's arrived.'

'Already?'

'Ossie's taking him out there.'

Moy stopped to think. 'Okay, I'm on my way.'

He stood up, grabbed his bag of golf balls and looked regretfully at the pine-trash, wondering how many balls still lay hidden.

But then he jogged off down the hill, past a water pipe they'd been meaning to fix since he was thirteen.

11

AN HOUR LATER, Moy arrived at the house on the end of Creek Street. A freshly shaved Metropolitan Fire Service investigator greeted him on the front steps. 'Sid Lehmann,' he almost barked, and Moy introduced himself as the lone detective of the mid-north wheatbelt.

'Nice little town, Guilderton,' Lehmann said. 'I was here a couple of years back.'

'A holiday, in Guilderton?'

'No. This boy and his mum, dead at the front door. She was holding the keys, trying to undo the deadlock.'

Moy decided not to think about it. 'So, what's the verdict?'

'Diesel. Mainly in the two bedrooms and the lounge. And the woman.'

'The woman?'

'She'd been doused in it. *Whoosh*. Which makes you wonder.'

'Christ, was she dead?'

The fire investigator smoothed his stubby moustache. 'That's why we need a coroner. Dead, or unconscious. We hope.'

Lehmann showed him into the lounge room, to the body—grey and featureless in the moonlight.

'Where did it start?' Moy asked.

The investigator led him to the front door. He pointed to a partly burnt match on the floor. 'My guess is he's knocked her out, spread the diesel and worked his way back here. Then he's stood outside and flicked it in.'

Moy sighed. 'Now I've got a job on my hands.'

'You certainly have.'

'No other explanation?'

'Well, she could've done it all herself, if she had a great sense of drama. But it'd be the strangest suicide I've ever seen.'

Moy attempted a smile. 'Anything else?'

'Give us a chance, Detective Sergeant. You leave your man here tonight and we'll be back in the morning.' Then he fixed Moy's eyes. 'Please don't go traipsing around.'

'Obviously.'

'There's a lot of disturbance already. Perhaps that's your Country Fire people…'

'Perhaps.'

'They weren't expecting a body?' Lehmann suggested.

'No.'

As Moy headed home he took another call from Gary. Ossie had just visited an old widow called Dorothy Olding who'd reported an intruder. Someone in her kitchen, she said. She'd got out of bed and heard someone running out the back door. Looked down the street and seen a small figure heading back towards town.

'Said it looked like a kid,' Gary concluded.

'Right. That's all? A kid?'

'Going through her fridge.'

Stealing food, at this time of night? He thought of the boy in the alleyway. 'Anything taken?'

'She said whoever it was had a good go at her orange juice. She was very annoyed. Said she'd paid top dollar. And some mint slices.'

'How did she know? She counts them?'

'Apparently.'

He pulled over in front of the first house on the way back into town. Someone would have seen something. As he got out he noticed a blind opening and a pair of eyes peering out. He walked up the front path and knocked. A man his own age, wearing a black AC/DC T-shirt and footy shorts appeared with a beer in his hand. He used it to scratch the tip of his nose. 'I know you.'

Moy took a moment. 'Commercial Hotel?'

'Spot on.'

It was his first week in Guilderton. He'd stopped by the Commercial for a beer, get to know the locals, try a bit of preventative policing. In the almost-deserted front bar he'd heard loud voices and applause coming from out the back. He'd gone to see what was happening.

A small group of men had cleared the tables and used cutlery to make a miniature racetrack on the ground. There were four babies in nappies and jumpsuits at an improvised starting line. One man gave a signal and the babies were off, crawling and tumbling along the beer-wet carpet. If one of them strayed across the cutlery a hand or foot would guide him or her back. The babies approached a finish line of folded napkins where four dads waited, calling, pulling faces and singing snippets of Wiggles' songs.

Eventually a tubby-looking boy crossed the line and the crowd roared as Dad turned to shake hands with his mates. Then the room quietened. Babies crawled under tables, dads exchanged cash.

Moy approached one of the fathers and said, 'Looks like a lot of fun.'

'Ladies' night at the footy club.' The man nodded towards the abandoned track. 'This is the crèche.' He leaned over and picked up his baby; eyed Moy defensively. 'It's not for money.'

Moy was surprised he'd been recognised. 'Well, I've never

arrested anyone for baby racing.'

Now, standing in the doorway at the far end of Creek Street, he smiled. 'How's the racing?'

'Good.' The man was unsure. 'That what you come about?'

'No. I's just wondering if you knew anything about this fire at the end of the street?'

The man took a deep breath. 'Right…a fire?'

12

MOY TOOK THE usual four hours to get to sleep. He avoided the Stilnox on his bedside table; they left him more tired the next day, and not in a way that translated to better sleep the following night. Just more tossing and turning, cursing himself for not being able to get even this simple thing right. Sometimes he'd get up at two or three in the morning and switch on the television. Abflexer and *Hey, Dad* did nothing much for his insomnia but they passed the time. Sometimes he'd try a walk around the block. Stand at the end of the driveway staring out across the paddocks.

Think of Charlie.

Eventually he'd go back to bed for two or three uncomfortable hours, sweat soaking his pillow, sheets kicked onto the ground as dark dreams squeezed themselves into what was left of the night.

This morning he was out riding with a boy who seemed to have his son's face and wiry body. They were following a path that ran beside a dry creek. The path was littered with leaves and the boughs of big gum trees hung low and heavy, brushing and scratching their faces. The boy was twenty metres in front of him. Although Moy pedalled hard he couldn't catch up.

'Slow down, my legs have had it,' he called.

'Hurry up,' the voice replied, fading.

Despite his anxiety to get to the boy, there was a feeling of euphoria as the cool breeze passed over his face and through his hair. He hurtled down a hill, no brakes. It was everything good and bad all at once; the feeling of wanting, but not getting.

When he woke the window was light. He felt glad for the sleep; happy he'd done it without the aid of his usual half-tablet.

Then he was asleep again. This time he was pulling into the car park of a hospital. The boy, still five years old, was lying on the back seat of his car, secured around the chest and legs by a seatbelt.

'We're there,' he was saying, searching for a park but not finding one, wondering why he was bothering anyway. He stopped in the middle of the emergency department car park. A security guard came over and said, 'Not here, you'll block the ambulance.'

He just ignored him. He got out and tried to open the back door. It was locked. He tried the driver's door but that was locked too. Then he saw his keys in the ignition.

'Fuck.' He kicked the front tyre and looked at the guard. 'It's my son.'

The guard seemed confused. 'You'll have to move the car.'

'*Look*,' Moy screamed, indicating. 'I can't.'

'You'll have to. There's an ambulance coming, it won't be able to get through.'

'Fuck, are you stupid? I've locked the keys in.'

The guard's face hardened. He stood up, twisted Moy's arm behind his body and pushed him against his car. Reached for his radio and called for help.

Meanwhile, Moy was looking at Charlie through the back window of his car. 'It's my son,' he pleaded, but the guard was unmoved.

'Christ, he'll die,' Moy said.

He woke. Opened his eyes and realised it was still early morning. He could hear cars and a lawnmower and smell porridge. There'd been no security guard, of course, and he hadn't locked his keys in the car. He'd found a park straight away and never blocked the ambulance.

His phone rang and he reached for it, knocking over the remains of a glass of water.

'That you, son?' A tired-sounding voice.

'Dad.'

'Look, I've got a bit of a problem.'

And then he heard the phone drop, George curse the *goddamn-piece-of-shit*, attempt to pick it up off the floor and say, 'Everything's coming back up the toilet.'

Moy sat up, rubbed his eyes and asked, 'What's everything?'

'Everything. Whatever's gone down, it's coming back up. Weeks' worth of it, by the look of things.'

He stood up, opened his blind and looked out at a pair of red-headed sisters walking to school. One of them noticed him in his boxers. She giggled and told her sister. 'I'll be there in half an hour, Dad.'

'What should I do?' George asked.

'What can you do?'

AN HOUR LATER, Moy and George were standing in the doorway of the toilet in the family home. Moy dared not venture in. The floor was flooded and the overflow, a mixture of pulped paper, shitty lumps and cigarette butts, had reached and soaked the hallway carpet.

'What a stink,' Moy said.

'What did you expect?' his father replied.

'What have you been putting down there?'

'Same's been going down there for the last thirty years, with no problems.'

61

'Well, you got one now. How much paper do you use?'

George looked annoyed. 'What's it matter?'

'Well…' He tried to think of how to say it.

'I use what I need to use.'

'What about the cigarettes?'

'I've always flushed them down…never mattered.'

'So, we call a plumber?' Moy asked.

'My arse. I know what the problem is.'

George led him outside, halfway up the driveway and stopped to point out a willow that grew on the other side of the fence. He showed him the roots that came onto his side and lifted the pavers he'd used as garden edging. 'Look. Right across the drive,' he said. 'And here, this is where the sewer runs.'

'Y'reckon?'

'I know. I've been waiting for this to happen. Ever since she planted that bastard thirty years ago.' He raised his voice. 'I told her not to. Not there. I said, why don't you plant it in the middle? Wouldn't listen.'

'Dad, ssh.'

'Won't bloody ssh.' He called louder. 'Now who's gotta pay three hundred dollars for a plumber?' And he quietened. 'Old cow.'

They stood together in the warm morning sun, Moy noticing the iron pulling away from the rotten fence posts. 'That'll need doing soon,' he said, indicating.

George looked at it. 'That's your problem, when I'm gone. Good luck getting any money out of her.'

Moy knew who 'her' was: Thea Miller, ex-nurse, widow and treasurer of the Guilderton Country Women's. She kept to herself, had a man in to do her garden and lawns, double-pegged her tunics, raked the gravel around her succulents and twice monthly vacuumed the carpet in her 1978 Premier. She generally ignored anyone she hadn't met prior to her fortieth birthday.

George shook his head. 'Only one thing for it.'

Five minutes later Moy was in the shed, wiping away spider webs as he moved through a jumble of old furniture, boxes and half-made cabinets George had lost interest in. He found the corner where the paints and chemicals were stored, lifted each tin and blew the dust from it.

'Bingo.'

He made his way back to George who in the meantime had used a stick to take the lid off the sewer access.

'There you go,' said Moy. 'Caustic soda.'

'Bung it in.'

Moy pulled back the lid and looked at his father. 'You want me to do it?'

'That's what you come home for, wasn't it? To help your old man?'

'Yes, that was the idea.'

'Well, off you go. That stuff eats anything. You wanna murder someone, that's what you use to get rid of the evidence.'

'I know, Dad.' He started emptying the powder into the hole.

'Fella in East Hay did that.' George sat down on a planter, remembering. 'His wife…and I think there was a kiddy. He thought she'd been on with another fella. You heard of that one, son?'

'No, Dad.' He emptied the last of the powder and replaced the lid.

'This fella at the pub had been bragging to his mates—I've had so-and-so's wife. But he never had. He was just a big mouth. So one of these blokes at the pub tells the husband and the stupid bugger believes him.'

Moy sat beside his father. 'I don't think that's gonna solve the problem,' he said, indicating the empty container.

'He strangled them. East Hay, yes. 1949…then, they say'—and he turned to his son again, smiling, as if he'd reached the punch-line—'he sawed them into small pieces, so they'd dissolve quicker. You ever heard of anything like that, son?'

'Yes, there was a case—'

George wasn't interested. 'There was a bathtub in the back shed and when they found it, it was full of jelly.'

'What about the bones and hair?' Moy asked.

'Some things persist.' George closed his eyes and smiled.

'Should we call a plumber?' Moy said.

'Suppose so,' came the whispered reply.

13

MOY DROVE TO Dempsey's Takeaway and bought three dim sims, bleeding oil into a bag that boasted *Proud Sponsors of the Guilderton Maulers*. As he ate he cruised along Creek Street, holding one of the dim sims with his fingertips. Minced meat emerging from what looked like an old war wound.

The radio nagged in his ear—slide guitar, nasal drone—and then the news update. It was the same voice that reported the fodder store specials, the demise of the Methodist tennis team and a fire at the impregnation plant, as if all these things could go together. Service times—Uniting, Anglican and Catholic, and then: 'Police media have just released details of a body washed up at Mangrove Point, south of Port Louis.' Moy held the dim sim between his teeth as he turned up the volume. 'The body, a tall, solidly built fella in his thirties, hasn't been identified. But, I suppose he will be…when someone misses him.'

These words rang in Moy's ears. *When someone misses him.* As if ultimately, everyone belonged somewhere. When, he knew very well, some people were never missed at all.

The low voice moved on to the more important business of lost rams.

Moy wondered what a dead body was doing in a swamp at Port Louis. The town was twice the size of Guilderton but half as interesting. Neat streets, all finished with diosma, leading down to a kelpy beach that kept going out for two hundred metres. Everyone agreed: not worth the drive. A Catholic town with seven churches, three Freemason halls and a 1950s feel. It had a Community Prayer Week every year when the locals shut up shop early to pray for the welfare of the town and its people.

When Moy arrived at the burnt-out house he noticed a Major Crime Investigation four-wheel-drive parked on the side of the road. Its back door was open and someone had unloaded cameras, bags and tackle boxes. There was a card table loaded with evidence bags, each holding small black objects: a remote control, sunglasses, knives, forks and jewellery.

He got out of his car, did up his top button and tightened his tie. Then he turned and noticed a farmer, sitting on an idling tractor in an adjacent paddock, watching him through a shelter-belt of sheoak.

'Got a minute?' he called to him, walking over to the fence between the shelter belt and the paddock.

The farmer got down off his tractor. 'Jo Humphris,' he said, extending his hand.

'Detective Sergeant Bart Moy, Guilderton police.'

'What's going on?' Humphris looked over to what was left of the house.

'You didn't notice the fire?'

'No, my place is a couple of clicks down the track.' He gestured to a hill that rose and dropped towards the horizon.

'But this is your land?'

'Yes.'

The farmer wasn't tall, and it seemed to Moy that he might be

66

shrinking as he talked to him. His breasts had formed udders that rested on a stomach straining to escape his flannelette shirt. He wore jeans, bare and white down the front where he'd wipe diesel and molasses from his hands. His boots had calcified, the brown leather worn thin and split beneath a layer of cow shit.

'You didn't notice anything?' Moy said. 'Yesterday?'

'No. Why you fellas so interested?'

'There was a woman inside.'

'Shit.' He raised his eyebrows and the white of his eyes caught the afternoon light. 'Who was she?'

'That's what we're trying to find out. You ever seen anyone in there?'

'No. Christ, no one's lived there for years. It's just a big rat trap…a ruin. We, I mean me and some of the other farmers around here, we've been trying to get the council to knock it down for years.'

'Right…so you don't think someone lost patience?'

Humphris stared at him, taking a moment. 'Na…these are sensible fellas. They wouldn't do that.'

'And you think they'd know someone was squatting?'

'Squatting?'

'Looks like it.'

'No, that's a bit of a mystery, Detective…Moy, was it?'

'Bart.'

'Good-o.' He shook his head in disbelief. 'Just lucky it wasn't earlier, before we got the crop in.'

'How's that?'

'You ever seen twenty thousand acres burn?'

Moy didn't really know how big that was. To the fence line? The horizon, the next town? 'So whoever was harvesting didn't notice anyone?'

Humphris squinted to see the house hidden in the scrub. 'No, you wouldn't, would you?'

'I suppose not,' Moy agreed, looking. 'Thanks for your help.' He took out his notepad and a pen. 'Jo, was it?'

'Yes. Jo Humphris. This is my road here, and this is where it ends, on Creek Street.' He pointed. 'You got any problems you come see me. Galbally, that's my place. We've had it for a hundred and twenty years.'

'Really?' Moy said, as he scribbled. 'The Moys used to have land, out past Cambrai. You heard of the Moys?'

'No.'

Moy turned to go, but stopped. 'By the way, what sort of car have you got?'

'Eh?' Humphris looked at him strangely.

'We're just trying to rule people out.'

'White ute, Toyota.'

'Good, that takes care of you.'

He started back through the scrub, jumped an irrigation ditch and passed through the gate of an old fence that surrounded the burnt-out house.

'Moy,' he said, greeting a sergeant in blue overalls, unbuttoned down to his breastbone, revealing a rug of curly hair.

'Tim Monaghan,' the towering figure replied. 'I was expecting you earlier, Detective Moy.'

'Detective Sergeant.' He looked at the sergeant's carefully trimmed moustache. 'My father's ill, I had to stop by. I assumed the firies were still going.'

'Gone. They're gonna send you a report. They came for the body, too. She's on her way to town.'

'That was quick.' He made the mistake of smiling.

'You'll need these.' The sergeant handed him a pair of feet covers. 'Looks like no one much has bothered.'

'Perhaps it was the CFS,' Moy said, pulling on the covers. 'They had two units, and they were all over the place.'

'None of your fellas?'

'Well, I'd hope not.' He wondered whether Monaghan's lips ever moved from the horizontal.

'We've got stuff crushed up everywhere in here.' The sergeant led Moy back into the house. 'It's like the Keystone Cops.'

Another investigator was taking photos of the floor in the lounge room. He'd set up markers and Moy was surprised to see that there were at least thirty points of interest around the room. 'What have you found?' he asked Monaghan.

'A few footprints, but fuck knows who they belong to.'

'Right, but nothing that might tell us who she was?'

'No.' The sergeant glared at Moy. 'We're still interviewing the possums. What about you?'

You prick, he thought. 'The closest homes are down the end of Creek Street. Nothing of much help. The fella that called it in was driving past with his kids, going into town for some bread and milk.'

'You've done the door-knocks?'

'Yes. I had a couple of constables work their way right along.'

'Nothing?'

'No.'

'Doesn't leave you with much.' Monaghan knelt down where the body had been. 'The fire investigator reckons she was covered in diesel. Don't know much else until the coroner's done. No stab marks, no strangulation.' He looked up at Moy. 'You finished your initial report?'

'I'm working on it.'

'Yeah.' He stood up. 'This way.'

Monaghan led him into the kitchen. They walked on a raised aluminium walkway that had been laid throughout most of the house. 'More prints here,' Monaghan said, indicating unburnt boards. 'Then there's ash, and more prints.'

They arrived in the kitchen and Monaghan indicated the sink, full of broken dishes, and a chicken carcass on a burnt chopping board.

'I could be wrong, but that's a lot of dishes for one person,' the sergeant continued.

'Maybe she wasn't houseproud.'

'Maybe.' He walked over to the sink and ran his index finger across some of the plates. 'All greasy,' he said, looking at Moy.

Moy shrugged. 'So, perhaps, whoever did it had tea with her first?'

'Maybe. That's what *you* gotta find out, DS Moy.'

'Right.'

'That's what the statistics show, isn't it? People getting knocked off by someone they know? So, if these were squatters…itinerant, probably. Unlikely to be local. You work it out. You get paid more than me.'

'Eat the chook, then have an argument?' Moy said.

'What about the diesel?'

Moy stared at the broken plates. 'I suppose I could start with the chicken shop?'

'Don't bother.' The sergeant held up a plastic wrapper. 'They roasted their own.'

And so the tour continued, with more suggestions about what he might want to consider next time, how there was a manual about securing crime scenes, easily downloadable.

'I'll do my report,' Monaghan concluded, as they returned to the front porch. 'You may be the only detective on this, at least for a while. But that's good, eh? You know all the locals, that's how you're gonna solve it. People don't just appear from nowhere and then disappear into thin air.'

MOY HEADED BACK to town. Light rain had fallen and dried. As he slowed for the intersection of Creek Street and Peyser Avenue his car skidded on a slew of loose gravel and ended up stalled in the middle of the intersection. He sat looking both ways but there was nothing coming. His heart slowed and he took a deep breath, pressing his foot to the brake before realising it was too late.

Then he heard the shriek of tyres from further along Peyser Avenue. He started the car and headed towards the tennis club where, it turned out, a pair of cockies' sons in a hot ute were busy with circle work on the newly resurfaced courts.

The ute had fat tyres and big rims, metallic paint and a pair of spotlights welded to a roll-bar. The driver, a peach-fuzzed teenager in a black singlet, was laughing, leaning into an ever-tightening circle as he called to his mate. There were a dozen or so skid marks covering all four of the courts. Moy could smell the rubber.

He pulled up on the side of the road and punched the number on the clubhouse into his phone. The club secretary answered and Moy asked him to come straight away. Then he got out and sat on the bonnet of his car with his arms crossed. Eventually the driver noticed him. Stopped; said, 'Fuck it,' and went back to circling. Moy stood up, and held his warrant card against the fence.

The ute stopped.

Moy walked over to them. 'Morning, lads.'

The driver turned off his engine and got out. 'Just a bit of fun.'

'Assuming you had *some* sort of intelligence, wouldn't you do this at night?'

The driver shrugged; his mate was trying not to laugh.

Moy took the keys from the boy in the black singlet. 'It's a very nice ute,' he said.

'Y'reckon?'

'Of course, those tyres are illegal, and the rims.'

A few neighbours, from homes across the road, had gathered to watch.

'I just don't get it,' Moy said. 'If you robbed a bank, you'd wear a mask, wouldn't you?'

'I dunno.'

'You would. Got a licence?'

'Yeah.'

71

'P-plates?'

'Yeah…' He looked. 'Must've fallen off.'

Moy couldn't understand why each new generation of farmers' sons just kept getting dumber. Supposedly they were better educated. The water, the food, the air didn't change. The schools didn't change, the shops. Nothing…nothing ever changed. So why?

'Well, I'll leave you to it,' he said.

'What, that's it?'

'Yep.'

'You're not gonna do anything?'

'No.'

'Well…okay, thanks.' He held his hands out for the keys.

'No, I'll take these. Mr Allen, he runs this place, he'll be here in a minute. He said he's happy to sort it out. Okay?'

They looked stunned. The boy kicked the tyre.

'Mr Allen, he's not a happy man at the best of times.' He got in his car and started it. 'I'll hold on to these,' he said, as he drove across the gravel.

There was policing and there was policing; he'd learned that in the early days. Gary had told him stories—about when he was a boy, growing up the son of a country copper in Mount Wilson. How back then the government didn't supply police cars, and how he remembered holding onto his seat as his dad chased crooks through the backblocks in the family car, mum holding her hat, his sister and him, still in his Sunday suit after a morning in the Baptist church. How, when one fella ran his car off the road, his dad got out, took him by the collar and punched him in the face. Said, 'Maybe you'll think twice next time.' Before getting back in the family car, straightening his tie and heading home for the Sunday roast.

The sun came out as he headed back through town. He passed George's house and saw him out with the plumber, talking.

He stopped. 'You okay, Dad?'

George stared at him, squinting. 'Who's that?'

'It's me, your son.'

'Oh…yes, I think it's fixed.'

A few minutes later he was back in his office. He pulled a drawing out from under his blotter. A house with a smoking chimney and a boy, a circle with stick legs and arms; trees with orange trunks, and two brown suns. A sort of hybrid dragon-stegosaurus roaming the neighbourhood.

Moy was watching Charlie colour the beast with a glitter pen. 'Is it a good one or a bad one?' he asked.

Charlie looked at him and bit his lip. 'Good.'

'Has he got a name?'

Charlie nodded. 'George.'

'Grandpa? Is Grandpa the dragon?'

He felt himself descending, his head dropping, his shoulders sagging, the shudders rising, the tears. He pulled himself together in case someone came in. Took a deep breath, wiped his eyes and slipped the picture under his blotter.

But he still saw the small face, and the wiry legs. The frown of concentration.

Gary Wright appeared, framed in the doorway. 'Coupla visitors out front.'

Moy lifted his head. 'Is anyone dead, dying or lost?'

'It's the baker from the Hot Bread Café. He's caught some kid stealing.'

'Some kid?'

Moy returned with Gary to the foyer. He shook the baker's hand.

'Robert Wyeth,' the baker said. 'I got something for you, Detective.' He used his hand to present a boy of maybe ten years old as if he were a prize on a game show. 'I just about had a heart attack chasing him three blocks.' He looked at the boy. 'Well, what yer got to say for yerself?'

The boy kept a head of dusty hair resolutely lowered.

Moy took the baker's arm and led him across the foyer. 'How about I leave you here with Gary? I'll take him and have a word.'

Wyeth thought about this. 'Okay. You can have him. I just don't want to see him back shoplifting.'

'Right. I'll let you know what's happening. He wasn't with anyone?'

'Not that I noticed. What sort of parent would let their kid…I mean, let 'em out of school, let 'em run feral?'

'We'll talk to the parents.'

Wyeth wasn't sure. 'Watch him, he can run. He woulda got away, but he turned to look back, and then he ran into a bus stop.' He studied the boy. 'It's probably not his fault. Probably the parents.'

Moy thought he could hear the baker's voice softening.

'Well, if there's anything I can do to help.' Wyeth took a deep breath. 'You listen to the policemen,' he said to the boy. 'You'll be okay…'

The boy looked up at him, refusing to concede anything. There was dirt, bark perhaps, in his hair. His lips were dry, scaly, and he kept licking them. Blue eyes floating in an ivory ocean and a fluorescent glaze. Moy waited for him to explain. But he just flicked hair from his eyes. Wiped his nose with the back of his hand.

14

TWENTY MINUTES LATER the boy was sitting in Moy's office, busy with one of Mrs Flamsteed's stir-fries. Moy had had it in the station freezer for months, squeezed in between the pies and Chiko Rolls. The boy smelled of disinfectant from where Gary had cleaned the grazes on his arms and legs.

'Enjoying that?' Moy asked.

There was no reply; just two eyes meeting his, searching the room and returning to the stir-fry.

'My neighbour cooks for me,' he said. 'She knocks on the door and if I'm not home she leaves it on the porch with a picture of Jesus.'

The phone rang; he lifted the receiver and replaced it. The boy raised the plate to his mouth and scooped the food straight in.

'Her name's Mrs Flamsteed,' he said. 'If I don't answer the door she walks around the house looking in all the windows.' He demonstrated, peering through an imaginary window with a squashed nose and pouting lips. 'And there's me, hiding behind the bed, or in the bathroom. *Mr Moy*, she calls. *It's just me…wondering if everything's okay?*'

Moy studied the boy's face. Nothing. No words; no smile. 'She's a strange woman,' he explained, but the boy just looked at him, eventually placing the plate on the table, wiping his chin and sitting back.

'Basil,' Moy said.

Nothing.

Gary knocked on the door and asked Moy to step outside. He said Wyeth had made his statement and left. Then he outlined how Wyeth had stood inside his shop watching the boy; and after a few minutes the boy had grabbed an apple pie from the clearance table in front of the shop and sprinted down the street. How Wyeth had chased him the length of Ayr Street, the boy ducking and weaving around shoppers before slamming into one of Guilderton's six bus stops.

Back in his office, Moy examined the boy's hands: the long, dirty fingernails; the grazed knuckles. 'You like living in Guilderton?'

Their eyes met and at last Moy noticed some expression, a squint. 'It looks like you get out on your bike,' he said, indicating the grazes. 'Or is it footy…or soccer?'

Nothing.

'You can talk…I'm here to help. No one can get in here. No one can touch you. You're safe.'

Just the hum of his computer. As he thought, Christ, what am I going to do with this one?

'The thing is, I gotta find out what's happened. I need to know who you are. You won't tell me? So I can help?'

The boy's eyes continued moving around the room, studying every feature. Eventually they settled on the old photo on the desk. Moy noticed his fascination, his eyes searching for some under-standing. 'That's my great-grandfather, Daniel Moy,' he said. 'His wife, Helen, and his daughter. She's dead, see?'

The boy looked more confused than shocked.

Storytelling, thought Moy. You could read kids with stories. 'See, after the girl died, Daniel and Helen decided they needed a photo of her, to remember her. So, Daniel went out to his stable to saddle his horse, so he could go to town and get a photographer. But when he got out there he remembered the damn thing had slipped a shoe.'

The boy moved his eyes between Moy and the sepia image.

'Daniel was pretty upset. He sat down in the hay and cried. But he wasn't easily put off, so he started walking to town. He didn't even go back inside to tell Helen what he was doing. Just got up... left. Didn't take any water or food. Nothing.'

Moy was watching Daniel set off from the farm, leaving the gates open, his shoulders slumped but his collar still done up, his tie tight, his vest buttoned.

'He walked through the heat. Into the northerly wind and dust. When his feet blistered he walked in his socks. And when they were just holes he went barefoot.'

Moy could see the blood, and Daniel's feet; he could smell his sweat and hear his whispers of pain.

'Then it got dark and he stopped to sleep under a gum tree. Two days later he walked into town, and the first person he saw he asked: "You know where the photographer is?"'

He waited, hoping the boy might want to know more, but his eyes continued drifting around the room. Moy sat forward. 'I reckon your name's Harry. Yeah, Harry? Or maybe it's Jebediah or Ezekiel. Is it Ezekiel?'

Gary Wright opened the door and stepped into the room, followed by Justin Davids. Moy stood up and shook the butcher's hand. 'G'day, Justin. I've got someone here I thought you might like to meet. Justin, this is...' They both turned to face the boy.

Davids stepped forward and squatted in front of the boy. 'How are you, mate?' he asked, extending his hand.

The boy sat motionless.

'Bit of a rough trot, eh? Heard you ran into a pole. Where'd it get you?' He waited. 'Doesn't matter. Mr Moy here, he'll fix you up.

We'll get some food into yer.' And waited. 'Luckily for you, I'm the butcher. You need a bit of red meat. Rib-eye? What do you reckon?' He looked at Moy, and knew what he needed from him. Then he cleared hair from the boy's eyes. 'We've met before. You were in the laneway, behind my shop, remember? I came out, saw you were having trouble.'

The boy grasped the handles of his chair. Knuckles white as his hollowed face.

'Was that your dad?'

The boy closed his eyes and dropped his chin onto his chest, his whole body trembling.

'Thank you, Mr Davids,' Moy said, indicating to Gary to take him out.

'You'll be okay, mate, you hang in there,' Davids said as he left the room.

Gary moved closer to Moy and whispered in his ear, 'There's something out here you should see.'

Moy turned to the boy. 'You okay for a minute?'

No response.

They went down the hallway and into the lunch room and there, on the table, was a near-new rug, a few packets of biscuits, a half-empty bottle of Coke and a few books.

'It was just a hunch,' Gary said. 'I thought, if he's stealing food…so I got Alex and Ossie to check all the laneways at that end of Ayr Street.'

Moy examined the rug, still with its price attached. It smelled of new sneakers and there were food stains—sauce-red and gravy-brown—and smears of dirt from where it had been spread out on the ground.

'There's a drainage ditch behind the park on Muenchow Road and he'd made himself pretty comfortable,' Gary said. 'You could see where he'd tried to start a fire.' He showed him a six-pack of matches. 'So what's his story?'

Moy shrugged. 'Won't say a word. Shock, I suppose, which makes you wonder what's happened once this fella's driven off with him.'

They looked at each other, thinking, but not saying.

'I better try again,' Moy said, taking the rug. 'You ring Family Services?'

'On their way.'

Moy returned to his office and placed the rug on his desk. 'You can have that,' he said.

The boy looked at him. Some of his colour had crept back.

'It is yours, isn't it?'

Nothing.

'I could go to a few shops and find out where it comes from, but then they'd just want me to lay charges against the...thief. And you're not a thief, are you...Ezekiel?'

Moy knew he shouldn't apply more pressure but he needed to know. 'So I won't do that...you can have it.' He pushed the rug across the desk just as the air horn sounded at Guilderton Primary.

'You don't go to that school, do you? We checked.'

He waited.

'But you must go to some school. Think of all the stuff you're missing. I noticed you found yourself some books. Do you like school?'

Silence.

'We should get you cleaned up, get you back, eh? Art, that was my favourite subject. Painted these big portraits, took them home, Mum and Dad said, Oh, that's so lovely, Bartholomew. See, that's my full name, Bartholomew.' He smiled. 'What were my parents thinking?'

He waited.

'Bet your name's not that stupid. Bartholomew. Moy. Sounds like an alien, doesn't it? Moy. I come from planet Moy.'

Laughing, from the lunch room.

'We could get you back to school tomorrow. Would you like that? We could buddy you up with someone. You'd soon be out kicking the footy. Or maybe it's soccer? You look more soccer. See, round head, these footy players have all got oval heads. The Guilderton Maulers—you heard of them? Bet you're a goalie? Long arms, long fingers. Although they're big blokes and you're thin as a rake. You could do with some more of Mrs Flamsteed's casseroles, couldn't you...or, no, you'd probably prefer a Big Mac, eh? Bet you're eatin' those all the time.'

He ran out of babble. Then he leaned forward and said, 'I know why you don't want to talk, and that's okay. Maybe if we find you somewhere to sleep...watch a bit of telly?'

But the boy just kept staring at him.

Gary Wright stepped into the room, put his hand on the boy's shoulder and said, 'Listen, good news. I've been talking to Mr Wyeth, and he's bringing around another apple pie. I take it you like apple pies?'

Pause.

'Mr Wyeth wants to say sorry,' Gary said. 'He got you confused with some other kid.' He looked at Moy. 'They're here,' he said. 'They've got someone to take him for a few days.'

15

LATER THAT AFTERNOON Moy drove to the backblocks on the southern edge of town. They were covered with acres of ruined cars and goats grazing weeds where someone had once tried to grow crops on dead soil. Everyone had given up on the south side of Guilderton. The council had put a road through one area and tried to flog blocks in what they called the 'Ayr Industrial Estate'. The land was cheap, and a few businesses had built factories—one, a pre-fab shed business, had closed six months after opening.

Moy stopped his car in front of a four- or five-hectare allotment that ran between the road and virgin scrub. He read the peeling words on a sign that was already leaning: *A New Suburb for Guilderton: Brentano.*

'Suburb'. Jesus. It had been the idea of the mayor before last. Every other wheatbelt town was doing it. One-dollar blocks. Arrest the population decline by promising young, hard-working families a big block to build their dream home; keep the builders, electricians and plumbers in work for years. Brentano would be a shining example for other towns: streets chocker with kids on bikes, mums out planting roses and dads in sheds stripping down lawnmowers and testing home-brew.

One-dollar blocks, Moy thought, surveying the acres of empty ground, dust blowing up between piles of rubble local builders had dumped.

His phone rang.

'Bart Moy?' a voice asked.

'Yes.'

'My name's Keith Gallasch, from the bowls club.'

Moy took a moment to think. 'G'day, Keith.'

'Listen, Bart, it's your dad…'

'What is it?'

'He's had a bit of a fall.'

'Shit, how is he?'

'Fine, don't worry, nothing serious. He just tripped on a gutter. There's a small cut on his head.'

Moy sat forward and sighed. 'He hit his head?'

'I wanted to drive him to the doctor but he wouldn't have a bar of it.'

'Tell him I'll be there in five minutes.'

When Moy arrived at the clubrooms, George was sitting in front of a picture window watching the competition, sipping a Jim Beam and Coke, holding a bloodied handkerchief to his head.

'How did you manage that?' Moy asked, sitting down beside him.

George looked him over. 'Why you got a suit on?'

'Cos I'm workin'.'

'Workin', in a suit?'

'Let's see what you've done.' He reached for his father's handkerchief.

'Get off,' George said, almost slapping his son's hand. 'It's nothing. Give it a minute and it'll stop bleeding.'

Keith Gallasch, a small man with a bulbous nose, came up behind them. 'If it's still bleeding it needs stitches.'

'Bullshit,' George replied, catching a drop of blood bound for his white shirt. 'Ten minutes.'

'We've got insurance,' Gallasch said to Moy. 'It's not like it'll cost him anything.' He turned to George, raising his voice: 'It won't cost you anything.'

'All right, I got a cut, I'm not deaf.'

'He's right, Dad,' Moy said. 'Let's have a look.' He tried again.

'Get off.' This time George did slap him. 'Just take us home, will yer?'

'I'm taking you to the clinic.' He took his father under the arm and tried to help him from his chair.

'I'm not goin' to no bloody clinic. No fuckin' stitches. I's kicked in the head by a bull and that didn't kill me. Not worried about a bloody graze.'

'It's a cut.'

'Stiff shit. Look, anyway, it's stopped.' He removed the hand-kerchief to reveal a four-centimetre gash, oozing slightly. 'I've got some Band-Aids at home.' He glared at Keith Gallasch. 'Or maybe the club could spare a few?'

Gallasch shook his head. 'I don't know, I'd rather you get it seen to.'

'Bullshit, it's stopped.'

There was an uneasy silence.

'Jesus, Keith, I'm not about to sue anyone.'

'I'm not worried about that.'

George smiled. Gallasch realised there was no point wasting any more time. He turned to Moy.

'Go on,' Moy said. 'You can't win.'

AS THEY CRUISED along Ayr Street, George studied his son's tie and jacket. 'Aren't you hot in all that get up?'

'No.'

'You look hot.'

They drove in silence past the locked-up stores. A dog was sniffing posts, lifting his leg and dry-pissing. The community radio station, operating from a shopfront, played music from a speaker on its verandah. Moy could hear the guitar twang and the nasal voice.

Who, Moy wondered, could possibly be listening?

'You should've gone with Keith,' he said to his father.

'Why?'

'He was only trying to help.'

George turned to him. 'The reason I bring it up,' he said, 'is every time you see a detective on the telly he's wearing a polo top and jeans.'

'Some, I suppose, if you're busting into houses and jumping fences. But if you're just asking questions.'

They passed the empty car park of the Country Target. There were a dozen trolleys left in a sort of Stonehenge arrangement. 'Then they complain when kids push them in the creek,' Moy said.

'Still, you wouldn't have thought a country copper would need a suit,' George continued. 'It's not like you're gonna be on telly any time soon.'

'What's that got to do with it?'

'You always look like you're off to a funeral.'

Moy slowed, indicated and turned. 'Perhaps I am,' he said.

'Whose?'

'Guilderton's.'

George touched the two Band-Aids stretched across his dressing. 'See. Fine.'

'You know, you shouldn't make it difficult for people.'

'Who?' George looked at him. 'You, you mean?'

'People. Whether it's you falling, or someone offering to help with the house.'

'Who?'

'You told me…that old girl from Foys.'

George crossed his arms. 'You want me to let her in the house?'

84

'Why not, if she's offered to help?'

'Help? She just wants to come and stick her nose in.'

Moy stopped at a T-junction and turned to his father. 'I've met her. She's not like that at all.'

'She's a gossip. Like the old thing next door. *How are you today, George? Fine, Thea.*'

Moy studied his father's face as the words trailed off. 'Not everyone's a pain in the arse, Dad.'

He drove off. 'The thing is, Dad, you're not getting any younger, are you?'

George looked at him strangely.

'With everything going on…with your balance. Your old legs.'

'Nothin' wrong with my legs.'

'What, the ground moved?'

'Don't get smart with me, Detective.'

'Dad…you're getting older. You're gonna have to swallow your pride occasionally.'

No reply; more feeling around on his forehead.

'Admit you may need help. Or else it'll just be…'

'What?'

'It'll just be me.'

'So?'

This time Moy didn't reply.

'Well? You came back to look after me, didn't you?' George said.

'Of course.'

'So?'

'I've got work too.'

'Everyone's got work. Doesn't mean you can't look after your old man.'

Moy was shaking his head. 'I didn't say I wouldn't.'

'It's an inference. *Get some help or I'll put you in that fucking nursing home.*'

'I didn't say that.'

'You don't need to.'

'I don't want to put you in a nursing home.'

'But you would.'

Moy bit his lip and looked at his father. 'That's why I sold up, and moved here, was it? To put you in a nursing home?'

George dropped his head. 'You started the conversation.'

'You fell over.'

'So fucking what?' the old man shouted.

They sat in the car, in front of George's house.

'Thing you forget is that I'm happy here,' George said, looking at what was left of his garden.

Moy just looked ahead. 'I didn't mention the nursing home.'

'Well, you have before.' His head fell back onto the padded rest and he said, 'You can't make a fella do what he doesn't want to.'

with you in a minute,' the assistant said to Moy.

'No rush.'

Moy sat down and waited. The smell of eucalyptus and cheap perfume radiated from the front of the store. It reminded him of ils—wrapped in foil and deposited in boxes, hundreds of them, th *Mrs Anne Moy* printed in economical letters on the front. His other making little piles of pills on a bench. Ten, twelve, even- ally fifteen—yellow, white and pink. By the time she was done e'd have to go back to bed, as George buzzed around asking if she anted tea or toast, mostly destined to be vomited.

The old woman finished, but then presented a new script. 'Does is have a repeat?'

'It is a repeat,' the assistant replied.

'Oh, so I'll need to go back to the doctor?'

'Yes.'

'And my gout medication?'

'You don't need a prescription for that.'

And the smell, again. Something, he guessed, to spread on a sore r insert up your arse; something to rub on a rash; or maybe, yes, nat was more likely, an antiseptic: something to tip in a bowl and oak your feet in. It was a smell he remembered from the oncology ard, drifting down the hallways they mopped and buffed every few ours. Mandarin, or pineapple. It was always there, as he buttered oast in the visitors' kitchen.

'Do you want to wait or come back?' the assistant asked the oman.

'Eh?'

'Do you want to wait?'

'What for?'

'Your medicine.'

The old woman looked at her strangely. 'Where else am I going o go?'

Toast. He was sure he could smell toast. And he could remember

88

16

THE FOLLOWING MORNING there were two[...] of rain. Within minutes the clouds had cleared a[...] appeared. George always put this sort of thing [...] shadow, and Moy always told him there was no suc[...] would ask how he knew. Had he studied meteo[...] farmed beyond Goyder's Line all his life? Or was [...] arse? One day, sick of his son's arrogance, he wen[...] and photocopied an article out of a *Britannica*. 1[...] put it in front of his son. 'See? *A dry area on t[...] mountainous area.*'

'Yeah, but this isn't a mountainous area,' Moy h[...]

George had just looked at him. 'The point is,[...] exist.'

'Not around Guilderton.'

Bart Moy was wearing jeans and a polo top, h[...] board as he stood at the counter of Bowey's Che[...] woman in a cardigan was arguing with an assistant ov[...] referring to receipts in a shoe box on the counter b[...]

carrying the plate in to his mother in the room with the recliner chairs and drips. Placing it on the table beside her and smiling and asking, 'Is that enough?' The clear bag, too, nearly empty (CAUTION CYTOTOXIC DRUG), and the pump that beeped every ten minutes for a nurse to come and press more buttons. His mother's face, and George spending hours on the same page of a magazine.

But mostly he remembered the plate of toast, still untouched, hours later, as his mother was helped from her chair, saying, 'Bart, take that back to the kitchen, the nurses are busy.'

Moy approached the woman at the counter, introduced himself and showed his identification. 'You've heard about this boy?'

'In the back lane?' she said, indicating a door at the back of the shop.

'Yes.' He looked at her name tag. 'Jay?'

'Quite young?' she asked.

'Nine or ten, perhaps. We've found him.' He showed her a photo Gary had taken of the boy before he left with the carer. 'Not familiar?'

She studied the photo. 'No.'

'Let's see,' the old woman said.

Moy showed her.

'Has he been taken?'

'He was, we've found him.'

'Good...parents'll be glad.'

Moy returned to Jay, and a hair comb holding back her fringe. 'Could I leave a copy?' He gave her the photo. 'He won't say a word, so we have no idea who he belongs to.'

The shop assistant was lost in a thought. She met Moy's eyes, took a moment and said, 'This is probably completely irrelevant.'

He leaned forward. 'Yes?'

'Just a thought,' she whispered, looking around. 'I open in the mornings.'

'Yes?'

'And I walk to work…I only live down Dawes Street. The thing is, I often see this car…'

He waited.

'Just cruising around.'

The old woman was sorting through her prescriptions.

'How often?' Moy asked.

'Most mornings.'

'What, just driving?'

'Yes.'

'And who's in it?'

The shop assistant closed her eyes. When she opened them she was even more determined. 'This man.'

'Yes?'

'And the funny thing is, I think I recognise him.'

'You do?'

'He's a teacher, at the high school.'

Moy leaned forward, splaying his hands on the counter. 'Are you sure?'

'As sure as I can be.'

'And this man, you know his name?'

'No.'

He stared into her small, brown eyes. 'And what sort of car is it?'

She stepped back. 'Goodness, I'm not sure, but it's an old-looking car.'

'Old?'

'You know, 1970s, or early '80s, with a box shape.'

Moy laid his folder on the counter. 'Like an old Falcon?'

'I don't know cars, Detective Moy. But it's big and he always drives around with his arm out of the window. You know how they do?'

'Who?'

'Young folk.'

90

'So he was young?'

'Yes…well, youngish, not old.'

'Thirty, forty?'

'Mid-thirties,' she guessed.

'What about his hair?'

'Brown, perhaps?'

The old woman stood up, walked towards the counter, picked a pair of reading glasses off a stand and tried them on.

'They're too weak for you,' the assistant said to her.

'At the high school?' Moy asked her.

'Yes.'

'How do you know?'

But she just smiled at him. 'It's a small town, Detective.'

17

IN THE EARLY part of the evening Bart Moy passed through the Flamsteeds' front gate, his arms full of casserole dishes, and knocked on the front door. Louise Flamsteed was out straight away. 'Let me help you,' she said, taking the dishes, disappearing into the kitchen. There was a sound of glass and crockery being rearranged.

Moy waited.

'Mrs Flamsteed?' he called down the hall.

More dishes; more rearrangement.

'Doug,' he heard her calling, standing (he imagined) at the back door, scanning their quarter acre of succulents and cacti for her husband. 'Doug, Mr Moy's here.'

Moy looked down the hall at the freshly vacuumed rug, the 1960s telephone table and a macramé pot-hanger overgrown with a maidenhair.

Mrs Flamsteed came trotting down the hall towards him. 'There was no rush,' she said. 'You could've held onto them.'

'I have some others, at Dad's house, and in the freezer at work.'

'No rush, I've bought a few more.'

'Not on my account?'

She tried to smile. 'Come in for a cuppa?'

'Thanks.'

Ten minutes later there were three cups of tea and a pot with a crocheted cosy cooling under the regard of a Virgin on the wall. A few inches below this was a tired-looking Christ slipping from his cross.

Doug Flamsteed, still in his overalls, snapped a biscuit in half and dunked it in his tea. 'Harvest nearly done,' he said. 'Paschkes at least.'

'Be glad when it's over, with the noise,' Moy replied.

'Low yield this year.'

Although Moy's cup was only a quarter empty, Louise Flamsteed topped him up.

'Thanks.' He could smell disinfectant again, this time laurel sulphate, a smell he always associated with the glowing lino floors at the RSL.

'Every year there's less rain,' Doug said. 'Global warming they reckon, who knows? Used to be they'd get thirty bushels to the acre, but not now.'

Moy wondered what a bushel was, but dared not ask. Flamsteed had once taught him maths and probably still thought him stupid. Still, he thought, forty years of metric and the world goes on like it's 1959. 'That's what they reckon,' he said. 'Every few weeks they open another power station in China.'

Doug looked at him strangely.

'Anyway,' Moy said, looking at the deputy principal, 'I was wondering, Doug, if you've got a teacher at your school who drives an old Falcon, or a Valiant?'

Doug massaged the tip of his nose. 'Alan Williams?'

'Yeah?'

'Teaches art. What's he done?'

'Nothing.'

Doug sat forward. 'He's a very good teacher. Did that mural on the girls' toilet, you seen it?'

'Yes.'

But Doug still wasn't happy. 'Why do you ask?'

'No, truly, it's nothing.'

'You wouldn't have asked if it was nothing.'

Moy felt himself back in Mr Flamsteed's year nine general maths class.

'So, he's kosher?' Moy asked, looking at Doug.

'Yes.' Pause. 'How official is this?'

'Not at all.'

'There's nothing he actually…?'

'No.'

Doug laid his biscuit on the table. 'About eight, nine years ago he took this year ten back to his place, after school, to show him some artworks, books or something. Anyway, shit hits the fan.'

'Doug,' Louise said.

'Parents put in a complaint to the Education Department, reckoned Alan was, you know, after this boy.'

Louise wasn't happy; she shook her head. 'That's all over.'

'This Alan Williams,' Moy said, 'he's not actually…suspect, in any way?'

'No…he's softly spoken, and wears these fancy shirts and tight pants. Not typical dress for a country teacher but hell, he's told me he's not a poof, and he wouldn't…well, as far as I know. No…he's okay.'

Moy was watching Doug's head rock back and forth. 'So the kid didn't actually complain?' he asked.

'No, just the parents. Kid said it was all a load of old…But you know, when you do something stupid like that, and it was probably just a lack of judgment, everyone's out to get you. And a place like Guilderton. Mud sticks.'

Yes, Moy thought.

94

Then he sat up, drained his cup of tea and asked, 'This boy's mother…name wasn't Jay, was it?'

Doug took a moment. 'No, don't reckon.'

'Well, thanks for the cuppa, Louise.'

'It's nice to see you, Bart. You must pop in more often. And… any requests?'

Moy studied the pink cosy. 'Ever tried teppanyaki beef?'

18

THE NEXT MORNING at two a.m. Moy was awake again, turning onto one side, the other, his back, as he tried to clear any thoughts from his head. Before long he gave up. Got up and walked out into his backyard; ambled over to the trampoline and fell back, bouncing a few times then settling. The air was cold, laced with sow's milk and oestrogen, traces of Mrs Flamsteed's braised steak.

'Watch,' he heard Charlie say. He watched as the boy jumped, tumbled and rolled onto the broken springs.

'Careful,' he said, 'you could crack a tooth on the side.' But he was already back on his feet.

'I can do a somersault.'

'No, I'm not sure.'

'I can.'

'No.'

But there was the small body, curled up in itself, turning in mid-air, landing on its feet, dropping to its knees and putting its arm around his neck. 'See?'

'Where did you learn that?'

'My first time.'

'Do you think you could do it again?'

'Course.'

The moon had just lifted above the horizon. Moy walked down the driveway and stood at his front gate. He was wearing a T-shirt and boxers torn down the front. His moon-shrunk cock kept popping out. He crossed the road towards the fence that was the very edge of Guilderton. Someone, possibly Paschke, had nailed dead foxes onto each of the fence posts by their tails. Some were fresh, some dried out, their pelts reflecting the moonlight. A warning, Moy guessed, to other foxes. Even the little ones, jiggling in the little bit of breeze.

He lifted two loose wires and stepped into the paddock. Soon he was walking, then jogging, across a hundred metres of stubble, looking back at his house and the glow of his television in the front window. He arrived at a second fence, pushed the wires down, climbed over and started walking through the wheat, up to his ribs in places. The land started rising and soon he was climbing a hill. A few minutes later he was at the top, looking down over Guilderton.

He studied the houses, and found his dad's place.

And then realised, and sighed.

Right, he thought. *That's easy.*

George Moy would never give up his plot, his house, his home. He'd done it once before and it had almost killed him.

Moy knew what he had to do. He'd pack up his little government house and move in with George. That way there'd only be one garden to weed, one kitchen to clean, one toilet to scrub. It would be their garden, and home.

That's what the old bastard's been thinking, he realised, studying the gutters; the window frames that would need scraping; the verandah that needed painting and the glass replacing.

He thought of his own place, glowing with insomnia.

Right. He'd made a decision. Raising his arms, he ran down the hill, his hands brushing the wheat heads. Soon he was overtaken by his own momentum; he tried to stop, but couldn't. His body was moving ahead of his legs, which meant the fall, when it came, was uncontrollable, broken only by the wheat closing in around him. Then he lay on the ground, trapped by a wall that shielded him from the world. Here, in a little amniotic pocket, he studied the stars again and realised that Charlie was still there.

He walked home through the wheat, turned off the television and went to bed.

Then he slept soundly, for an hour, before the phone rang.

'Yes?' he said, fumbling, wanting to say, *are you fucking kidding me? Four-fucking-forty-one?*

'Yeah, Bart, it's Jason.'

'Jason…what's wrong?'

'This woman from FACS, the carer…'

'Who?' He sat up, focusing on indistinct shapes around the room.

'Deidre, the woman looking after the kid.'

'Oh.'

'She's just called…says she's having problems with him, and can someone come and get him.'

Moy slid his feet onto a floor carpeted with clothes and junk mail. 'What problems?'

'She didn't say.'

'Can't she wait for the morning?'

'Apparently not.'

Moy rang off, pulled on some track pants and grabbed his keys. A stray dog watched him as he passed the Rotary Park at the end of Gawler Street; apart from that there was nothing. Just long shadows cast by floodlights in car parks and loading bays, the street-light silhouettes of branches and leaves.

When he arrived at the small, pink house the front light was on. He stood at the partly open door. 'Hello? Deidre…you there?'

A woman came out of a room and up the hallway to greet him.

98

'Hi, Bart?'

'You okay?'

'No.'

He studied her pale face and noticed her clothes were soaked. She, too, was wearing track pants, but they were loose, hanging from wide hips. 'He's tried to get away three times,' she said.

'When?'

'Once out the back, once when I took him down the street, once when I was in the shower…oh god.' She turned and bolted back down the hallway, slammed a door. He listened as she vomited, eventually spitting and flushing. He heard her wash her hands before re-emerging.

'The Chinese near the Wombat Inn,' she said, attempting a watery smile.

'What did you have?'

'Short soup and lemon chicken. Undercooked. I thought it tasted a bit strange.'

The boy appeared in the hallway, looked at Moy and then shot back into his room.

'You're gonna have to take him,' Deidre said. 'I'm not up to it tonight.'

'That's okay, he can come with me. I've got plenty of room.'

'I nearly got him talking once. Scooby Doo came on. I think he may have a bit of history with Scooby Doo. I asked him, who's your favourite, Shaggy or Velma, and he nearly answered…He wanted to.'

'Okay. Let's get him home.'

Deidre led Moy into the boy's room, decorated with soft toys and a collection of Buzz Lightyears. The boy sat on the bed fully dressed, his hair combed and his face washed. He was wearing a white shirt and a jumper she'd bought him that afternoon. Knee-length shorts, almost Edwardian, revealing two knobbly knees above long socks and leather shoes.

'Well, a new boy,' Moy said, but he didn't lift his gaze.

'He's all ready to go. Bag packed, the lot.'

Moy noticed a bulging backpack.

'So,' he said, but the boy wouldn't look up. His back was straight, as if someone had been on at him about posture. His feet sat together and his hands were clamped tightly in his lap.

Moy sat next to him. 'You remember me? Detective Sergeant Moy...Bart...you can call me Bart. Remember, Bartholomew? Curse my parents. There's no way you could have a name as bad as that?'

The boy looked at him, then back down at the rug.

'I can look after you for a while, eh? So you don't get sick.' He pretended to vomit. 'See, look, peas, corn...yesterday's Froot Loops.'

He took the backpack and offered his hand. Instead, the boy just stood, walked out of the room and down the hallway.

'I hope you feel better,' Moy said to Deidre, as they followed him.

'I hope he comes good.'

As they drove through the quiet streets Moy glanced over to the passenger's seat. The boy's new pants were draped over legs that were mostly bone and tendon. His new jumper was too long—he could see Deidre had tried to turn up the sleeves. He studied the boy's hands: skin wrapped around long, bony digits, his discoloured nails cut back.

'I bet you've never been out at this time of night?' Moy asked, before he remembered. 'It's the best time of day.'

He turned down the radio.

'Looks like Deidre had everything nice. Still, I have a neat little...bachelor pad. Unfortunately you won't find any fruit or vegetables in my fridge, but there's plenty of chocolate.'

The boy looked at him, then back at the road.

He stopped and waited at a deserted T-junction. 'You know, this is an unmarked police car,' he said, indicating the comms screen on the console. 'If you look very carefully you'll see that I have lights, and a siren.' He gestured towards the warning lights at the front on the dash, and hidden by louvres on the back window. 'So?'

A horn sounded behind him: the newsagent's van. He moved off, still looking at the boy. 'You can turn them on if you like. There's no one around.'

The boy looked at him, unsure.

'Go on.'

The small hand reached out, slowly at first, looking at Moy for approval.

'It's fine, we can't get in trouble…we're the police.' He studied the boy's face. He noticed how he bit and licked his lip.

The boy switched on the lights and looked around. The whole street turned red and blue, lit up in ribbons of light that bounced back, drowning out street lights and delicatessen neon.

'Good, eh?' Moy said.

The boy couldn't help it. He smiled.

'What do you think of that?' Moy asked, but the boy remembered and his face hardened as he stared out at the lights.

'We could pull someone over. How would that be?'

No. He'd retreated again.

'We could book someone for speeding…that's always a laugh.'

Someone's front door opened and a head popped out. Moy switched off the lights. 'Neighbours aren't happy. Shall we go home?'

The boy's hands came together, forming a ball and returning to his lap.

They turned a corner and headed home along Gawler Street. The boy leaned forward. Moy looked at him. 'Are you…'

He vomited in one long stream that struck the airbag panel and sprayed back over both of them, splashing the seats and doors, consoles and radio, dripping down onto the floor. The boy sat back in his seat and wiped his mouth.

Moy braked hard, stopping in the middle of the road. 'Shit,' he said, wiping the spray off his hands.

The boy just sat there, motionless.

'You don't think you're going to do it again?' He planted his foot and they shot off down Gawler Street. 'She didn't tell me you had Chinese too.'

The boy shook his head.

'Ah…' Moy smiled. 'Not even a spring roll?'

Headshake.

'That's just fantastic, young man.' He handed over a tissue. 'Now we're getting somewhere. You didn't have Chinese food? Nothing?'

Again. Negative.

He pulled into the driveway. 'We, my fine, feathered friend, are developing a clear line of communication. Aren't we…Colin, was it?'

The boy just looked at him.

'No, you're not that easily fooled, are you? It's not Colin. You never said Colin, did you?'

He switched off the lights. 'Well, un-named young man, carefully step out of the car and make your way to the front door.'

Moy fumbled his keys, aided only by the little bit of light coming up over the eastern horizon.

'This has been an interesting night,' he said. 'And it's not over yet. If you want to go to the bathroom and throw those clothes out into the hall, I'll put them in the washer. I have a big hot water tank, so you can shower for an hour if you like.'

19

MOY WAS WOKEN by the sound of dishes. The air in his room was warm; it was already mid-morning. When he went out to the kitchen the boy stopped washing up, looked at him and then continued.

'What a great helper.' He sat down at the table.

The boy was wearing the boxers and T-shirt Moy had left outside the bathroom for him earlier that morning. The boxers were too loose. After racking each clean dish the boy had to reach down and hoist them up.

'I bet you're ten years old?' Moy said. 'Or maybe nine? Eight then…surely not eight?'

The boy looked at him, unhappy. He finished washing the dishes and started drying them.

'Leave them,' Moy said, but he kept working.

'That was quite a spectacular effort last night, young Ezekiel. How on earth d'you fit so much food into such a little stomach?'

Nothing, except the sound of spoons and forks settling in the drawer.

'I used to eat a lot…still do, all the wrong foods. You can get away with it until you're thirty, then you get this enormous belly, see?' He patted his stomach. 'Fibre, that's what you need, a young man like you.'

Moy stood up, fetched two bowls from the drying pile, searched the cupboard for a box of All Bran and started preparing breakfast. 'Here, bran, you like bran? Keeps you nice and regular. You know what that means, don't you?'

The boy looked at him.

'It means you're able to do your *business* every day. That's important, your *business*.' He gently poked the boy in the ribs. Once he'd filled the bowls he fetched the milk from the fridge and smelled it. 'Wait a minute. Tummy bug, milk, not a good combination? What do you think?'

The boy shrugged.

'Risk it?' Moy placed both bowls on the table. The boy finished drying, hung the towel over the back of a chair and sat down. He waited for Moy—then they started eating.

'I know this place isn't much, but it does the job,' Moy said. 'It's a copper's house…a government house.'

He noticed how the boy filled his spoon, drained the milk from the bran then ate.

'We, I mean my dad and I, moved to Guilderton when I was twelve. We used to live on a farm.' He studied the boy's small fingers and guessed he wasn't a farmer's son. 'I used to nurse the lambs. If the mum had twins she'd only look after one. The strongest one mostly…and she'd leave the other one.'

The bran tasted stale. He hadn't eaten cereal for years. Breakfast was generally a coffee and danish from the Hot Bread Café.

'I had a vegetable patch, and we used to get tomatoes, hundreds of them.' He looked at the boy's wide eyes. 'I bet you've grown veggies? Probably not tomatoes…you look like a zucchini man. No? What about carrots, or peas, there were a few of those in your

104

business.' And smiling. 'No…the *other* business.'

The boy grinned.

'That's it,' Moy said. 'Things aren't that bad, eh?'

The boy's head dropped. He let his spoon fall into his bowl.

Right, Moy thought. Guess they are.

'Anyway, I was very sad when we had to leave the farm. It was a good life.'

Silence.

'And Dad had to sell off the sheep, and that year's lambs.'

He touched the boy's arm. 'I bet it's Wolfgang. Wolfgang, isn't it?'

Eyes, peering.

'Barry…Gavin, Kenny, Trevor. They were the names in my day. Now everyone's Keanu. Christ, I hope you're not a Keanu, are you?'

The boy shook his head again.

'Thank God. Anyway, then we arrived in Guilderton. And I had to go to the primary school. You know what they did to me on my first day?'

'No,' the boy replied.

'No?' Moy forced his face to remain neutral. 'Well, a whole gang of them chased me into the toilet, and I locked myself in a cubicle. Then they started spitting over the top, going outside and getting rotten fruit to throw in at me, wetting big wads of toilet paper and throwing them in…disgusting, eh?'

The boy screwed up his face.

'Horrible kids, weren't they?'

He nodded.

'Then one of them climbs up on the divider between the toilets and says, how you going, Moy? Sarcastic, like that. *How you going?* You know, kids back then weren't so clever. But I mean, first day, trapped in the dunny, what would you have done?'

A smile.

'Well, I tell you what I did. I picked up the toilet brush, shoved it down the dunny and started flicking you know, *business* water. Right in his face.'

The boy giggled, and this time Moy could tell his voice was clear and high-pitched.

'*Get stuffed, Moy*, he says, like that. *Get stuffed*. But there's me, flicking more and more water at him.'

The boy was laughing, doubled over, wiping his eyes on his new T-shirt.

'What do you think about that, Wolfgang?'

The boy had stopped laughing, but he smiled.

'It's good to see you laughing. You don't know how good that makes me feel, Professor Vomit. You're a big fan of toilet humour, obviously. That's good. So am I. We can spend long hours farting. You enjoy a good fart, I take it?'

The boy shook his head.

'Rubbish, I bet you do. I bet you could fart for hours.'

But the moment had gone.

'The thing is,' he began, slowly, 'you might want to stay with Deidre, but if you'd prefer, you could stay with me for now?'

The boy's head tilted. He took a moment and then nodded.

'Fine, well that's easy. So, my name's Bart, what's yours?' He extended his hand.

The boy wouldn't be drawn.

'Ah, I'm pretty clever, Wolfgang. I'll get you yet. I am a detective, you know. I find out things for a living.'

He took the boy's hand and shook it anyway.

'I'll check with Deidre, see if it's okay, eh?'

Their eyes remained locked.

'Just for a while, mind you, until we find Mum and Dad.'

Something went out behind the boy's eyes, and it was all over.

20

MOY SAT ON a bench in the middle of the back lawn. He held a cigarette, but hid it from the boy. Took a puff, turned away, exhaled. 'How many?' he called.

The boy was using an old squash racket to hit a tennis ball against the side of the house. Moy was impressed. 'You play for a team?'

He was good, the heartbeat rhythm, the determination not to miss a shot. Moy watched him biting his bottom lip, focusing on the ball like it was a personal challenge. 'We've got a club, if you like. Or badminton. I played badminton.' He wondered if he should tell him: George watching him every Friday night, coaching from the side, becoming angrier.

What was the point? As if he'd care about racket sports in Guilderton. 'I'll give you a game. What do you reckon?'

Nothing except the regular thump resulting from an unvarying parabola; never harder, softer, longer, shorter. As if the formula worked, and had to be honoured.

Gary Wright walked down the drive, stopped and watched the boy. 'Impressive,' he said.

The boy didn't stop.

'Nearly as good as me. Wimbledon champion, 1978. *Just* beat Connors. But it was a tough game.'

Nothing.

'Course, you won't find it in the history books…but I won. Do you believe me?'

The boy took a step back and nearly missed. Forward, and re-established his rhythm.

Gary made his way over to Moy.

'You're so full of shit,' Moy said.

'*Me?* How's it going?'

'Signs of life.'

They watched the boy. Moy said, 'He's gotta get sick of it soon.'

'I tried both motels,' Gary said. 'That fella, what's his name, Gale, Gage, he's got something on with that Asian bird.'

'It's his wife.'

He smiled. 'Yeah? She's a good worker…all day, washing sheets. They're actually *married?*'

Moy didn't care. 'Nothing?'

'Said he had a family with a couple of kids, but they were younger.'

The boy stopped. He looked at them. Moy hid his cigarette and said, 'All done?'

He went in.

'Doesn't trust me,' Moy said. 'Maybe I look like someone…'

Gary watched him go. 'Got me thinking.'

Moy offered Gary the cigarette. He took a puff then returned the stub, which Moy snuffed out on the bench.

'About two years back.' He took an envelope from his pocket and removed a rubber band that was holding it together. 'Probably no connection.' Then he took out a pile of colour photos. 'They were left in the pub.'

Moy looked at each of the photos as Gary handed them to him.

They'd been taken at the local pool. Children, boys mostly, in the water, on the grass, the change rooms. Two shots were dark, like they'd been taken in a corner. They showed more than the others.

'Just left in the pub?' Moy said.

'Russ handed them in.'

There was a long pause, as Moy thought how this might fit in.

'I never knew.'

'Don't know lots of things about this place, Detective. They've been sitting in the safe. We asked around, no one knew nothing. So we guessed we got a kiddy fiddler somewhere.'

'You guessed? Could be a photographer.'

Gary just looked at him.

'Know the kids?' Moy asked.

'Locals.'

Moy studied the envelope. There was a picture of a silo in the top corner, with the words *Stow's Fabrications: Sheds and Silos*. He looked at Gary and said, 'What's he got to say for himself?'

'Dunno.'

'No one ever spoke to him?'

'It's not like you'd put them in your own stationery.'

'But you said *got me thinking*. About who?'

'No one…coincidence. The age of the kids in the photos. And Roger Federer over there.'

Moy placed the photos back in the envelope, put it in his pocket and stood up. 'Watch him for thirty minutes?'

'My day off.'

He walked away. 'You can tell him about the time you captained Australia A.'

When he arrived at Stow's a silo was being loaded onto the back of a truck. He asked for the manager and was shown into his office. A short man with an open shirt and a gold necklace greeted him. 'Bill Stow.'

'DS Moy.'

They sat down and Stow said, 'You lot after a silo?'

Moy looked at him and wondered. Why would you put photos in your own envelopes? He noticed his leather hands, and strong arms, and guessed he wasn't the type. 'Stow's have been round a while?'

'We have.'

'My dad had some of your silos.'

'Everyone has.' But he wasn't going to waste time on small talk. 'Someone stolen somethin'?'

'No...no.' He took out the envelope and showed him. 'One of yours?'

Stow looked carefully. 'Ten years since we used them.'

'It was found in the pub a couple of years back. Full of photographs...kids.'

Stow understood. 'Fuck.'

'At the time, apparently, nothing much was done. Not that you could do much.'

'Someone at the pub mighta seen.'

'Too late now. Don't s'pose you'd know anything that might help?'

'No.' Wondering if this was really a stationery issue, or something deeper. 'So, you're saying someone here...'

'No, Mr Stow. Just, there's so little to go on with these sorta things.'

'Right.' But he kept looking at him. 'Why you asking now?'

'Well, it's complex, but we've found an unclaimed kid.'

'What, someone's bringing them into town?'

Moy knew he'd said too much. Could see the front page of the *Argus* in the morning.

'No one's bringing kids to Guilderton or...anything like that. I just came on the off-chance.'

Stow stood, approached a filing cabinet and pulled out a drawer. 'A to F,' he said. 'These go back forty years, but out back there's a dozen boxes with all our old orders.'

Moy understood. You couldn't solve a crime with an envelope.

'I don't know what I can say, Detective. Unless you want to take everyone's number and ring them. Might take you a couple of months. Then you gotta think what to say, eh?'

Excellent. Another prick trying to do his job for him. 'Anything you can think of, Mr Stow. Wouldn't like to think there's someone in town who'd hang out in change rooms.'

'Every town's got one of them.'

'Have they?'

Stow stopped, refusing to be drawn. 'This unclaimed kid prob'ly just needs a belt around the ears. Someone's looking for him.'

Him, Moy thought. 'Yes, she'll probably be claimed soon.'

Stow sat down. He looked at the envelope. 'You could check it for fingerprints.'

'We could.'

'But it's prob'ly seen a few hands.' He waited with an *anything else?* expression.

'Keep your eyes open,' Moy said, reclaiming the envelope. 'You're well connected, eh? Speak to a lot of people?'

'It's not a question you ask, is it?'

Moy walked out through a cathedral-sized shed where two men were welding. Silos. He guessed that's what you could do with a body. He remembered the story, years ago, of the kid who'd climbed a ladder, looked in, fallen in. And drowned, wheat and its dust filling his lungs as he choked down the grain. Less than a minute, then silence. And it took them weeks to work out where he was.

He looked back towards the office and Stow was watching him. He raised his head in a final farewell. He was convinced the man was no photographer, but he wasn't sure he had no idea.

21

MOY BRIEFED GARY, who told him he was wasting his time. The kid had run away. The parents didn't want to report it. They were scared of what he'd say about them. The boy was still deciding if he should turn on them.

After he was gone, Moy stood at his kitchen window watching the boy hanging their freshly washed clothes on the line. He noticed how he took a shirt from the basket, climbed a chair and pegged it out. Guessed he'd been taught well; could almost see someone standing beside him, telling him what to do.

For those few minutes there was nothing but the washing—vomit-free pants and shorts, socks and undies—all from the little piles Moy had left sitting around his house for weeks, until, when he was out, the boy had gathered them in a basket. 'He's quite a little worker,' he said to Deidre, clutching his phone.

'He is,' the carer replied. 'So...you're sure about this?'

'Yes,' Moy said, watching the boy drop a sock, climb down to retrieve it and return to the job. 'We seem to get along...I think. I'm not saying you didn't—'

'No, no,' she said, coughing. 'But I'm quite happy to have him back.'

'Give us a few days. Not sure what the rules are but…it's not like anyone's gonna say anything.'

'Don't be so sure.'

'*Guilderton?* Headquarters don't know we exist. I used to fill in all the forms, but now…'

'You're mandated?'

'Yep, I'm mandated.' And he wondered whether he was, or what it meant.

It was one of the consolations of country policing. He knew it suited his own gluey state. Not that he didn't try. He did. *Every day in every way I'm getting better and better.* But things were missed. Like the Crowley file. He thought he'd forwarded it to the drug section. Then again, it hadn't come up on the courier's list. But he must've. Perhaps. And he wondered, where else could it be? In the vegetable section at the supermarket? In with the magazines in the doctor's waiting room?

Deidre still wasn't sure. 'Aren't you busy with all your investigations?'

'I can work around it. Anyway, he's company.' He looked at the boy, thinking. 'And I can talk to him, and ask him questions.'

'He's talking to you?'

'A few words.'

'Great.'

The boy finished, and stood staring at the half-full line.

'If I can get him to trust me he's more likely to open up,' he said.

'Have you got some clothes?'

'No.'

'I have a few things—'

'I'll take him out, he can buy what he likes.'

And then he stopped, thinking. Charlie's clothes, where were they? In boxes, at Megan's place? Or did they give them away? Some of them at least? No, Megan would never have done that. So where were they? Then he thought—what does it matter? They'd be far too small.

'Something practical,' Deidre was saying. 'Summer clothes. Shorts and T-shirts, polo tops.'

Moy looked up and smiled. There, on the hoist, turning in circles, was the boy; holding on to one of the support bars, stretched out, his feet a few inches from the ground; kicking his legs, laughing, turning circles until he slowed, at which point he'd put his feet back on the chair, push off and start again.

'He'll be fine,' he said.

'Let me know if you need help.'

'I will.'

And then he rang off. He walked from the house and made his way out to the hoist. Grabbing the supports, he started turning the line's metal arms. 'How's that?' he asked, but the boy was just laughing, giggling. 'Are you feeling sick?'

No reply.

'You will soon…we'll have another pile of vomit to clean up.'

He pushed harder and the boy's legs flew out, collecting him in the side of the face.

'Sorry!'

'That's okay.' Then he spoke loudly. 'Should I keep going?'

'Yes.'

He pushed. 'More?'

'Yes.'

'Sure you're okay?'

'Yeah, I'm good.'

Moy just watched him fly, seeking but never finding a straight line. The greaseless axle ground. Then the stem of the hoist cracked and the whole line toppled. Wires flew through the air as struts bent, collapsed and sent the boy flying onto the grass. He rolled, sat

114

up and looked at Moy. 'Oh no,' he said, and Moy came and sat next to him. 'You okay?'

'Yeah.'

'Nothing broken?'

'No.'

And they just looked at each other. 'Do you think they'll make me pay for it?' Moy asked.

The boy nodded.

'I'll say it was like that, shall I?'

A smile.

'That's what I'll say…it was like that when I got here, eh?'

A shrug.

'Or, I could say, this nasty little thief broke in…and when I caught him, I had to torture him.'

Moy tickled the boy's side. The boy pulled away, giggling.

'Yes, that's it. I had to torture him until he admitted breaking my washing line. Go on, you young thief, admit it.'

Moy was tickling with both hands and the boy was rolling about on the uncut grass, laughing, curling up to protect his midriff.

'I'm waiting,' Moy said. 'All you've gotta say is, it was me. Go on.'

No response. The tickling continued.

'Go on.'

The boy was kicking the grass and his shoes left brown skids. His eyes were closed. 'Get off,' he squealed.

'*It was me.*'

'It wasn't.'

Moy stopped. The panting boy looked up at him.

'I'll have to charge you,' Moy said. 'And there may be prison time involved.'

The boy giggled and hit him lightly with a fist.

'My son used to ride the hoist. Used a chair to get up, then realised he couldn't get down.'

'Where is he?'

Moy sat forward, his arms on his knees. He looked at a distant geranium, overgrown with weeds. 'He's...gone.'

'Where?'

'Gone.'

'When's he coming back?'

'Looks like you can speak,' Moy said. He squeezed the boy's knee. 'Now maybe I get to know your name?' He extended his hand once again. 'I am Bartholomew Moy...and you?'

'Isn't he coming back?'

'Wolfgang, wasn't it?'

'Bart?'

'You're using my name...I should be able to use yours, don't you think?'

'He's not,' the boy said, choosing not to shake Moy's hand.

Moy turned around. 'He died,' he said.

And the boy was gone again.

THEY FIXED THE hoist, straightening the stem and propping it up with an old ladder. Then they filled two buckets with warm water and disinfectant, found a few old sponges and went out to the car. The boy was straight into it, wetting the vomit stains, wiping them, rinsing his sponge and starting again. He cleaned the dashboard and started on the carpet. Moy worked from the driver's side, slowly wetting and scrubbing, picking flecks from the radio. There were several minutes of silence before he said, 'It looks like your mum taught you well.'

No response.

'How's that, Detective Moy?' he asked himself. 'Well,' he answered, 'I don't have to ask you to do anything.'

There was another minute of silent scrubbing.

'Your mum would be very pleased with your efforts.'

Silence.

'Or maybe your dad?'

The boy looked at him angrily.

'Maybe not.' He stopped to think. 'Dad's not around, perhaps?'

'You keep my dad out of this.' His face hardened and he clenched his fists. 'You just want to solve your case, so you can get on with something else.'

Moy stood up and came around to the boy's side.

'So you can put me in a home, and forget about…'

He knelt, held his arms, but he pulled away.

'Get off! Don't touch me!' He was shaking. He picked up a bucket, went to throw it over Moy, but stopped. Instead, he ran inside, went to his room and slammed the door.

Moy followed. He stood in the hallway. 'You okay?'

No response.

He didn't know what to say. To keep prodding and poking, opening barely healed sores, invoking a father who might have been capable of anything. 'If I came in, we could talk?' He guessed it mightn't be so simple. 'I'm sorry,' he said. 'I don't know anything about your dad.'

Silence.

'You there?' He went into the room. The window was open and the boy was gone. He stepped forward, looked out and called, 'Come on.' Then he ran from the house, around it, tripping on a bucket of water. 'Where are yer?'

Nothing.

To the top of the drive. Looking down the road. The boy was further along, standing outside the plumber's house, waiting.

'You coming in?'

The small figure darted across the street, into the paddock on the edge of town. As Moy followed he watched him flatten wheat, fall, stand, run towards a distant harvester.

'I said I's sorry,' he called. He could see the boy was wounded; just had to run.

Arriving at the fence, Moy climbed over. Stood standing, searching.

But the boy had gone.

'I know…it's none of my business,' he shouted, over the sound of the approaching harvester. 'Come on, show yourself, it's dangerous.'

The driver was watching him.

'This is silly…I'm sorry.'

Then, a muffled voice. 'Go away!'

The harvester was eating the crop. It turned, came back, and Moy held his breath. There was no point risking it. He waved at the driver but he just looked at him strangely.

'Please,' he called. 'What do you want me to say?'

Nothing.

The harvester turned again. This time it would come close. Moy ran into the wheat, searching. *You little shit.* But he knew there was more at stake. He wasn't a foster carer. It'd be hard to explain.

He turned towards the harvester and waved. It slowed, stopped, and the driver got out and called, 'What's wrong?'

'Could you wait a minute?'

The farmer watched as Moy searched. Then, he looked back towards the fence. The boy emerged from the wheat, slid between the wires and ran back up Gawler Street.

Moy waved at the driver. 'Lost dog.' He struggled through the wheat, hurdled the top wire and ran after him. Back up the road, across, into the Flamsteeds' yard.

The boy had picked up a shovel. He was swinging at knee-high aloe, taking off lizard-tongue leaves.

Moy held him. 'Stop it!'

He twisted to release himself but didn't have enough muscle. Moy ripped the shovel from his hands and threw it down. Then, Mrs Flamsteed was standing on her porch.

'All under control,' Moy called.

She didn't respond. She knew he was reliable.

Moy wrapped his arm around the boy, lifted him and carried him from the yard. 'Sorry,' he said, as he went. 'We'll get them replaced.'

The boy fought to get free. Moy took him in, put him on his bed, pointed a finger in his face and said, 'Not an inch.'

The boy just glared at him.

'Got it?' He knew there'd need to be tough love first. Car washes weren't going to do it.

Then he went to the shed, found a hammer and nails, and stood on the outside securing the window. As he did he looked at the boy, but he didn't look back. He said, 'I can remove these, any time.'

He looked across the road. Mrs Flamsteed was still on her porch, watching.

'All tidied up?' she called.

22

THE PROBLEM WAS solved with pizza. Moy ordered three. Garlic bread. Coke. A conversation at the door with the delivery boy. 'Looks like I'll have to eat them all myself,' he said, turning towards the door of the spare room. 'My son, he's too sick to eat.'

He sat in the lounge room, feasting. A few minutes later he heard the boy's door opening, then saw a shadow in the doorway. 'Help yourself,' he said. 'I got tropical. You like pineapple?'

The boy came in and knelt down in front of the boxes on the coffee table. He took a slice and started to eat.

'I poured you a Coke,' Moy said.

The boy chewed a few times, waited and swallowed.

'Thank you, Detective,' Moy said. 'That's okay.'

'Thanks,' the boy managed.

'That's okay.'

After they'd eaten and drained nearly a litre of Coke, Moy said, 'Do I owe you an apology?'

The boy looked at him. 'Was the lady angry?'

'No. She's got plenty of plants. Said she understood. Still...'

'What?'

Moy fetched pen and paper, and helped him compose the note. *'Dear Mrs Flamsteed…'*

'I can write it by myself. I'm not five years old.'

'You never told me how old you were.'

'Nine.'

When he was finished he crossed the road, by himself, and placed it in her letterbox.

He returned and Moy said, 'She'll be over with one of her saints.'

The boy had seen them on the fridge. 'For me?'

'Yeah. But I'll keep her at the front door. I'll tell her you went down the street for some milk. Unless, of course…'

The boy grinned. 'My uncle was into Jesus.'

Moy knew better than to try again. Instead, 'I suppose I should go do some work.'

'What about me?'

'You can come with me.'

'To work?'

Moy shrugged. 'I don't think you're ready to start school just yet, are you?'

'No.'

They both got changed. When Moy emerged from his room the boy was putting the pizza boxes in the bin.

They backed out of the driveway in the lemon-scented car, cruised along Gawler Street behind a truck full of pigs, its tray dribbling shit, and past Civic Park on the way to the station. 'What's your favourite music?' Moy asked, tuning from station to station. Eighties double-plays…Bing Crosby.

'Don't know.'

They settled on the squawk and mumble of the police radio.

Then the boy looked at Moy and said, 'Patrick.'

Moy kept his eyes on the road. 'Patrick?' He stretched his right hand across his body. 'I'm Bart…nice to meet you.'

Patrick lifted his hand from his lap. Slipped his fingers and palm into Moy's. Then Moy closed his hand and they shook.

'Do you have a surname, Patrick?'

The boy looked back at the road.

'That's okay. One step at a time. It's a nice name, Patrick. Very Irish. But you're not Irish, are you? I mean, what would an Irish person be doing in Guilderton? No, that's quite a start. I feel like I know you now.'

They pulled up in front of the station. Patrick sat back in his seat, his hands sliding down, and squeezing his legs. His teeth closed on his bottom lip and he looked at Moy strangely.

'Let's go,' Moy said, climbing from the car.

Patrick sat motionless, staring down into the black comms screen.

'You coming?'

They went in through the double glass doors, postered with an ad for a Blue Light disco and a man named Sidney Barrett, wanted for the murder of his wife and mother-in-law. Patrick walked slowly, looking around—at the fan clunking above the waiting area; the aquarium, full of murky water and plastic seaweed; a coffee table with magazines and a Rubik's cube with most of its coloured stickers peeled off. Moy approached the desk where Jason Laing was busy counting the number of fines in an infringement pad.

'This is Patrick,' Moy said, his voice filling the empty room. 'Patrick, this is Constable Jason Laing.'

Patrick lifted his head and looked at the policeman. Laing studied the boy's face. 'Hello, Patrick.'

No reply. Patrick looked down at the lino and the black marks at the bottom of the counter where thousands of boots had scuffed the wood.

'Patrick's staying with me,' Moy said.

Laing leaned forward, although he was no closer to the boy.

'Are you sure that's something you want to do, Patrick? This man hasn't cooked a meal since 1986.'

'Thanks very much. At least we don't have cats sleeping with us.'

'That's not my fault,' Laing replied, attempting to meet the boy's eyes. 'It's my wife, she loves cats.' He leaned across the desk. 'That's what happens when you get married, Patrick…be warned.'

Moy looked at him, the kindergarten teacher with the bobbed hair on the tip of his tongue; Laing shot back a glare. Patrick (if that was his name) watched them with a blank expression.

'Well, you look after yourself,' Laing said. 'Detective Moy will find your parents in no time. He's very good, despite what everyone says.' The phone rang and he answered it.

'Come on,' Moy said, taking Patrick around the shoulder and leading him towards his office. As he went Laing covered the mouthpiece and said, 'Oh, Superintendent Graves rang. He was wondering why he hasn't got a report on—' he indicated the boy. 'And the fire.'

'Thanks, Constable.'

'Thank you, Detective.'

Moy took Patrick through into the hallway. 'You find this place a bit…intimidating?'

'No.'

'Any of these fellas would help you, you know. All you gotta do is ask.'

They got to a room with a steel door. Moy produced a fistful of keys he used to open a seam of locks. 'This is the armory.' He walked inside and switched on the lights. Patrick followed him in, his eyes lighting up at the sight of three shotguns, two pistols and a rifle locked in a cradle. There was a silver cage, itself locked up, full of old pistols, rifles and shotguns. 'These are the ones we've confiscated,' Moy said, shaking the cage. 'They have to be sent to town, to be destroyed.'

The boy had seemed fascinated with Moy's revolver, snuggled into a holster on his belt. He'd studied it, his mouth open with anticipation, plainly resisting the temptation to ask if he could hold it.

Now he looked at the cradle with the guns and said, 'Have you ever had to use them?'

'Not these, but back in town, there were times...'

'Like what?'

'Well, there was this dad, and he'd locked himself in his house with his wife and kids...' He stopped.

'And what happened?'

'What happened? Nothing, he gave up.'

'You didn't have to shoot him?'

'No.'

'You should've.'

Moy looked at the boy, looking at the guns. 'Why's that?'

'If he was threatening them.'

Moy could hear Laing whistling from the front desk. 'But he gave up. Everything was okay.'

'I suppose.'

'Of course, we don't put up with violent people. If we can just work out who they are.'

'Sometimes you know,' Patrick said, looking at him.

'What do you mean?'

But the boy's head just dropped.

'So there's a violent person?'

No reply.

'But it's not someone you know, is it? Someone from Guilderton, for instance? Someone you've met today?'

Nothing.

'The thing is, if you told me, I'd have him in here like that.' He clicked his fingers. 'Or if it was someone close, we could go and have a talk.'

The boy worked at a hole in the lino with the tip of his shoe.

'Someone you know, someone in your family?'

Silence.

Moy switched off the lights and locked the door, and they continued down the hall. He entered a code on a keypad and another door opened. They walked into a room made up of three small cells. The cells were clean, with tiled floors and fold-down beds that had been made up with fresh linen and rugs. Each had its own stainless steel toilet, a single roll of paper and a hand basin.

'This is where we put the bad guys,' Moy said. 'Or sometimes, on nights, we have a sleep here.'

'You do?'

'The beds are quite comfy. Try one.'

Patrick stood staring at the closest cell, its door wide open.

'Air conditioning, heating, everything. We have meals sent over from the Wombat Inn. If this was a motel it'd be two hundred a night. What do you think?'

Patrick was still looking, unsure.

'Come on,' Moy said, going into the cell, sitting and then lying on the bed. 'It's mainly for the farmers who get on the grog.' He stopped again. 'It's like a cubby house.' He motioned for Patrick to come in.

Patrick took a few steps, looked up at the bars and then crossed the threshold.

'See, you could decorate it: lava lamp, the whole lot.'

Patrick's face twisted. He dropped to his knees, fell forward and crumpled into a ball.

Moy knelt beside him. 'You okay?'

'Please…'

'Should we take you out?'

But the boy just kept crying.

Moy picked him up and carried him from the cells. He draped him across his shoulder, entered the code and left the room. When he had him in his office, he lowered him into a chair. 'Hey,' he said, but Patrick just sobbed, fighting for breath.

Laing stepped into the office. 'Everything okay?'

'Fine,' Moy replied.

The constable just waited.

'Fine.'

Laing left the room.

Moy sat beside the boy. 'I'm sorry about that. It wasn't such a good idea, was it?'

A vacant stare. Moy looked around. Picked up the old photo on his desk and held it for a while. 'I didn't tell you what happened to Daniel Moy, did I?'

Patrick shook his head and sniffed.

'See, after all that walking, the photographer wouldn't go with Daniel.'

Pause. 'What do you mean?'

'After walking for two days the photographer wouldn't go with Daniel, to take the photo of his daughter, Lizzie. So Daniel said, listen, she's my only daughter, and she's gone. Me and my wife are worried we won't remember what she looked like.'

'But you've got the photo,' Patrick said.

'Wait, I'll explain,' Moy replied. 'Daniel was in tears…he was a broken man. As the photographer carried on he sat in a chair and cried like a baby. Eventually he stood up and pleaded with the man. You want money? How much money? I only want one photo. But this photographer, he just kept on with what he was doing. You listening? Daniel asked. You listening to me? And then he got angry. He saw this knife on a bench and grabbed it. Then he held it to the photographer's throat. You will come with me, he said, calmly.'

Patrick looked closely at the photo. Studied the expression in Daniel's face.

'Next thing,' Moy said, 'this photographer's son comes in the room and Daniel lets go of the photographer and grabs the boy. He takes the knife and holds it to his throat.'

Patrick's eyes widened; Moy could see him picturing the boy, his face screwed up, his hands trembling and his knees weak.

Moy talked in a whisper. 'Right, pack your camera, and let's get going, Daniel said. He held the knife to the boy's throat as the photographer went outside and got his cart ready. Then they set off for Cambrai, the photographer driving, and Daniel sitting in the back with the boy, his neck all nicked and bleeding, blood on his shirt.'

Patrick settled back in his chair. Looking, Moy thought, like someone was reading to him from a book. He took the photo and looked carefully.

As the boy contemplated the image, Moy's inbox rang its little bell. Moy knew he should ignore it, but hoped it might be something useful: the boy's father discovered, the whole mystery solved in the click of a mouse. He opened the email and there was a message from Superintendent Graves at Port Louis: 'DS Moy—Is this a familiar face? He was found washed up at Mangrove Point. Early 30s, brown hair, greying on sides, 171 centimetres…'

He opened the attachment and studied the face. The young man's body had bloated in the ocean, and his skin was red and flecked with broken capillaries. He had three or four days' worth of stubble. His hair was wet, full of sea grass.

'He was found like this, naked. Looks like he'd been wearing a ring and earring, both removed.'

Moy studied the dead man's flat chest and stomach, and his white skin.

'I suppose you won't recognise him, but I wondered if someone there might. He's not a local. Coroner's coming tonight but they reckon he's been in the sea for twelve hours.'

Moy saw the lifelessness most in the hands, the fingers. The way they might have, but never would, move or twitch or form a fist.

Doesn't ring a bell, he replied, but I'll forward to the fellas here.

23

PATRICK WAS STILL not talking, but Moy had a lead. Sort of. He left the boy in the lunch room in front of a television documentary about seals and set off towards the south-east corner of Guilderton. It was a little enclave hemmed in by roads named Oxford and Cambridge, Margaret and Elizabeth, running off the central spine of King Edward Terrace. But there was nothing regal in the scribbly gums and stunted eremophilas; the roads worn away and colonised by grass; blue metal footpaths and humming transformers.

He pulled up in the driveway of a house on the far end of Cambridge Street. Fibro, with a tenuous brick veneer cladding, most of the fly-screens hanging loose. He walked up the drive past a half-buried fish pond full of brown water and what looked like a carburettor. At the edge of the scoria stunted cacti survived the Armageddon that had laid waste to the front yard.

He went to the front door and knocked. And waited. A neighbour stared over the fence. 'Hello, do you know if Mr Williams is at home?' he asked.

Blank face.

'Alan Williams? Does he live here?'

The man said nothing and went inside. Moy knocked again. 'Hello, anyone home?'

He took a few steps across the verandah, past a box of old *National Geographic*s and looked in the front window. 'Mr Williams?'

There was a table with plates and mugs and breakfast cereal. A lounge suite and a coffee table covered with magazines. There were clothes on the floor, and a suitcase with a collection of airline tags attached.

He walked around the side of the house, standing on his toes to look in the higher windows: a bathroom (with frosted windows, latched); a spare bedroom (a single bed with a bare mattress, a dresser, a wardrobe); the main bedroom (a double bed, another wardrobe, open, full of neatly hung clothes); the toilet; and a third bedroom (empty, marks on the carpet showing where furniture had once rested).

His phone rang. 'Shit.' He fumbled for it and answered with a whisper.

'Guess who I just got a call from?' George said.

'Dad, I can't talk now.'

'You been goin' behind my back.'

'What?'

'You know.'

Moy continued whispering. 'Dad, I'm in the middle of something.'

'Speak up!'

He raised his voice slightly. 'I'm with a suspect, Dad.'

There was a short pause.

'Well, I'd like a word when it suits.'

'Fine. I'll pop around later. I've got some news, and someone for you to meet.'

'Who?'

'Later.' He hung up and switched off the phone.

The shed door was locked, so he looked through the louvred windows and saw dozens of boxes, taped up and stacked on top of each other. There was a lawnmower and he could make out one end of a train set on an old door resting on trestles.

He looked around the yard. Tall grass growing through the remains of a vegetable patch. 'Fuck.'

'Can I help you?'

He turned to face a woman in late middle age, her hair up in a bun, one eye compressed in what he guessed was the legacy of a stroke.

'Detective Sergeant Bart Moy,' he said, producing his warrant card. 'Guilderton police.'

'Yes?'

'I'm looking for Alan Williams.'

'That's my son.'

'He lives here?'

'You know…why are you asking me?'

Moy shrugged, uncomfortably. 'You live with him?'

'Are you asking or telling me?'

'Asking.'

'In that case, no. One of the neighbours called me.' She looked at him with contempt. 'So?'

'I didn't catch your name?'

'Naomi Williams.'

'Naomi…you might have heard, last Monday, a young boy—'

'Oh, goodness me,' she said. 'You're making some very… tenuous connections.'

'No…I didn't even know about all that business.'

'There was no *business*, Detective. A few paintings. And a town full of very bored people.'

'I wouldn't necessarily argue with that, Naomi. But the thing is, this woman claimed to have seen Alan driving down Ayr Street when the boy was taken…by a man she *said* looked like your son.'

Naomi closed her eye and slowly shook her head. 'That was very convenient. She got a good look?'

'She wasn't sure.'

'No, she wasn't, was she? But that's enough reason for you to come and…snoop?'

He stared at her. 'Well, yes, in a case of possible child abduction.'

Moy could see her jaw tensing. 'Seeing how Guilderton has decided that my son's a paedophile?'

'No.'

'Yes, he is, apparently. He brought a student home. The student told everyone, all we did was look at some art, but that's beside the point. Only a paedophile would *lure* a student back to his house.'

Moy was lost for words.

'So that's why you're looking in the shed. Alan got that child—'

'We found him.'

'So *he* would've told you to come here?'

A long pause; the sound of the fly-screen tapping.

'I think I'll put in a complaint about you, Detective.'

'I'm sorry you see it that way.'

Naomi turned, found a key in her pocket and opened the shed. 'Come in,' she said.

They both walked into the shed. She switched on a light. 'You can come out now,' she called.

'Listen, Mrs Williams, it's not about what I think,' Moy said. 'It's just my job, to follow up on everything.'

'Rubbish. Did you ring Alan?'

'That's why I came—'

'You were trying to be clever! As with everyone in Guilderton you assumed—'

'I didn't know about your son. I've been in the city for the last fifteen years.'

She stood her ground; then she turned and indicated the writing

131

on the sides of the boxes: *paints*; *small canvases*; *brushes*; *sketchbooks*; *charcoals and pencils*.

'See, after all that business he just didn't feel like continuing,' she said.

Moy was scanning the shed. 'I could imagine.'

'Now he just gets up and goes to work.'

'It's a small town, isn't it?'

'And getting smaller, it seems.'

He shook his head. 'Okay, I'll be honest, Naomi, I acted very stupidly.'

She looked at him, her face calming.

'I thought, maybe…What can I say?'

'Sorry would be a good start.'

'Sorry.'

Naomi's eye was clear and bright. 'And I bet I know who saw Alan near this boy?'

'I can't say.'

'It was the mother—her name's Silvia.'

'No, I can tell you. Her name wasn't Silvia.'

'Or her sister, the boy's aunt—Jay.'

Naomi stared at him, and knew. 'See, you listen to gossip, Detective.'

'I didn't say…'

'You listen to gossip…'

Yes, in fact. It was his job. He said nothing.

'The thing is,' Naomi said, finally, 'Alan drove me to town last weekend and shouted me a ticket to *King Lear*. He took an extra day off school and we drove back on the Monday afternoon.'

'*King Lear*?'

'So, he might've taken him. Assuming he went missing after that.'

'No.'

'When was it again, Detective?'

132

Silence.

'Mrs Williams, I'm sorry. I suppose I'd complain about me too.'

Naomi stepped forward, took his hand and attempted a smile. 'Perhaps it's best if we all start again.'

'Yes.'

'Almost like you'd never been here, Detective Moy.'

24

MOY SAT BESIDE his father at the small dining table in the old man's kitchen. Patrick sat in a smaller chair, his hands under his legs, occasionally looking up at the stooped man with his big ears and hairy nostrils.

'We're looking for Patrick's parents,' Moy told George. 'Until then, he's staying with me.'

George looked the boy over. 'You speak?'

'He's a bit shy.' Moy placed another crossword book in front of the boy. 'You can do these?'

Patrick picked up a pen and started writing.

George glared at his son. Moy stood his ground, his arms crossed.

'Well?' the old man asked.

'What?'

'Is there something you'd like to tell me?'

Moy shrugged.

'I had a phone call earlier on.'

'Good.'

'Don't get smart.'

'Who was the phone call from, Dad?'

George stopped to think. 'Janice…Janet? Either way, she was from the nursing home. She was after you, but she must have got the numbers mixed up.'

Moy didn't know what to say. 'I was gonna tell you.'

'You were?'

'It was just an inquiry.'

'He's put down your name, she says.'

'There's a three-year waiting list.'

'I told you—'

'Dad, what if you had an accident? What if you couldn't look after yourself?'

George pointed his finger. 'You were going to…' He trailed off, looking at the boy. 'You got many, Patrick?'

Patrick's eyes drifted from the old man to the page.

'Bit old-fashioned, eh? Words. No Facebook here.'

'I'm not on it.'

'And, what's it called, the box thing?'

'Xbox.' He looked at the old man. 'It's good. I can play…' Then returned to the crossword. 'I can do these, too. Here, the most common element, silicon.' He indicated.

George checked. Maybe the boy had a head for facts.

Moy knew his father wouldn't let it go. 'Dad…I'd never willingly put you into one of those places.'

'Is that why you came home?'

'That's not fair.'

'I can tell you one thing, you'll never drag me out of here.'

'I don't want to.'

'Once is enough. This is all we've got to show for a hundred years of killing ourselves. Land. Only a little bit, I know, but enough for some grass and weeds.'

'Dad.'

'You'll never drag me out of here.'

Moy knew these words were raw. He could still remember the swearing and kicked walls from thirty years before; his father pacing the empty rooms of their farm house. Although he couldn't remember what he said, he guessed it was along the same lines: land, and history, lost; banks as a sort of cancer that ate into honest people's lives; relief, at least, that his ancestors weren't around to see it. He could remember the moving van and the boxes of books and toys, and worst of all, the empty sheds and yards.

And then, attempting to convince his dad that it was time to go. 'It'll be great, won't it, walking into town?'

'Yeah…'

'Come on then. The movers will need us to open the new place.'

Moy knew how hard it was for his dad. The actual moment of leaving. 'Dad?'

'Christ, son, they'll wait.'

Back in the kitchen, Moy said, 'Anyway, it doesn't matter. I've made a decision. I'm gonna move in with you.'

George wasn't sure. 'You never said anything about this.'

'I'm saying it now.'

Patrick looked at Moy with a sort of *does this include me?* expression.

'Easy done,' Moy said, looking at both of them. 'There's no lease and I'll be saving a hundred and eighty a week. We can use that for a gardener, or to get the place painted.'

'You don't want to.'

'There's only one lot of dishes to clean, one afternoon lost vacuuming.'

'But you don't *want to.*'

'Why not? I can put up with you. I have for forty-two years.'

George just stared at him. 'Maybe *I'm* not so sure.'

'You gotta decide.'

'I got things how I like them.'

'So? We can work around you. Like Dad and Dave.' He looked at the boy. 'What do you think, Patrick?'

'Good.' He turned to George. 'I can help you with your crosswords.'

'So that's the plan,' Moy continued. 'I pack up my few things, hire a trailer. Few of the fellas at work will help. There's plenty of space if we clear out the bedrooms.'

'They're full of my stuff.'

'Stuff you don't use. A bike machine you haven't sat on for thirty years. There's plenty of room to store your *stuff* in the shed.'

'What if I don't want it in the shed?'

'What if you don't want to go to a nursing home?'

George sat up. 'Don't play your bloody detective tricks on me.'

There was a long pause as they stared at each other, as Patrick scribbled letters across the page.

'I'm not useless,' George said.

'I didn't say you were.'

'I can still look after myself.'

'Didn't say you couldn't.'

Another long pause.

'Well?' Moy asked.

'I get the last say.'

'Of course.'

Moy smiled, convincing himself as much as anyone.

HALF AN HOUR later the three of them walked down Ayr Street. George stopped to rest on his walking stick. Moy was beside him, his hand near but not touching his father's arm. Patrick walked behind them carrying a string bag with George's few groceries.

'So, Patrick,' George said, 'what's happened to your parents?'

'Dad, you remember the story, about the laneway?' Moy asked.

'Yes.'

'Well, that's Patrick.'

'So what was that all about, Patrick?'

'Dad.'

'What?' He couldn't see the problem. 'Best thing's to talk about it.'

'*Dad.*'

'Some fella givin' you a hard time, was he, Patrick?'

Patrick stopped. The two men walked a few steps before they realised. They turned to him. 'You okay, Patrick?' Moy asked.

George just stared at him, studying his eyes, his small ears and freckled nose. 'He's okay,' he said.

'Patrick?'

'Come on, boy.'

'Dad.'

'What?' He shook his head, turned and hobbled on.

'Come on,' Moy said to Patrick. 'He takes a while to get used to.'

They continued and Moy returned to his father's elbow.

'The thing is, Patrick,' George continued, 'I've been in this town a pretty long time and I know most people.'

'Dad, Patrick's not local.'

'Well, Port Louis, Sandringham, Close's Beach.'

Moy stopped in front of the entrance to Turner's Shop. 'How are you off for clothes?' he asked his father. 'Socks, jocks, singlets?'

George looked at him. 'I've got enough clothes to see me out.'

'Shirts? That one's only got four buttons.'

'There's another job for you, when you move in.'

They continued.

'You leave him with me, I'll get him talking,' George said to his son.

'It's not that easy.'

'It is.'

'A few days ago he wouldn't say a word. Now he talks to me. You've gotta give him time.'

138

George flicked his hand, as if there was a fly. 'I know all that,' he said.

'He needs to know he can trust you.'

'Why couldn't he trust me?'

Moy walked around a pram left in the middle of a footpath. 'Maybe he will.'

A thought occurred to George. 'You're not doin' this because you need a babysitter?'

'FACS was looking after him. I asked to have him. But it might be nice, mightn't it? If I gotta go off somewhere?'

'It might be…but I'm an old man.'

'You're not that old.'

'Old enough.'

'For a nursing home?'

He glared. 'No.'

'Well, this will be good…bonding.' He looked back at Patrick. 'Eh, Patrick, Dad says you two can hang out. Says he'll take you to bowls.'

'Did not.'

'He'd love that, wouldn't you, Patrick?' He looked at his father. 'Imagine all the old girls, with their paws all over him. You'd be the most popular man there.'

'Too old for that.'

Moy stopped outside the chemist. He looked at Patrick and asked, 'Can you look after Dad for a minute?'

Patrick nodded, took George by the arm and led him to a bench.

'I'm all right,' the old man fussed, reclaiming his arm.

But Patrick persisted, sitting beside him and holding his walking stick.

Moy went into the chemist, walked down the soap and shampoo aisle and emerged at the front counter. 'Remember me?' he asked the assistant.

'Yes, Detective Sergeant. How did it go?'

'It was Alan Williams, wasn't it?'

She looked confused.

'The man in the car. The old car you told me about. It was Alan Williams?'

'Was that his name?'

'You know it was.'

'Pardon?' She looked indignant. The pharmacist was listening from the dispensary, slowly typing.

'He taught your nephew, didn't he?'

'Did he?'

Moy glared at her. 'You've wasted a lot of my time.'

'I don't understand.'

'Alan was with his mother, in town. He had an extra day off school. They were seeing *King Lear*.'

The assistant just shrugged. 'All I know is I saw this man, several times.'

'You're sure?'

'Yes.'

'I could charge you.'

She took a step back. 'Excuse me?'

But Moy almost laughed. '*King Lear*. Shakespeare.' He left the shop, upsetting a table of half-price cologne.

25

AFTER MOY DROPPED his father home he decided to take Patrick along Creek Street. There's something I've missed, he kept telling himself.

As they drove they passed paddocks full of stubble. Moy noticed a pair of tall silos: *Stow's Fabrications*. He wondered if this was the farmer who'd misplaced his photos. Then felt the usual exhausted futility. What could you do? Knock on the door, ask if he had a camera?

Moy's arm extended out of the car, tapping on the roof. 'You gotta understand,' he said, 'George is gonna do his best to scare you.'

'Why?' Patrick asked.

'It's just how he is.'

'Why?'

Moy shrugged. 'I suppose there weren't a lot of Disney movies when he grew up.'

'So?'

'He was out bagging wheat when he was nine.'

Patrick was confused. 'How's that make him grumpy?'

'He's not grumpy.'

The boy was staring at him.

'Back then you didn't have time to stand about discussing your problems.'

'Doesn't mean you gotta be grumpy.'

'No,' Moy agreed. 'Maybe they wanted to come over strong…manly.'

'Why?'

'To show each other they could do the job.'

'What job?'

'Shearing sheep, welding axles.'

'So he's grumpy because he had to shear sheep?'

'Yes, exactly, because he had to shear sheep.'

Patrick still wasn't convinced. 'But you reckon he'll stop being grumpy?'

'Yes.'

'When?'

'A couple of days, a week…never.'

When they reached the far end of Creek Street the houses spread out. Moy noticed an old shed on the backblocks. Turning down a gravel road he coasted and stopped his car at the end near a patchwork iron shed. There was a weedy yard full of old washers and stoves, bed frames, mattresses and forty-four-gallon drums. And what looked like the remains of a bus, completely overgrown with vine. 'What a dump,' he said.

Patrick was quiet, his face set hard.

'Someone's collected a lot of crap. I can't believe the council would allow it.'

'Can we go?' Patrick said.

'You okay?'

'I don't like it.'

'It's just rubbish. I should have a look.'

'Can we go?'

Moy looked at him, thinking. 'Have you been here before?'

'No.'

'It's just a shed…and a heap of junk.'

No reply.

Moy got out. 'You okay?'

Nothing.

'How about I lock the car?'

'No,' he shot back, lifting a hand, with five outstretched fingers.

Moy walked into the yard and noticed a fence, its rusted wire and posts hidden by grass. He walked through the rubbish on his way to the shed. There was a path of sorts winding through it all. He noticed a few mice dart from under a tea chest. When he got to the opening, or what passed as a door, he called out, 'Hello, anyone around? Police.'

Silence.

He looked back at Patrick and waved. 'You okay?'

The boy didn't respond.

Moy hauled aside an old mattress that was being used as a sort of sliding door. Stepping inside, the smell hit him straight away. Stale oil, unwashed clothes and rotting food. There was enough light to see piles of junk. Six- and seven-foot high columns of pots and pans; wet newspapers and magazines; shelves (fallen, clinging to the old wood of the shed) full of broken irons, lamps, a record player and a collection of everything electronic ever bought, sold or stolen in Guilderton.

'Hello?'

He followed another path that moved among the junk. It brought him to the centre of the shed where there was a bath and, inside it, a mattress with a depression where someone had recently slept. Beside the bath-bed was a pile of rugs. It seemed to move. He knelt down to look at it, unsure if it was a trick of the light.

Fleas. Millions. Jumping about in the last bit of light.

He stood up and stepped back.

'Hey,' a voice said behind him.

He turned and a fist connected with his jaw, sending him flying. As he fell he upset a pan full of fat sitting on a Primus stove.

'Christ,' he said, sitting up, feeling his face and noticing blood on his hand.

'You fuckin' thief,' he heard the voice growl, before a foot hit him on the side of the head, knocking him to the ground. He was groggy, unsure of where he was or what was happening. He managed to look up and see an old man in a grey parka and overalls standing over him.

'Police,' Moy said.

'My arse.' The old man went to kick him again.

He shielded his face with his arm, grabbed the old man's leg, pulled it, and heard him fall back onto a pile of cartons.

'*Police*,' he repeated, sitting up, spitting blood from his mouth and noticing Patrick's face above the man. Then he heard fists, and a series of punches. Little hands connecting with bone. He stood up, took a few steps and tried to pull Patrick off.

'No,' the boy shouted, as he hammered the old man with both fists.

'Come on,' Moy said. 'Stop now.'

Patrick stopped, rolled his head and said, 'Leave him alone.'

Both the old man and Moy looked at the boy.

'He was just looking,' Patrick said.

'In my house,' the old man replied, sitting up.

There was a short pause as all three caught their breath. Moy felt his lip and realised it was split. 'You've just assaulted a detective,' he said to the old man.

'And you've just broken into my place.'

Moy could see that he only had a few teeth, and that his lips were turned in. He had a flat nose, brown eyes and grey skin.

'You come to steal from me,' this man said, running his hand through his matted hair. 'This is private property.'

'You live in this mess?'

No reply. Patrick stood with his arms crossed, glaring at the old man.

'This isn't healthy,' Moy said. 'The place is full of fleas, you shouldn't be here.' He noticed a pile of books on a bench beside the bath-bed; a candle; the remains of a meal.

'I was here first,' the old man said.

'What do you mean?'

'When I built this shed sixty years ago there was no one for miles. They come and built their places around me.'

Moy moved and felt his jaw. Nothing seemed to be broken. 'Why did you hit me?'

'You broke in.'

'I was investigating. I thought it was a shed, not a house. I could charge you.'

'And I could call the police.'

'I am the bloody police.'

'How was I to know you weren't a stealer?'

Moy looked at him and realised there was nothing to be done. The old man stared at Patrick and said, 'I remember you.'

Moy looked at them both: the old man, squinting, trying to remember; Patrick, moving away, dropping and turning his head.

'I seen you,' the old man said.

'You have?' Moy asked, looking at them both.

'Yeah.' He kept looking at Patrick. 'Out with your brother and your mum.'

Moy stared at the boy.

Patrick turned away from them.

The old man looked at Moy. 'I seen 'em walkin' down here... down Creek Street.'

The boy turned, took a few steps and ran from the shed. Ducking and squeezing between the towers of junk, pushing back the mattress. He disappeared into the night.

'How old was the other boy?' Moy asked.

'Not much older than this one.'

He stopped to think. 'Can I come back?'

The old man shrugged.

'Listen, I'm sorry, I shouldn't have come in…I didn't know.' He extended his hand. The old man took a moment and then shook it. 'Sixty years I been here,' he said.

'I know.' He followed the path out, knocking over a rag bag that spilled open and blocked the junk corridor.

He emerged into the night and saw Patrick sitting in the car. After walking through the yard he stood looking at the boy. Then he looked up. Creek Street. He could smell smoke; and see the yellow and red blocks of Lego half-hidden in the ashes. He looked back. Their eyes met but the small head dropped again. Once he was in the car he said, 'We better watch out, that place was full of fleas.'

No reply.

'That was a nice thing you did, Patrick.'

Patrick just closed his lips, and licked between them.

'So, what happened, you saw him coming in and followed him?'

Nothing.

'He could've given me a black eye, or worse…he might have had a knife.'

The old man stood in the doorway looking at them. Then he picked up the mattress and laid it across the door.

'Thank you, Patrick,' Moy whispered, and their eyes met. 'I know I should say you shouldn't have done it, but every bit helps, eh?'

'I don't think I hurt him,' Patrick said.

'No, but you've got a decent fist. Good punch.' He felt the boy's right bicep. 'See, it's all that pizza I've been feeding you.'

'And fried chicken.' The boy took a deep breath. As his eyes slid away, Moy thought he saw relief there.

146

26

THEY DROVE WITH the races. Belmont. *All ready, lights, they're off, Precious Gem out quickly, followed by Beltane Lass, two lengths…* in a drone that perfectly matched the weather, the landscape, monotone, with the occasional bump and depression. Moy could see Patrick looking into his lap, fiddling with the trauma, fingers locked together, pushing and pulling on the meaty bits of hand.

'What were you buying?' Moy asked.

Patrick looked up at him but decided it was a trick.

'Milk? Bread? Or was she taking you for fish and chips?'

No reply.

Moy wondered whether he should back off. He was risking four days' work. Back where he started, or worse. But the clock was ticking. He thought he knew where the mother was. But what about the other boy?

'Did you often walk into town?'

Patrick looked up. 'I've never seen that man.'

'But he's seen you.'

'It must've been someone else.'

'He seemed pretty sure.'

'He was wrong.'

'So you've never lived around here?'

The conversation slowed over a cattle grate. Stopped. They drove on.

Moy knew this changed everything. No longer the runaway. No longer misplaced, or unwanted. 'Was that your brother?'

Nothing.

'Bit taller? Look a bit like you?'

Patrick waited.

'Quite a walk, into town? Specially if you had to carry groceries.'

He dropped his head.

'Now I'm looking for two, am I?'

'No.'

'Well?'

Beltane Lass finished four lengths ahead of the field. Moy switched off the radio.

'So, here's a scenario. It might have nothing to do with you. Brothers. One's taken. The other knows that if he...says anything... but *he* mightn't understand that the *police* can get to anyone.'

Patrick looked up. This seemed to concern him. *The police can get to anyone...*

'At this point, time is of the essence. Know what that means? Every minute matters.' He watched for his reaction. 'It's time, Patrick.'

'It's just me.' But he didn't look up.

'Who was the woman, and boy?'

He glared at him. 'Me!'

'No.'

They were giving correct weight. Only a dollar fifty for the win.

'You gotta give me something, Patrick.'

Patrick clicked his seatbelt, reached for the door and opened it. Moy braked hard but the boy half-tumbled to the ground, got up and walked back along Creek Street. Moy pulled over, got out and called. 'Patrick.'

Patrick kept walking. Moy ran, then slowed, then walked beside him. 'Stop.'

He continued.

'Okay, my mistake. He was old. Must be a hundred kids live along here, eh?'

Patrick's withering look said he knew it was another trick.

'They've all got a mum. I'm sorry. When he said it, I just thought…'

Patrick stopped and looked at him. 'I'd tell you, wouldn't I?'

'Yes.'

'You should believe.' He turned and headed back for the car.

Moy left a good ten metres, and followed. When he got back in they were loading the next twelve horses. As they drove, he said, 'That old fella needs some help.'

'Leave him be.'

'I could tell Deidre.'

'He probably just wants to be left alone.'

Silence. *They're off. Clean start.*

'He might need glasses.'

But Patrick just closed his eyes.

THEY DROVE TO the IGA on Humbolt Street and spent twenty minutes flattening boxes. Patrick took them out to the car and stacked them in the boot. Eventually they were jammed in tight—thirty, forty, maybe more. They drove home, unloaded the boxes into the hallway, stacked up against the wall under a Heysen gum-scape. The afternoon sun, coming in the bubble glass beside the front door, had bleached the trees and hills calcium white.

Moy assembled the first box and fastened it with tape. He carried it into his bedroom and stood staring at the mess. Clothes all over the floor. He wondered whether he should try and fold them, stack them in the box, and cover them with the shirts and undies in his drawers.

No, he concluded, clothes should come last. So he turned to the improvised bookcase he'd made beside his bed: a series of four planks supported on either side by bricks. *Finnegans Wake*, the first seven or eight pages read and reread a dozen times. He threw the book into the box and returned to the shelf. *Sons and Lovers*. Judging by the scuffed pages he'd read three chapters before asking himself if he really cared.

Patrick walked slowly into the room balancing a cup of coffee he'd filled to the rim.

'That for me?' Moy asked.

Patrick was biting his lip. 'I made it strong.'

'Good.'

He placed the coffee on a table beside the bed and Moy leaned over to sip it. Patrick sat down, looked at him and asked, 'What will they do with the old man?'

'There's nothing you can do. It's how he wants to live.'

Patrick couldn't understand. 'Why?'

'It's what he's used to.'

'But he could get used to a nice place, if someone found it for him.'

Moy sipped more coffee. 'Did you sugar it?'

'One. Three spoons of sugar isn't healthy.'

'You're my mother?'

'You'll get diabetes.'

'Who says?'

'Mum…' He stopped.

'What else does she say?' Moy asked.

The boy bowed his head.

'Patrick?'

Nothing.

'You still don't want to tell me who the other boy was?'

'He would've been covered in fleas,' Patrick said.

'Who?'

'The old man.'

'Patrick…' He waited. 'What else did your mum tell you about?'

'You could at least take him to the station, and let him use the shower there.'

'I could.'

'And then you could get a pest control person…'

Moy tried to think of a way in, but couldn't. Instead, he took a small photo album from the bookshelf and turned to a random page, halfway in.

'Ha,' he said, looking at a photo of himself, aged seven or eight, bare-chested and broad-shouldered, standing in front of a silo his father was bolting onto a concrete slab. 'Look at me there. I'm not fat.'

'Is that George?' Patrick asked, studying the bent-over figure in shorts and singlet.

'Yes. We bought that for the cattle feed, but I don't know that we ever used it.'

And there, in the background, a woman, standing with her arms crossed.

'Who's she?' Patrick said.

'My mum.'

'Does she live here?'

'She's dead.'

Patrick didn't seem surprised.

'When I was twelve,' Moy said, waiting for some sort of response.

But Patrick wasn't interested. 'George was bigger there.'

'Yes, people shrink as they get older.'

He looked at the photo of Moy, and then at the older version. 'You're not shrinking.'

'No, I mean…after about sixty.'

'Was he grumpy back then?'

'I suppose…although not so much. You've got more to be grumpy about as you get older.'

'Like what?'

'Like…things not going the way you planned.'

Patrick didn't understand. 'But doesn't that mean that kids should be the grumpiest?'

'Well, perhaps, but they haven't had time to make plans.'

'Yes, they have.'

'Like who?'

Patrick stopped short again, refusing to be drawn. He returned to the photo. 'He had muscles then.'

'He did. And what about me? No pot belly.' He patted his stomach. 'This, my boy, is what you have to look forward to.'

'Not if I don't eat chips all day.'

'You will.'

'I won't.'

'Maybe you were taught well?'

'Yes.'

'She sounds like a smart woman, your mum…?' Moy let it hang but Patrick took the album and continued looking. There was another photo of Moy, twelve or thirteen, dressed as a sort of budget Prince Charming, wearing felt slippers, beige tights, a short tunic and a cap decorated with feathers. 'That can't be you?' he asked.

'It is. What do you think?'

'What were you doing?'

'It was a school production. *The Little Mermaid*.'

'You're wearing makeup.'

'Yes, including lipstick, if I'm not mistaken.' He squinted to see. Patrick looked at him strangely.

'What?'

'Couldn't you have been a fish or something?'

'I didn't want to be a fish. I wanted to be Prince Charming.'

'Yuck.'

'I was expressing myself…I was experimenting.' He lifted the lukewarm coffee and sipped. 'You're not from a theatrical family I take it?'

'No, I've never seen a show.'

'Just the telly?'

'Yes.'

'And what about your brother?'

Patrick glared at him. 'I'm not one of your criminals.'

Moy was taken back. 'I didn't say you were.'

He continued searching the photos. 'You just keep asking.'

'I want to help.'

'You just want to…solve it, so you can get on with something else.'

Moy sat forward. 'That's not true. I want to help. Maybe that means solving it.'

Patrick looked at him, closed his lips and studied another photo. 'Who's he?'

'That's Charlie.'

Charlie was four, fresh-faced and blue-eyed, sitting on a rug painting a picture of a train.

'Your son?'

'Yes.'

They both examined the photo.

'That was bad luck,' Patrick said.

'Yes.'

And he glanced up, although his head was still down. 'Do you miss him?'

'Yes.'

'It's a nice train.'

'It is. I still have it somewhere…' He took another album from the bookcase, opened it, found a poster in the back and flattened it out on the floor. It was the same train, hurtling through a landscape of box houses with cotton smoke coming from their chimneys. Patrick compared the half-finished version in the photo with the finished painting. 'He did a good job. Except…'

'What?'

'There are no people.'

'Maybe he never finished it.'

'Or maybe he didn't want people. They're hard to paint.'

They both sat, studying the smudged paint.

Moy was standing in his driveway, holding his son, trying to open the back door of his car. It opened and he laid Charlie across the back seat, secured him with a seatbelt, closed the door and got in the driver's side.

The engine was still running. He selected reverse, shot back up the driveway (crushing the soccer ball) onto the road, changed gear and took off with a puff of tyre smoke. He became airborne over a rise, crashed down to the road and continued. 'Charlie, can you hear me?' But he knew it was best to keep going, towards the road that led to the highway that took him to the hospital.

There was a roundabout, but he didn't look right. Instead of slowing, he pushed his foot to the floor and the car roared. 'One minute, Charlie, one minute…hold on.'

He slowed for the highway but didn't give way. As he turned a pack of oncoming cars had to brake to avoid him. Then he planted his foot again. 'Hold on, Charlie.'

When he looked at the photo Charlie was still painting the train.

'What happened?' Patrick asked.

Moy tried to smile at him. 'It was an accident.' He studied the blue clouds and yellow birds.

'But what happened?'

Moy looked at the boy and understood, at last, why he wouldn't talk about his brother.

27

THE NEXT MORNING, already warm, as Moy paced up and down his driveway. 'This other boy might be his brother, or a friend,' he said, into his phone. He moved it away from his mouth, cleared his throat and returned to Superintendent Graves. 'I've got no way of telling.'

'Every home?'

'Yes.'

'Schools, motels…pubs?'

I'm not completely fucking stupid.

'Footy club, scouts—'

'Listen, Superintendent—'

'It seems you've got a different crime now. If there *was* a brother. Patrick might have been threatened.'

Moy took a deep breath. Nothing annoyed him more than remote-control policing. 'Things are progressing,' he said. 'I'm happy with the way Patrick's opening up.'

Patrick. Sitting at the kitchen table, looking out at him, raising a few fingers as a token wave, grasping his texta and returning to his portrait.

'You don't actually know who the boy is?' Graves asked.

'Yes, I do.'

'Patrick? That's what you know? Assuming he's even telling you the truth.'

'The way I see it,' Moy said, watching a crow on the fence, 'is there aren't many options. He's just a very scared boy. I don't think formal questioning would achieve much.'

'I'm not suggesting that,' Graves shot back. 'I'm not completely insensitive.'

'I didn't say—'

'I just don't want to be in this situation in a month's time.'

Moy took a moment to consider his response. 'I think he's starting to trust me. I think there's something he wants to tell me.'

'Well?'

Moy studied Patrick's face, the way he bit his lip as he worked, stopped, turned his head to assess his progress, then continued.

'Here's how I see it,' the superintendent said. 'If you could just tell him everything's okay, but we need his help. Say this isn't something that can go on and on.'

'I can't pressure the kid.'

'If you want me to arrange for him to go to town, see a shrink, find a foster family? Maybe that'd give him some sense of normality. Maybe the problem's that he's still where it happened.'

'I don't think...'

'The threat is too close.'

Moy knew he had a point, but wouldn't say so.

'I think that would be a disaster. I don't think those sort of changes would be good for him.'

'Well, get me something.'

Moy stopped himself from barking back down the phone. *Get you what? He's a kid, for God-fucking-sake.*

156

'I just need a bit longer,' he said, as he crushed broken concrete under foot.

'You're not a social worker, Bart, you're a detective. This goes against the grain.'

'A bit longer.'

There was a short pause, and then the superintendent said, 'Righto, keep me informed.'

There was no goodbye, no conditions, no threats—just the implication that the boy, who was now looking up at him, would be taken away, fed into some machine and processed for information.

Moy stared back at the crow. It flew away. He went back inside the house, turning over his options. There were books full of procedures that helped you solve crimes. He remembered studying them for his first detectives exam. Cross-matching stories. Phone number analysis. But it was all a distant haze. He guessed he must've been good at it. Promotions. Commendations. But that was all before he backed up his driveway. Now there was just the occasional complaint; the raised eyebrow. *Why didn't you enter his name on the database?* I did…didn't I? *We could've saved twelve months' work if we'd known.* Right, I…

Can't seem to put things together, he thought. Pedal faster and go slower. But I'm dealing with it…*Every day in every way…*

Later, as they sat eating lunch, Moy looked across the table at Patrick. He hoped he didn't have far to go. If the boy told him everything (the crime, who was at home, who did the bashing and burning) then all this time would have been well spent. He knew what he should do next. 'I'm quite stumped, with this fire,' he said.

Patrick looked at him. 'What fire?'

'The house, on Creek Street…not far from where that old fella said he saw you and your…friend.'

Patrick looked down, studying the cuts he was making in his pie. 'Don't you know what happened?'

'I thought you might know something, seeing how you lived

around there.' He waited. 'You did live somewhere…close?'

Patrick stood up, scraped the rest of his pie into the bin and went into the next room to watch television.

Moy fetched another box, took it to the lounge room, taped it together and started packing DVDs. As he worked he said, 'Do you want to help?'

Patrick just stared at the screen, trying to make sense of other crimes, other people's problems.

After ten minutes of packing Moy stretched and said, 'I'm getting a bit sick of this.'

No reply.

'Maybe we should go for a drive. There may be ice-cream involved.'

'I can help you pack.'

'Later.'

Moy picked a random route through town: Civic Park, Ayr Street, King Edward Terrace back to the showgrounds. The boarded-up sideshows were being cleaned, painted and stocked for the annual show. A few men were welding sheep-yard panels. Some of the rides and the steel superstructure of the ferris wheel had already arrived. 'Ever been to a country show?' he asked.

Patrick shrugged.

'It's a lot of fun. Preserves and tractors and monster pigs…big as cows, I kid you not.'

'Pigs?'

'Yes. Genetically engineered. Enough bacon for a whole city. And cows like elephants. Not natural. Still, that's what it's all about. Increased productivity. Even the pigs have to fall in line.'

'What makes them fall?'

'It's an expression. They have to get bigger.'

Then they went onto the oval, driving around the circumference for no particular reason. 'See, this is my exercise,' Moy said. 'Four circuits…and look at me, still fat.'

'We could try jogging.'

'You could. It's much easier this way.'

'You're a disgrace, Bart,' the boy said, beaming.

Moy turned to him. 'Bart? That's a bit disrespectful. What about Mr Moy? Or Detective?'

'Bart…fart.' He giggled.

'Hold on, that's it. I'm placing you under arrest for—'

'Bart fart.'

Moy reached for the boy's hand. 'Where are my handcuffs?' As he started searching his belt the car veered left. He braked but the front fender made contact with one of the posts supporting a boundary rope. Closing his eyes, he smiled. 'They never check.'

He continued along RM Williams Way, across the train track and back onto Creek Street. Then he saw a familiar-looking jogger: early twenties, slim, bike pants. He noticed how she hovered above the road. Her trunk, too. Like you could get your hands around it. And tear-drop breasts that slept in a sort of leotard.

'I reckon you fancy her,' Patrick said.

Moy turned to him. 'Pardon?'

'You were looking at her.'

'I look at everyone.'

'Not like that.'

'I'm a detective. It's my job.'

Patrick smiled. 'You should stop and talk to her.'

'Why?'

'You could pretend you're looking for someone.'

Moy shook his head. 'You think I fancy her?'

'I don't *think*…'

'I should stop and talk to her?'

'Get her phone number.'

'How old are you, exactly, Patrick?'

'Old enough to know.'

Pause.

'I wasn't even looking.'

'You were.'

They passed a tractor.

'About an eight,' Patrick said.

'You're scoring women? You're nine years old.'

'So?'

Moy tried the radio but there was nothing worth listening to. Then Patrick asked, 'Where are we going? Are we going back to see him?'

'See who?'

'The old man.'

'Do you want to?'

'I'll wait in the car.'

Moy looked at him for a few moments. 'I just feel like some fresh air.'

They kept on, and the last few houses petered out. 'Should we go back?' Patrick asked, moving about in his seat, clutching his seatbelt.

'Why? Is there something wrong?'

'No.'

Moy felt he shouldn't, but something was leading him on. He knew there'd be a psychologist somewhere who'd have a problem with his approach but he sensed it had to be done. He sped along the road, past virgin scrub. 'Feel that wind on your face, eh? That's the good thing about this job.'

'Bart...'

'No one watching over your shoulder.'

'Can we go home?'

'No one telling you what to do.'

'Bart!'

Moy slowed as they approached the house.

Patrick looked at the ruin and dropped his head. 'Please?'

'What's wrong?'

160

'I don't want to be here.'

'Why?' He pulled over and stopped. 'It's a beautiful bit of country.'

'You did this on purpose.' He glared at him.

'Did what?'

'Brought me here.'

'This road?'

The boy pointed to the house.

'That's the house,' Moy said. 'The one I'm confused about.'

'Why did you do this?'

'I thought I'd show you.'

Patrick stared at him. 'Why?' He clenched his fists and started punching him.

'Hold on,' Moy said, grabbing his arms.

'You knew,' Patrick screamed, pulling away from him.

'Knew what?'

'That I lived there.' He stopped, relaxing his arms and sinking back into his seat. 'With my mum, and my brother.'

Moy took a few moments. 'Your mum?'

'Yes, you knew.' His face was full of anger.

'I suspected.'

'*You knew.*'

Moy felt bad. 'I'm sorry.'

'It's too late to be sorry.' He opened his door and ran. Sprinted across the road into the scrub. Moy got out and chased him through paperbark and spiny acacias. 'Patrick! I said I'm sorry.' He looked around but couldn't see him. 'Patrick!' His words settled in the scrub. Then, twenty or so metres away, he saw him climbing a eucalypt.

He ran towards him, watching him grasp the trunk and pull himself up. The boy arrived at a branch and sat on it. Standing up, he hugged the trunk again and continued climbing. Another five metres and another branch.

'Patrick, get down. You're gonna fall.'

He continued climbing. There was a long stretch of naked trunk. He got halfway and looked up. Then he dropped his head to check on Moy.

'Patrick!'

Another branch. This time he climbed a series of limbs that rose like a spiral staircase. Now he was high above the earth. He seemed content and sat down in a fork that sagged beneath his weight. Then he looked out across the wheatbelt.

'Patrick, this is stupid.'

Moy guessed he was high enough to kill himself. He had no idea if this is what he had in mind, or whether he was just making a point. 'Are you gonna talk to me?'

Patrick looked down. 'I don't need you.'

'You can look after yourself, eh?'

'I didn't ask you to look after me.'

'I know.' He wanted to reach up, to hold him. Thought of climbing but realised he'd never get off the ground. 'That's quite an effort. You like climbing trees?'

Patrick looked down with disdain. 'I can keep going.'

'I know you can.' He waited a few minutes, looking up at the boy who was looking out towards impossible horizons. He wouldn't look down.

'I make stupid decisions,' Moy said.

Patrick looked down at him, as if to say, *I noticed.*

'I'm an idiot.'

'I don't *need* you.'

A few more minutes. It was as if the boy was welded to the tree.

'Right,' Moy said, realising. 'I'll be in the car then.' He turned and walked off.

Twenty minutes passed before the door opened and Patrick climbed in.

'Quite an effort,' Moy said.

No reply.

'Point taken.'

Patrick looked at him. 'That's nothing. I climbed a power pylon once.'

28

THE FOLLOWING DAY Moy received a phone call from the Port Louis police.

'Just wondering if you know anything about this body?' Detective Sergeant Susan Carey asked.

Doing the rounds, Moy guessed. He remembered her from the academy. A square-faced woman who topped every exam, ran fastest, asked the most questions. He cleared his throat and attempted to speak in clear, detached words. 'Ah...the body? Mangrove Point?'

'That's the one.'

'No, not yet.'

Then she asked if they had any missing persons, unsolved domestics, drug crops?

'We've got a body in a burnt house, but I'm still looking into that.'

'Well, our man still hasn't been claimed. We got the autopsy report back and it says he's been whacked on the back of the head with something flat. A shovel, or spade, perhaps?'

'Nasty.'

'A single fracture to the skull. And there was soil under his fingernails, and pine pollen in his hair and eyebrows.'

'No one like that reported missing here.'

He could feel her burrowing into his head. There was tension in his neck, and he used his fingers to soften his muscles. *Solve your own friggin' case. I've got my own problems. Tell me who the burnt woman is, where she came from, where the missing kid's hiding. Or buried.* 'Gotta go,' he said, tired of playing along.

He put his phone in his pocket and took a deep breath. There were a hundred thoughts trying to pierce the endless fog in his head, and none of them connected. All he could think was that he wanted to get away from Guilderton, its gravel footpaths and experimental roads. The smell of the police station, its faintly blue fluoro lights, piles of papers like gas bills, except they weren't. The lost, dead and dying. Screaming out for attention, like a blown globe or uncut lawn. Multiple jobs—dozens—but none of them he felt up to.

Fuck it, he thought.

'Patrick!'

THEY LEFT GUILDERTON behind. The grey streets and shop-fronts, the granite Anzac and the smell of burning wood; the café, with its plastic flowers and pipe loaves. As they drove, Moy chose to forget. Memories that filled every room of his house. Weeds in the garden and in the cracks in the driveway. 'It's a nice bit of country,' he said.

'Not many trees.'

He guessed this wasn't something a wheatbelt kid would say.

'They cleared them a hundred and fifty years ago.'

'I know.' The boy played with his seatbelt.

'But they couldn't get all the stumps. So after they'd planted the wheat someone invented a plough that would...'

'I know,' Patrick repeated, looking at him. 'The stump-jump plough. We went to this museum...'

The edges had crumbled so Moy drove in the middle. A fresh-water pipeline followed the gist of the road, stretching across valleys on a viaduct that looked rusted and weak. The steep hills were bare and rocky; the low slopes and plains yellow with wheat. Moy noticed that Patrick wasn't interested in the scenery. His eyes would move from his lap to the mid-distance, back to the dashboard, the radio, the clouds.

'This is Guilderton's water,' Moy said, indicating the pipeline.

Patrick looked at him, lost in a thought. 'Where's it come from?'

'A big reservoir, off to the north. The highest ground in the district.'

'Is there enough water?'

'I assume. It's not New York, is it? Six or seven thousand people.'

'Five thousand, eight hundred and eighty. It's on the sign as you come into town.'

Moy ran over a dead fox with a smear where its head had been. 'These little buildings are pump houses,' he said, indicating a small brick structure through which the pipe passed. 'There's one every few kilometres.'

Patrick looked at him again. 'But you said the reservoir was built on high ground. Why do they need pumps?'

'Maybe it's not high enough.'

'There's lots of pump houses.'

'There's a lot of water.'

'And a lot of gravity.'

Moy stopped to think. 'I'm starting to see you're a clever young man.'

Patrick studied the ripe wheat. 'Tom was smarter,' he said.

'Tom?'

'Don't be stupid, you know who Tom was.'

'Your brother?'

No reply.

'Was he older than you?'

166

'Yes.'

Moy was determined to take it slowly. 'Tell me about him.'

'What?'

'Tom. What was he like at school?'

'He used to teach me my tables. Dad said he had a photographic memory. You could take a list of words, as hard as you like, and put them in front of him. Maybe five or ten minutes later you could test him…a hundred per cent, every time.'

'That'd be handy for crosswords.'

Patrick stopped, thinking about what he was saying. 'He remembered all of Dad's phone numbers. Dad used to call him Teledex, but Tom got angry, so he stopped.'

There was a long pause. Moy was willing to wait. He watched an eagle searching for thermals or perhaps thinking about eating what was left of the fox. 'Sounds like you really got on with your brother?'

The reply took a few moments. 'Sometimes he was okay…other times he was a giant pain in the arse.'

'I suppose all brothers are.'

'Did you have a brother?'

'No. Just guessing. From what I've heard.'

A road-train thundered past. Moy held the wheel tightly, avoiding the edge, the gravel, the rollovers he'd seen, the flattened panels and crystals of glass in the dirt. 'He was a year older than you?'

Patrick shrugged.

'You don't know?'

'Of course I know. He was my brother.'

They passed close to a harvester busy on the edge of a paddock, its driver half-asleep at the wheel. Moy waved but he just sat forward, trying to work out who he was. 'I don't mean to be nosy.'

No reply.

'I know I shouldn't have taken you to your house. I just thought it would help. I just thought, the sooner we can work out…'

'Who I am?'

'Your family. It's strange. You talk to me, but you won't tell me anything.'

Patrick looked back in his lap.

'But if you just told me, I could help you. Your mum, your brother…your dad. Where was your dad?'

'I don't want to talk about him.'

'Why?'

'I don't.'

Moy realised he'd done it again. 'Fine, I can be your dad, for now.'

'You're not my dad,' the boy shot back. 'You're nothing like my dad.'

'How's that?'

'You said you wouldn't do this. You said you were sorry.'

'I was about to say *I can look after you*, for now. But at some point we've gotta sort this mess out.'

Silence; for a full minute, perhaps more, as Patrick turned his head and stared at the door handle.

'I just think you'd be happy if we could sort it all out,' Moy said.

But Patrick had retreated again.

A FEW KILOMETRES later they were inside Bundaleer Forest, the light and warmth of the day fading. The pencil-straight pines extended out in geometrically perfect rows, the bottom half of each tree shaved clean, its branches left to rot on the forest floor.

'This is the stuff they use for house frames,' Moy explained, driving slowly.

'It's spooky,' Patrick said, searching for the last bit of sun through the tree tops.

They spent an hour driving around. Moy found a wrecked car

but it was old, colonised by birds. He stopped at the rangers' station but no one had seen anything for weeks. At the top of a hill, he stopped, switched off the engine and sat listening. 'Hear it?'

'What?'

'Nothing. Listen, absolutely nothing.'

'You can't hear nothing.'

A crow followed the curve of the road and flew into the trees, disappearing into darkness. As it went, so did its cry, and the sound of its moving wings.

Patrick was looking up into the auditorium of man-made nature, along the rows, through the blocks of cold air between the trees. 'It smells like new furniture.'

'The pine oil,' Moy said.

They got out of the car, walked around and sat on the bonnet.

'You know, this is as far as you can get from Guilderton, without actually…'

'Escaping?' Patrick suggested.

'Come on, we'll see what you're like with a club.' He walked around to the boot, opened it and produced a two-iron and a bag of golf balls. 'You play?'

'No.'

He found a clear spot, produced a tee from his pocket, set up a ball and handed Patrick the club. 'Go on.'

'I can't.'

'Of course you can. Just give it a big whack.'

Patrick took the club, stood beside the ball and swung. He missed, but tried again, and again, eventually nicking the ball, which dribbled through the leaf litter before stopping a few metres away.

'Good shot,' Moy said. He took the club, placed another ball on the tee and stood beside it. 'Now, here are a few hints. Side on to the ball, thus far back. Hold the club further up, like so. Keep your eyes on the ball, extend all the way back and…' He swung, contacting the ball's sweet spot. It flew up, along the road, entered the forest and collected a tree trunk.

'Not bad,' Patrick said.

Moy handed him the club. He set up another ball and the boy got into position. Then he swung, and missed again. 'I'm rubbish.'

Moy knelt down and adjusted the boy's feet, turned his body to the correct angle, moved his hands and pushed his head down. 'Now, keep your eyes on the ball,' he said. 'It doesn't matter where it's going, just whether you can hit it.'

Patrick tried again. This time he hit the ball with a solid *thwack* and it went flying. It descended, landed on the road and rolled down the hill.

'Excellent,' Moy said. 'You're quick on the uptake. Want to try again?'

Forty-five minutes later the bag of balls was nearly empty; the afternoon becoming darker and colder. Patrick had hit nearly every ball. There were little white dots littered across the landscape.

'Do you want me to pick them up?' Patrick said.

'Don't worry. We can get more.' He reclaimed his club, teed up and stood in front of the ball moving his hips. 'It's all in your posture,' he said. 'You've just gotta stick your bum in, like this.' He stood straight, stretching his neck and sucking in his gut. Then he swung wide, missing the ball completely.

Patrick broke up. 'It's still there.'

'That's how *not* to do it.' Moy took the last ball from the bag, placed it on the broken tee and hit it to the far end of the forest. '*See.*'

They set off, following a different track. Piles of harvested timber sat on churned-up ground between forest and bush. This scrub dropped into a valley that seemed to stretch for miles. The track took them to the lowest point in the landscape, and a water-hole at the end of a creek. Moy drove as close as he could, then stopped. 'What d' you say?'

'What?' Patrick said.

'A swim?'

He wasn't sure. 'In there?'

'Why not?'

'Wouldn't it be full of…dead stuff?'

'Come on. This is our big adventure, isn't it?'

Patrick almost grinned. 'Yours, perhaps. It'll be freezing.'

Moy could tell that Patrick liked the idea, but wasn't sure about the logistics. 'There's no one for a million miles.' He got out and ran down the hill towards the waterhole. He was thinking of stripping as he went, throwing himself in and splashing about, but then thought better of it. Arriving at the water's edge, he slipped off his shoes and socks, pants and shirt. 'Come on.'

Patrick was walking down the hill towards him. 'You won't go in.'

'Wanna bet?'

Moy turned and walked into the water. Jesus. He stopped, eyes watering. He'd guessed it'd be cold, but not how cold. Still, he felt the boy's eyes on him and willed himself forward. He got up to his knees before he stopped. 'I'm not doin' it alone.'

Patrick was standing at the edge, the brown water lapping at his shoes.

'Come on.'

The boy thought about it, then took off his own shoes and socks. He stepped into the water; kept walking, up to his ankles, higher.

'You gonna take your gear off?' Moy said.

Patrick looked at Moy's bowling-ball belly and meaty arms; the hair across his chest and his small nipples.

'Well?' Moy asked.

He walked in further.

'Come on, take your pants off. I'm not lookin'.'

Patrick stopped, deciding.

'You don't wanna drive home in wet clothes.'

He turned and walked back to the muddy shore.

'Come on,' Moy said. He followed the boy out of the water, grabbed his shirt and tried to remove it.

'No!' Patrick said, pulling his shirt down, backing away.

Moy looked at him, confused. 'I just thought…don't you wanna come in?'

There was no reply.

'That's all I was doing.' He stopped, remembering. The bathroom door being locked, checked, locked again. Patrick's habit of doing up his top button, until he was told, 'You're gonna be hot like that.'

Patrick turned and headed back up to the car.

'You can just swim in your pants,' Moy called.

He reached the car and got in. Moy walked from the waterhole, gathering his shirt and slipping it back on, finding his shoes and socks, soaked brown by the lapping water.

On their way home, as the car glided along the empty road, as the sun spread itself out across the horizon, Patrick said, 'My mum…'

'Your mum?'

'I suppose she was burnt, in the fire?'

Moy took a deep breath. 'What makes you think—'

'That's enough.'

Moy drove on, waiting for an answer, a way out. 'You've already guessed, haven't you?'

Patrick returned to the mid-distance. They drove in silence until they arrived back in Guilderton.

Then Patrick looked at Moy and said, 'I'd like to thank you, for looking after me.'

29

MOY CLOSED THE door and turned to face the toilet. There was piss on the seat, dribbling down onto the floor, where it had formed a yellow veneer. He used a fistful of toilet paper to wipe it clean. He dropped his pants and sat down. Looked at the streaks of dried shit on the wall. 'Jesus.'

When he was finished he washed his hands using a wafer-thin slice of soap with a few greying pubic hairs embedded. Then he made his way out the front door, along the garden path to his car. 'So, are we ready?' he asked his father.

'I've been waiting.'

Moy looked at Patrick. 'How are your muscles this morning?'

'Okay, I guess.'

Moy had hired a twelve-foot trailer from the local BP. He'd spent the previous evening (as Patrick kept him supplied with coffee) loading it with bed-slats and boxes, drawers and a few pot plants. He'd loaded his two wardrobes, fridge and washing machine using a sack truck from work. When he'd finished he tied the whole lot down with a too-short rope that had come loose on the journey.

'The big day,' he said.

'What?' George replied.

'The prodigal son returns.'

'Who?'

'Me. Don't I get a welcome home? It's been a long time.'

George didn't know what he was talking about. 'What, you think I bought champagne?'

'Did you?'

'Christ…Where do we start?'

Moy loosened the wing-nuts on the tailgate. 'You're not doing anything,' he said.

'My arse. I'm not useless.'

'I didn't say you were, but I got it all on, so I can get it all off.'

He dropped the tailgate and unhooked the wire doors to the cage that surrounded the trailer. Then he used a board to make a ramp. 'How about you supervise?' he said to his dad. 'Give Patrick the small boxes and tell him where to put them. I'll take the big stuff.'

'Nonsense, I can help. My brain might be shrinking, but I've still got muscles.'

Moy opened the boot and retrieved the sack truck. 'I don't want anything broken, or strained. Let's just keep it simple.'

'Come on,' George said, shaking his head.

'Listen, Dad, now I'm back you can take it easy. That's the whole point, isn't it?'

'I thought it was so you could stop paying rent?'

'No, it's to help you. What's the point if you're gonna…' He stopped. 'You need to *listen*, Dad.'

'It's my house.'

'Ours.'

'My rules.'

'No.' Moy lifted the first box onto the sack truck. 'Compromises.'

'I'm not changing a thing. What's in that box?'

Moy read the words Patrick had scribbled on the top. 'Utensils.'

'In the kitchen.'

'Some of it we can work out for ourselves.'

'You asked.'

'Fine.' He turned to Patrick. 'Maybe you could start with the bed slats. Two at a time.' He pulled two lengths of wood from the trailer and balanced them in the boy's arms.

'The back bedroom,' George said, and Patrick walked down the drive, carefully avoiding a wind-chime hanging from the porch.

When he was gone George said, 'You never told me there was another kid.'

Moy loaded a second box. 'Where did you hear that?'

'I just did.'

He shook his head. 'It doesn't take long, does it?'

George didn't seem surprised. 'You're the one going around asking people.'

Moy wondered who: Rebecca Downey, Mrs Flamsteed? Perhaps Jason's wife or girlfriend. Any one of a dozen people who'd let something slip in the café, the Wombat Inn or Fred Hoyle's yoga group at the Institute.

'His name is Tom,' Moy said. 'Patrick won't tell me anything else.'

'Why don't you make him?'

'What, smack him around the head with a phone book?'

'You say, I need to know, and I need to know now.'

Moy adjusted the sack truck. 'It doesn't work like that.'

'Tell him if he doesn't help you'll send him to town, and they'll find a place for him to stay.'

'Dad...'

'What?'

'He's screwed up. We don't know what happened.'

'All the more reason.'

Moy studied his father's face, but couldn't work him out. 'His mother's dead.'

175

'So?'

'He knows we found her, in the house. Listen, if you're gonna live with him you'll have to show some compassion.'

George looked surprised. 'I do show compassion. Plenty of it.'

'Maybe this wasn't such a good idea.'

'You wanted to do it.'

They stared at each other. Eventually Moy said, 'I'm trying to think of you.'

'I'm all right.'

Another long pause.

'No, it's sensible,' George said. 'No point payin' for that place when there's room here.'

Patrick re-emerged from the house and returned to the trailer. He stood with his arms out, waiting for more slats. George loaded him up with another two. 'How you coping?'

'Fine.'

'Can you manage three?'

'Two'll do,' Moy said.

'He can manage three,' George insisted, taking another plank and placing it in the boy's arms. 'It'll make the job quicker, won't it, Patrick?'

'I suppose.'

'Off you go.'

Moy followed him in with his first load of boxes. 'If there's anything George says that you're not happy about, you tell him… or me.'

'I can carry three.'

'Not just that. Anything. Sometimes he's pig-headed.'

'I'm okay.'

Moy unloaded and returned to the trailer. 'That toilet of yours,' he said to his father.

'What?'

'How often do you clean it?'

'Often enough.'

'Books?' He loaded another four boxes onto the sack truck.

'The lounge. There's plenty of room on my shelves. What's wrong with my toilet?'

'Listen, you've got to—'

'No one's ever got sick from a toilet.' He shook his head. 'It's just those dirty bastards coughing all over you in the shops. Or those fuckin' Asians, not washing their hands after they have a bog.'

'You haven't even got soap.'

'Listen, I've been quite happy here these last thirty years.'

'Okay.'

'Doing things my way.'

'Sorry.'

Patrick re-emerged and they fell silent. George loaded him with the last three slats. 'See, hardly heavy now, are they?' He looked at his son.

'No.' The boy turned and walked off.

'As long as you don't mind if I...standardise things,' Moy said.

'Standardise?'

'Like soap, clean towels.'

Patrick looked back at them.

'Go about your business,' George called, returning to his son. 'I don't care if you have fresh towels every morning, and flowers, and ironed hankies...just don't go on about it.'

Patrick came out and took a heavy box from George, carried it a few metres up the driveway and stopped to rest. When he picked it up it slipped from his fingers and fell with the muffled tinkle of breaking glass. He looked at George, but the old man hadn't noticed. He picked it up again, climbed the three steps onto the verandah and dropped it again, knocking over a pot of petunias. It broke and the seedlings scattered across the concrete. He put the box down.

'What are you up to?' George said, hobbling up the drive onto the verandah, followed by his son. He stood looking at the small plants, the shards of broken pot and the soil. 'Bloody hell.' He bent over and picked up a petunia.

'I didn't mean to,' Patrick said.

'How did you manage…?'

'He didn't mean to, Dad.'

George looked at the small figure, his hands clenched. 'If it was too heavy, you should've said.'

'I was going okay until I tripped.'

George shook his head and collected the seedlings in his palm before dropping them in disgust.

Patrick waited for him to explode. 'I can help fix it. I saw some pots out the back.'

'What's the good of that? Once the air gets to them roots…'

'I'll buy you another punnet,' Moy said.

George took a deep breath to calm himself. 'Right, inside. You can wash up.'

'He didn't mean to,' Moy repeated.

But George just glared at the boy. '*Now.*'

AFTER LUNCH, WITH the trailer unpacked and both bedrooms full of boxes, Moy went to the shed and found another pot and a pair of old trowels. With Patrick's help he scraped the soil from the tiles and filled the pot. As they worked he said, 'You know, he will come good.'

Patrick just looked at him, unsure. 'I didn't mean to do it.'

'Of course not. Old people just explode, like volcanoes.'

They soaked the soil with water from a bucket. 'If he gives you trouble just think: you poor old man, I understand. Then walk away, wait an hour or so, go back and see how he's going.'

'Does that work?'

'Mostly. Sometimes he needs a day or two.'

Moy made a hole with his finger, planted the first petunia

and compacted the soil. 'Go on.' He handed one to Patrick, who repeated the process.

'Whatever you do, don't start an argument. He'll just get his back up.'

Patrick moved on to his second and third seedling. 'Was he like this when you were a kid?'

'Worse. He used to have a very short temper. Once, I remember, something happened in the traffic—someone cut him off, or didn't indicate. So there he was, flashing his lights, tailgating him.'

Patrick was almost laughing. Moy knew he couldn't stop now, even if he had run out of story. 'So, Dad followed him all the way to Port Louis.'

'Port Louis?'

'Yes, just cursing him. *You bastard! Pull over!* And when this fella finally stopped…'

'What happened?'

'He storms out of the car, and Mum's saying, George, get back in, don't be so stupid.'

Patrick was sitting forward, the last petunia clutched in his hand. 'Your mum?'

'So Dad marches forward and it's this little old lady. And she says, have you been following me? Like that. *Have you been following me?*'

Patrick started laughing.

'And Dad says, Oh no, Missus, I's just comin' back from the shops.'

Patrick made a hole and put the last petunia in. He pressed around it with his fingers and Moy watered the flowers. 'There, finished,' he said, standing, looking at the seedlings. 'As good as new.'

Patrick stood next to him. 'You think they'll survive?'

'Of course. Now I'm gonna sweep out the trailer. How about you put on the kettle and make me and Grandpa a cup of tea?'

30

THE NEXT MORNING, the first they were all together in George's Clyde Street house, Moy was up early sitting in his bedroom at his computer. He'd closed his dad's door, put on the kettle and made a coffee. Then came the dishes, scrubbed, scalded and put away. He'd returned to his room, stopping and surveying the boxes, the names of the products crossed out and relabelled with *BM's DVDs*; *my clothes*; *old elec equip*.

He'd spent half an hour setting up his computer on a desk made from the planks and bricks of his old bookcase. Started his old machine, connected to the internet and checked his emails. Nothing much, just work. Stuff (he guessed) a better cop would be onto straight away—reports, requests—as well as spam about cheap hotels and a photo of seventeen nuns in a mini.

In the end he'd drifted back to the news: some footballer out three weeks with a hamstring, a new tax on cigarettes, a boy dead after waiting fifty-seven minutes for an ambulance.

He clicked onto the story and studied the boy's face: freckles, and fine black rings around his pupils. The child, still in his pyjamas, was sitting beside his bed, playing with toys.

He knew when I needed a hug and I knew when he did, his mother had said.

Moy felt unable to take his eyes from the boy's face.

A spokesman for the ambulance service. *We received a call at 12.47 and the first unit was dispatched two minutes later.*

Moy tried to make out what the boy was playing with. It was a plane, two wings and a broken propeller.

The address we were given was Forbes Avenue, but in the rush to respond our paramedics read this as Forbes Street.

Missing wheels.

By the time they'd realised their mistake it was 1.07, and by then, I believe, the parents had rung a second time.

And a red lump which, he supposed, was the pilot.

We extend our sincere apologies to the family. Both paramedics have been stood down pending the results of an investigation.

The mother explaining how she tried, for thirty or forty minutes, to get a ball of plasticine out of her son's throat. How she patted his back and squeezed his chest, but he kept turning blue.

Moy looked out of the window. The blinds were half-closed and the early morning was dark, split into small Cartesian moments. The blue and white of the sky pulsed with energy. He sipped his coffee and wondered how many people it would happen to again today. A hundred, a thousand?

'Good morning,' Patrick said, appearing behind him.

Moy clicked off the screen, and turned. 'Hey, Patrick, sleep okay?'

'Sort of.' He winced, moving forward. 'I think I heard George snoring.'

'That's something you'll have to get used to. Along with several other…issues.'

'Like what?'

But before Moy could provide the details his phone rang. It

was Gary Wright. 'This place is turning into a hive of excitement,' he said.

Moy took a moment. 'Please tell me, nothing major?'

'I don't think…but you better take a look.'

THEY DROVE PAST Civic Park, along Creek Street and turned onto Dutton Street. Halfway along there was an empty block with a tall sculpture sitting in the middle of weedy ground. It was granite, sitting on a plinth: a single stem of ripe wheat in the shape of a man, a farmer with broad shoulders and a sort of earless, mouthless head. And growing from the head, ram's horns, turning in concentric circles that (a plaque explained) represented the rhythm of the seasons, the circle of life. 'It's called *The Australian Farmer*,' Moy said.

'What is it?' Patrick asked.

'It's like a…shaft of wheat, with a head.'

'Why?'

Moy shrugged. 'Symbolic.' He slowed past it. 'The council wanted something to attract the tourists, but I'm not sure it worked. I've never actually seen anyone looking at it.'

'It's ugly.'

'Everyone wanted a new toilet in Civic Park, but this is what they got.'

When they arrived at the end of Dutton Street, Bryce King was waiting for them. There were no homes this far along, just piles of rubbish and rubble that locals had dumped. Weeds and grass had grown up through most of it but there was one pile, part broken furniture and clothes, part ash, that looked fresh. Moy and Patrick got out and greeted the constable.

'Someone's had a bonfire,' King said, pointing.

'Who found it?' Moy asked.

'Fella down the road. I asked him, he said it wasn't there last week.'

182

Moy added the days. 'So, he reckons last Tuesday, Wednesday?'

'About then.'

'Exactly?'

'He couldn't say.'

Patrick stepped forward, staring at the pile.

'What is it?' Moy said.

Both men watched as he walked forward.

'Patrick?'

No reply.

Patrick approached what was left of the partly burnt junk. When he reached it he stopped, knelt down, held the arm of a half-burnt jumper and pulled it from the pile.

'What is it?' Moy asked, coming up behind him.

'It's mine.'

The arm was red and green. Mud-soaked. There was a shoulder, and part of the chest, but the rest was singed or burned away.

'It's our gear,' Patrick said, looking at the pile. 'See, that's Tom's parka.' He indicated a mostly melted nylon jacket draped over a cricket bat. It had burned from the inside out, leaving a glazed shell. There were a few toys, charred shoes, the burnt-out spines of several books, a soccer ball with its side split open and a small tub of Lego, its contents melted into a chromatic glob.

'Anything you can salvage?' Moy asked, but Patrick didn't reply. He stood up, white-faced, and stepped back from the pile. Then he sat down on a lump of old concrete.

Moy picked up a stick, stepped into what was left of the fire and started moving the objects about.

Meanwhile, Bryce King came up behind Patrick. 'Don't worry about that lot, we can get you new stuff.'

Moy rolled the soccer ball through the ashes. He noticed some writing on it. Leaned forward, wiped the ash and read the words *Patrick Barnes*. He looked up at him. At last. Not that it made any difference. All of the hard work had already been done.

'You don't want to have a look?'

Silent headshake.

A bag of marbles, intact; a fishing reel, the line and rocker cover melted; a CD, sitting between two partly burnt books, protected: *J. S. Bach, Preludes and Fugues.* Turning to Patrick, he held it up. 'You've got good taste.'

Patrick stood up, came over and took it from him.

'Yours?'

'Dad's. He left it behind when...'

Moy wanted to ask, but stopped himself. 'You like Bach?'

'Yeah...Mozart's better.' Patrick looked at the pile. 'He's in there somewhere.'

Moy and Patrick Barnes drove back towards town, past the Australian Farmer, unclipped yards smelling of wattle and wood fires and a rubbish truck labouring along Jenner Street. As a Bach prelude played, Patrick sat with his eyes closed, tapping out a musical pulse on his knee.

'Did Dad play music?' Moy asked.

'No.'

'Was that his fishing reel?'

'Yeah...he bought it, and said he was gonna take us and he never did.'

Moy throttled back, waiting.

'I wasn't that interested anyway.'

'I suppose you'd have to live somewhere near an ocean, wouldn't you?'

'We did.'

'Really?' He waited for a name. 'Where, Port Louis or somewhere?'

Silence, as they continued along the damp road. Patrick seemed to think something, then dismiss it. 'Anyway, Dad went away...'

As seconds, and minutes passed.

'Why was that?'

'Mum didn't say. I suppose he had to.' He looked at Moy to confirm this.

'He probably did.'

'Why do you think?'

'Work, maybe?'

Patrick looked forward. 'Maybe.'

The notes tumbled faster and faster, spilling out of the window. Patrick just kept staring into the distance, trying to find other reasons.

31

THEY WENT HOME for a late breakfast. George acted as a sort of housemaid, filling their bowls with cornflakes, bran, wheat germ, a handful of fruit medley. As Patrick watched him work, he bit his lip; not only was it inedible, but there was so much of it. George covered his creations with milk and looked at Patrick. 'Sugar?'

'Yes, please.'

He placed the bowl in front of him. 'There you go.'

'Thanks.'

Moy had got used to his father's concoction. He'd learned to hold his breath, chew with vigour and swallow fast. 'Thanks,' he said to George, taking his own bowl.

Patrick, sitting on his hands, stared at the small mountain of cereal. George looked at him. 'What's wrong?'

'I don't know if I can eat it all.'

'You haven't even tried.'

He dug down to the cornflakes, collected a spoonful and began. Meanwhile, George wiped his lips with the back of his hand. 'You don't talk much,' he said.

'Dad,' Moy warned.

'You always feel better when you talk…when you share things. It's the way people work, isn't it?'

Patrick just looked at him, and tackled the bran.

'Dad, can't we just eat our breakfast?' Moy asked.

'Just making conversation.'

George opened a crossword book, one of a dozen or more on the table. He took a minute to study a clue. '*Lighter than air*?' he said.

'Hydrogen,' Moy replied.

'Yes.' He smiled, writing down the letters and looking back at Patrick. 'For instance, you never mention your father much.'

'*Dad.*'

Patrick moved the sultanas to the side of the bowl. He looked up at the old man.

'What sort of job did he do?' George asked.

Patrick stared at him, unsure. Eventually he said, 'He was a designer.'

'What did he design?'

'Brochures…stuff you get in the mail. Before they were printed.'

Moy finished his cereal, and studied Patrick's face.

'Like Target? K-Mart?' George asked.

'I suppose.'

George sat back in his chair, pleased with himself. 'That sounds very interesting.'

'He hated it.'

'Oh?'

'He wanted to do something else, but there was nothing he could do. He tried mowing lawns for a while but couldn't make any money.' He searched his breakfast for more cornflakes.

'And where did you live?' George asked, looking sideways at his son.

'In the house…that burned down.'

'No, before that.'

Patrick realised what was going on, sat back and glared at George.

'When you lived with your dad?' George continued. 'Was that before you came to Guilderton?'

Patrick swallowed the last of the cereal he was willing to eat. 'What about your dad?' he dared.

'Don't worry about my dad.'

'Or your grandad? Wasn't that Daniel?'

'I showed him the photo,' Moy said to his father.

George shuffled off, muttering. There were a couple of minutes of distant huffing before he returned, and handed something to Patrick. 'This is the only other photo the photographer took that day,' he said, as if attempting to prove that family stories, no matter how difficult, were always worth telling.

Patrick studied the backdrop of scrub and drought-baked hills. 'That's Daniel Moy,' he said. 'With…?'

'With his arm around the photographer's son,' George managed. 'I always thought it was curious. Daniel had just threatened the photographer and his son, that boy, with a knife. Then he'd forced them to drive back to Cambrai in their own cart.'

'So why is Daniel standing with the boy?'

George leaned back. 'Well, this is how my father told it,' he said. 'As they drove back, Daniel started talking about Elizabeth. How she could make the sweetest soup with nothing more than turnips and sheep shanks; how she was pitch perfect, and could sing every song in the key the composer had intended; how she could make you feel happy, just by looking at you, by smiling, by saying, it's all just a bit of bother, isn't it, Dad?'

Patrick studied the two faces.

'And after all that,' George continued, 'Daniel just sat there, his knife in his hand, staring at the floor of the cart. Then he said to the boy, what's your name, son? and the boy said, William, sir. Then Daniel asked him if he wanted to be a photographer, like his father, and he said, perhaps…perhaps a policeman. Then, all of a sudden,' George continued, 'Daniel stood up and threw his knife into the bushes. I'm sorry, he said. Turn around and head back. It was a stupid thing to do. But the photographer said, no, I'll take your photo. I'm sorry your girl's gone. And he flicked the reins, and they started off again.'

Then George told him how Daniel, the photographer and the photographer's son had stopped for a rest on the way to Cambrai. How they'd sat on a rock, and drunk water from a canteen, before the photographer suggested a picture. 'The thing is, Patrick, my father once told me, just as this photo was being taken the photographer was thinking of asking a favour of Daniel Moy.'

'A favour?'

'Yes. When William wasn't listening, the photographer said, Mr Moy, I feel, already, I can trust you. And Grandad said, you do do you? Why's that? And the photographer replied, only a very good parent would do what you've done.'

Patrick was waiting, hanging off every word.

'Then the photographer said, Mr Moy, I have to travel to Sydney, for four or five weeks, and I need someone to look after William.'

Patrick sat forward. 'But Daniel had just had a knife to William's throat?'

'True. But that's what the photographer had come to think of Daniel, in those few hours. As they went they talked, and they struck up a bond. I suppose they discussed family and farming and photography and how hard it was to make a living. And then—they were mates. One minute there was a knife, and the next, mates.'

'And did he agree to look after him?'

'Of course. The photographer said, in return, I'll take all the photos you want.'

'What happened then?'

'Well, no one likes to tell the whole story. Do they, Patrick?'

32

MOY DROVE BACK to work, past the Bryan Moroney Public Pool and what was left of Klinger's old service station. He could still remember pulling up as a child. George, cigarette in hand, getting out to fill their car. Some sunburnt teenager would pop the bonnet, check the oil and ask if he wanted a top-up. And George would drag on his Winfield and say, 'Leave it, I haven't got time.'

He slowed past the Jack Dawes Crèche and Kindergarten.

Yes, my God, it is, he thought, studying the man in work pants and black boots, a windcheater pulled over his uniform. He was talking to a much younger woman who was leaning against a car, laughing.

Jason, you dirty bastard.

He slowed and pulled up on the opposite side of the road. Then he killed the engine and slipped down into his seat, watching. The girl stood up and crossed her arms. She said something and playfully pushed him. He pretended to fall back before holding her shoulder. She smiled. Looked around. Kissed him. Then he dropped his head and whispered something to her.

Soon it was all over. Perhaps it was the epilogue to a secret lunch at the teacher's house. Perhaps they'd been alone together in the kindy, swapping saliva under a Dorothy the Dinosaur poster. Either way, Jason Laing held her arm, but stopped himself from kissing her again, perhaps remembering the wife and kid and the mortgage he had no intention of repaying. He got into his car and drove off and the girl went back inside the kindy.

And Moy remembered, just as clearly as the smell of fifty-fifty petrol, how quickly the love faded. How, in the end, it was sacrificed to rates and early starts, lawns mowed and gutters cleaned.

He drove back to work and settled behind his desk. He studied the lumps of Blu Tack where his photo had been and listened to the thud of a football from the primary school oval. Someone asking Gary for an application for a gun licence. A kettle boiling. He massaged his forehead, took hold of his mouse and started navigating through the police database.

HELEN JANE BARNES
BORN 9/7/1974
AUSTEN JAMES BARNES
BORN 10/6/1971
MARRIED 1/10/2001
ISSUE 2
THOMAS JAMES BARNES 3/11/2003
PATRICK JAMES BARNES 17/4/2004
CALLOUT FOR DOMESTIC DISTURBANCE. NO ACTION TAKEN.

That was it. No record of parents or grandparents, brothers, sisters, uncles or aunts. It was as though they had just appeared, lived some sort of secret life, moved into the mouse-infested shack on the edge of town, pissed someone off, and suffered. Try as he might, Moy still couldn't put meat on their bones, dress them, arrange them and move them through the world. They were phantoms, living on the fringes of a town where no one kept secrets for long.

Constable Laing came into the office, placed some files on the desk and looked at Moy. 'You look tired.'

'Not half as tired as you.'

'What do you mean?'

Moy shrugged. 'You had a job down the kindergarten?'

'So?'

'Just sayin'…you look tired.'

'You watchin' me?'

'Just happened to be driving past.'

Laing waited. 'Community relations.'

'Yeah.'

'What?'

Moy looked up. 'None of my business.'

'*What?*'

'It's not too late…'

'Say it.'

'Think what you're risking.'

Laing looked as if he was biting back a retort. He said, 'Detective Sergeant, you know how hard it is to get the whole story.'

'Yeah?'

'The life of a country copper.'

'How's that?'

'Lot of dust, little bit of justice. It's not so much the law, is it? More a sort of compromise, between the could and the should. You know?' He almost winked. 'What we do, and what we write in that bullshit.' He indicated the files. 'You gotta work out what's important, Detective.' Waving a finger, he drifted from the room.

Moy stopped to think. Had he just been put in his place? *I'm the detective.* He wondered whether he should call him back in, dress him down. He opened his desk drawer and found the kids' book stashed at the back. *Mr Slow.* He leafed through. New Year's before he'd opened his presents. Easter before he'd written his thank-you notes. Laing had given it to him as a birthday present. With a cake, in the staff room, with everyone gathered around. They'd all laughed. He'd laughed along. But he wondered now, was this really what they thought of him? Later, a copy of *Mr Forgetful*. But that was somewhere in the mess at home.

Respect. He'd had it in town. But maybe this is what his colleagues thought of him now. He looked at Mr Slow, his big white moustache and yellow nose, and felt a pang of recognition.

MOY CAME AROUND the back. He tripped on a bag of fertiliser and walked past the kitchen window. He heard voices from inside the house. 'Thirty years, maybe,' George was saying. 'No guarantee it'll work anymore.'

'Can we try?' Patrick asked.

Moy stopped, and looked in the window. He could see that his father had cleared the kitchen table, fetched his old train set from the shed, and set it up on the dining table.

'Perhaps you could be an engineer,' Moy heard George say.

'No,' Patrick replied.

'You've got your civil engineers, who make bridges and roads, chemical engineers...petrol and the like.'

'I wouldn't be smart enough,' Patrick said.

'Report card no good, eh?'

Moy could see how Patrick was looking at George. He was fascinated how the two interacted, how they ebbed and flowed, talked over each other, waited, laughed.

'Or maybe a pilot?' George said.

Moy could see the detail of their bodies, and clothes, highlighted by the glare off the venetian blinds.

'No? What about a copper?'

'That'd be okay, I guess.'

'A detective?'

'No, the ones with the dogs. Did you know they get to keep

them? Take them home…and when the dog's too old, they live with them.'

'No?'

Patrick had finished the track: an elongated oval, stretching a half-inch or so over the edge of the table. He took the tunnel, wiped it down and positioned it next to George. Then he started with the legless, headless farm animals, allowing them to graze the cracked melamine. Every animal was dusted, wiped and positioned carefully. Spots were tested and rejected; angles considered; distances varied.

'Or maybe you could be a designer?' George continued. 'Like your dad.'

Patrick didn't look up from his menagerie. 'Dad always said, you learn the job in a month and then you just keep repeating it for the next thirty years.'

George shrugged. 'That's most jobs. Farming, for instance. Once someone shows you how to vaccinate a lamb…or fill a seed box. Doesn't mean it's not worth doing. You like eating bread, don't you?'

'But some jobs are different.'

'How?'

'Farmers get to see things grow, which is kind of cool.'

'Cool?'

'Yeah…but when you get a brochure, you look at it once, then you put it in the bin.'

Moy smiled. It was like watching a couple of kids play. His father, he sensed, had allowed himself to become happy, almost.

'So Dad eventually threw it in?' George asked.

Patrick frowned. 'Threw it in?'

'Gave it up? Quit?'

'No.'

'But what about when you moved?'

Patrick took a few moments. 'He didn't come with us.'

'Ah.'

'Coming to Guilderton, that was Mum's idea.'

Moy tapped on the window. 'Looks like you two are having fun?' he said. Then he came inside, and stood looking at the evolving diorama. 'Bloody hell, where did you find that?' he asked, leaning against a cabinet that still displayed the best of his mum's crockery.

'I don't throw nothin',' George explained.

'I know,' Moy replied. 'Good to see you two getting along.'

'He's no trouble.'

'Best to keep busy, isn't it, Patrick?' Moy asked.

The boy looked up at him.

'Patrick Barnes.' Moy stepped forward, pulled out a chair and sat down. 'The funny thing is, you've got the same middle name as me: James.'

Patrick's jaw tightened, and he played with the trees.

'And the same as your brother, and father…Austen.'

Patrick placed his hands in his lap.

'Austen James Barnes. And your mum, Helen, but you've already told me that.'

'What's your point?' George said.

'Nothing. Just saying, I managed to find out. Bit of muckin' around…but I managed to find out.' He stared at the boy. 'Patrick?'

'What?'

'You could've saved me a lot of time.'

'Bart,' George said.

'I told you,' Patrick shouted.

'Not enough to help you. See, that's the thing. You want me to find out where Tom—'

'Bart!' George insisted.

'Dad, thanks.'

'Tom's gone,' Patrick said.

'Gone?'

'It's too late. Whatever I say now, it doesn't matter.'

195

'It's not too late.'

'It is.'

'How do you know?'

'He wouldn't have kept him for that long.'

'Who?'

'The man…the men.'

'Why?'

'Cos I got out, and ran away, and he said if I told anyone he'd kill my family…'

'He? Who's he?'

'The man in the car…'

Moy took a moment, dissecting Patrick's words, looking for something tangible. 'You got out, and ran away?'

Patrick spoke slowly, looking at the ground, remembering. 'The shed had a dirt floor, and there was a little bit of light coming in, through the roof.'

Moy waited, silently.

'I could hear pigs.'

Scraps of information. Moy willed the boy to speak, to say something specific, to pinpoint the geography.

'I remember, I moved close to Tom and asked him what he thought the man had done to Mum.'

'And what did Tom say?'

'He said she'd be okay. I said, but he hit her. He just told me to be quiet.'

There was a short pause. 'What was in the shed?' Moy asked.

'Bags…grain, fertiliser. Shovels and spades in an old chest. I crawled to the door and pushed it but it was locked. So I went back to Tom and he said, we've gotta get out.'

Moy and George were watching the boy.

'So it was my fault.' And he looked at Moy. 'My fault we haven't found him…that he's…'

'What?' Moy asked.

196

'Dead. That he's dead. That everyone's dead—Mum, Tom—that everyone's...' He trailed off. George put his hand over the boy's, held it, squeezed it, and felt the plastic shape.

'The more you tell me...' Moy continued.

'I have.'

'Like where you're from, and why you came here.'

Patrick reclaimed his hand.

'There's a lot of missing information,' Moy continued. 'The Barnes family is a mystery. But you, you could tell me why.'

'I shouldn't have run off,' Patrick repeated. 'Tom told me to. I didn't know what to do, I just kept running. And when I went back, later, he wasn't there.'

'The shed?'

'Yes, on the farm, with the pigs. See, he came to get Tom, because I ran away. He warned me...I should've...' He looked up. 'That's when I came back to town...'

Patrick stood up and bolted, knocking over his chair as he ran from the room. Moy looked out of the window and saw him going into the shed.

'What's all that about?' George asked.

'I'm sick of waiting.'

George moved in his chair, shook his head and sighed. 'I just about had him talking.'

'What?'

'Why his dad didn't come with them, when they came here.' He plugged in the transformer, connected the wires to the contacts, switched it on and listened as it buzzed. 'Thirty years...sounds like new.'

'He didn't say?'

'No.'

George carefully lowered one of the locomotives onto the track.

'I thought if I made him face up to it,' Moy said.

'I think you were right before. You're just gonna muck him up

197

even more.' He adjusted the current and the loco moved off. 'Look at that.'

'Great.'

'Go out and see him. Tell him the train's workin'.'

Moy followed the loco's progress around the tracks. It jumped and almost came off at a bad join. But then kept going. 'Used to seem bigger,' he said.

'Go on.'

Moy went out, across the yard of fat hen and wild radish, into the dark shed. He looked at Patrick. 'You okay?'

No reply.

'George has got your train going.'

The boy looked up. 'I know.'

'Come and have a look.'

Patrick sat, undecided.

'I've done it again,' Moy said.

Patrick wiped his nose on the back of his hand and said, 'What?'

'You know…misjudged.'

'What?'

'My…parenting skills.'

Patrick scowled at the choice of words, but let it go. 'I can't look you up on a computer,' he said.

'I know.'

They could hear the buzz of the loco from inside the house. Patrick smiled. 'He wanted to do it.'

'Yeah, nothing changes. Like when he first put it together… There's me: Dad, can I have a go? *In a minute, son, I gotta make sure it works.*'

Patrick laughed.

'*Yer muck around, it'll just blow up.* And me: Dad…?'

'*Dad?*' Patrick sang.

'*Dad, can I have a go?*'

'*Shut up, son.*'

'Y'muck around, it'll just blow up.'
And from inside the house: 'You two comin' in or not?'
As they both tried to stop laughing.

33

AGAIN. ONE, TWO, three a.m. Hours of rolling from side to side, face down, sweating. Eyelids clenched. Face sore with the effort. Rug between his knees, no rug, window open, closed. Nothing. Just a clear, waking mind, and Charlie, buried at the bottom of the bed-sheets.

Come out, he said. I gotta make the bed.

Charlie, Megan echoed, coming into the room. I've got to leave in seven minutes and you're still in your jarmas. Turning her gaze to Moy. He's still in his pyjamas.

I know, dear, I'm trying.

Charlie, she shouted. Now! She removed his sheets. What happens if you're late?

Charlie sat up. I don't want to go.

You're going. Fiddling with a pearl earring.

It's boring.

So what?

Can't I stay home?

Who's gonna look after you?

He looked at his father.

I've got an afternoon shift, Moy said.

Till then?

No.

Till lunch?

No, Megan added, putting her hair in a tie. Now, get your stuff.

Charlie kept looking at his dad.

Well, maybe a few hours, Moy said.

Megan looked at him. He's booked in for the day. We've still got to pay.

I know, but just for a few hours.

She shook her head. Fuck.

What?

After she was gone, Charlie sat on the lounge eating chips, kicking his feet in the beanbag and smiling. Thanks, Dad.

Eleven o' clock, okay?

Twelve? Lunch? We can make omelettes.

Moy stood looking out the window. He studied the paling fence, coming away from its frame, hanging as if just about to fall, although it had been that way for years. The shed door moving in the breeze, catching in the grass. Walking out to the dining-lounge, he sat in George's chair. An old recliner; the foot-rest broken years ago. It was covered with a towel that smelt of old farts.

After sitting for a few moments he said, 'What's the point?'

He stood up, walked into the laundry, found the spray-on cleaner and went into the bathroom. Then he set to the toilet, cleaning the bowl with a shit-flecked brush, wetting the sponge and wiping every square inch of ceramic. He flushed. Exchanged the sponge for a new one and started on the sink.

George stormed out of his room. 'What are you doing?'

'What's it look like?'

'You woke me.' He stopped, staring. 'I'm not gonna have this shit going on.'

'Sorry.'

'You haven't heard a word I've said, have yer?'

'What?'

'This is my place.'

Moy's fingers were on the trigger of the spray bottle. '*Our* place,' he said.

'Bullshit…mine.'

'If it's yours, you clean it, buy your own food, drive yourself to the doctor.'

'Been doin' it for fifty years.'

'Don't,' Patrick said, coming out of his room.

'You'll turn this into a nursing home,' George shouted.

'George,' Patrick insisted.

'Keep out of it.'

'You don't want a nursing home?' Moy asked. 'You want a hovel, you want—'

'I don't care about—'

'Stop!' Patrick called, stepping between them.

There was a short pause. 'You two argue about everything. It's not like anything's that bad, is it?'

They both looked at him.

'It's not like anyone's…gone.'

'What's it…four-twenty?' George asked his son.

'I couldn't sleep.'

He shook his head and returned to his room. Moy looked at the boy. 'It's either this or stare at the ceiling.'

Patrick left him alone, stripped back to a few basic fears, confused about how he should carry on. Eventually he stood, went into the kitchen and made a coffee. Returning to his room, he sat down and started working. A flick of his hand and the coffee tumbled, spilling over a pile of manila folders containing reports and photos, statements and marked-up maps. Some of it flowed under the keyboard, and over the edge of the plank onto the carpet.

'Shit,' he said, standing, feeling the coffee on his legs. Darting into the bathroom, he grabbed a couple of towels and started blotting up around his improvised desk.

There was no space on his bedroom floor so he went into the hallway. He opened the folders and, one by one, took out the sheets, dried them off and lined them up on the floor. After he'd done about a dozen documents, Patrick appeared. 'Can I help?'

'Could you keep doing this? Most of them are just wet around the edges. It won't take long.'

He returned to his bedroom, finished cleaning up and got dressed. Then he heard the boy take a sharp breath. There was silence, small feet running down the hallway, the fly-door slamming. He went into the hall and stood looking at the sheets of paper, some already dry, scalloped around the edges. One was sitting by itself in the middle of the hallway. Picking it up, he looked at the face of the man who'd washed up at Mangrove Point.

He folded the sheet in half, walked down the hall and from the house. 'Patrick?' he called, as he stood on the porch.

No reply.

'Patrick?'

He noticed the shed door was ajar. Jumping down he walked slowly through the ankle-high grass. 'Patrick?' He went inside, climbed over a fallen bike and stood staring into the corner. 'You okay?'

The boy had finished crying but was taking long, difficult breaths.

'Watch for spiders,' said Moy. 'You still upset?'

'No.'

'I wondered what had happened.'

'Nothing's happened.'

He sat beside him. The iron bit into his back so he leaned forward, took the folded sheet and opened it out. 'Maybe you know this fella?'

Patrick studied the face. 'No.'

'You sure?'

He grabbed the sheet, screwed it up and threw it across the shed. Moy just waited, looking at him.

'What?' Patrick asked.

'Should I leave you alone?'

Shed silence. Objects still, rusted and gathering dust. No breeze. Warm air rising, encountering the roof and turning down in a kero-scented convection. Patrick said, 'He was the man who came to our house.'

'When was that?'

'That morning.'

'The day of the fire?'

Patrick stretched out his legs and sat back. 'He came back, and me and Tom had to run.'

He told Moy about the figure in the hallway, the pushing and shoving.

'It was him.' He pointed to the piece of paper. 'He was shouting at Mum, and Mum was shouting back, and Tom tried to help.' He stopped, staring at the floor.

'I bet you were scared. This fella…he was violent?'

'He hit her, and she fell over, and her head…I screamed at him, I said, leave us alone, but he just stood there, looking at me.'

'And what about Tom?'

'He was sitting on the floor.' He looked at Moy pleadingly. 'The man…I hit him but he just pushed me away and I fell down too. Then he knelt down, looking at Mum.'

'Like he was checking if she was okay?'

'He kept feeling her neck and her hands.'

'What, her pulse maybe?' Moy asked, holding his wrist.

'I think…perhaps. Then he stood up and looked at us, like he was angry. Tom said, you better not have hurt her, and he just shouted, shut up, like that, over and over.'

There was a long pause as the boy got his breath.

George came out onto the porch and called, 'Bart, where are you?'

Moy waited, then heard his father go back inside.

'He was angry, Bart. I thought he was going to…Then Tom said, run, and we both stood up and ran out of the house. He came after us but he wasn't that fast. We went into the bush and just kept running until we couldn't go any further. So we stopped…'

Moy was waiting patiently. 'So you ran all the way to town?'

No reply.

'This must have been early?'

'It was. We were running through the bush and it was hard to see but Tom knew the path really well.'

'So you made it to the laneway?'

Nothing.

Moy shrugged. 'That's enough for now, eh?'

Patrick just looked at him. 'We were so scared she might not get up.'

34

MOY WENT DOWN to Mango Meats but Justin Davids was off on a delivery, so to fill the time he worked the shops again. He walked down Ayr Street, stopping to look in store windows. The Guilderton Retravision had 42-inch plasmas, surround sound, near cost, easy finance. One was showing an old black-and-white movie: a boat load of survivors floating in the Atlantic, as the radio operator, eyes ablaze, told the captain he hadn't had time to put out an SOS.

Must go, he thought, pulling himself away from the window, wanting to see how it ended. They would be saved, he guessed, but not before the most problematic passengers were strangled or drowned. Then there would be room for the other survivors. Neat, simple justice. The sort that always seemed to elude him.

He went into the store, talked to the manager and soon the mystery man's face, complete with pollen-crusted eyebrows and reef-shredded cheeks, was doing a circuit of the white goods showroom.

No one had seen him before. An old woman, visiting from Fortescue, claimed he looked like her daughter's ex-boyfriend but that, she explained, was twenty years ago. The accounts clerk had seen him somewhere, perhaps the IGA, perhaps playing for the Guilderton Maulers, but then said no, I'm thinking of someone else.

He tried Webb's Tyres and the Commercial Hotel before returning to Mango Meats. 'Is Justin back?' he asked a young man, busy making sausages.

'Justin,' the lanky teenager called, before turning to Moy and asking, 'You're that detective?'

'Yes, that detective. You're new?'

'Ray Foster. The new apprentice. I would shake your hand.' He showed him his meaty hands.

Justin Davids appeared from the cool-room. 'Sorry I was out.' He opened the display cabinet and placed a tray of premium mince at the front.

'You look busy,' Moy said.

'So-so. Got your man yet?'

Moy produced the photo of the Mangrove Point body and placed it on the counter. Davids took a moment before looking up. 'That's him,' he said.

'You sure?'

He squinted and tilted his head. 'I reckon. Stood there lookin' at him. What happened to him?'

'Washed up on the coast.'

'Couldn't happen to a nicer fella. You don't know who he is?'

'No idea. Nothing on him.'

Foster glanced at the picture then stepped forward. He picked up the image and studied it. 'That's Alex Naismith,' he said. 'He used to play for the Maulers.'

Moy noticed the young man's deep brown eyes. 'Naismith?' He took a pen and paper from his clipboard and scribbled the name. 'Seen him around lately?'

The apprentice wiped his hands on a towel. 'Year before last... Div Four. '

'That's it?'

'I didn't know him that well, just to say g'day. Worked around the place. Odd jobs, whatever was going.'

'You know who he worked for?'

'A fella named...John Preston. Did a couple of harvests for him.'

'John Preston?' Moy wrote this second name.

'He had a farm on the Port Louis Road. Sold it. Moved to town.'

Moy stared at him, thinking. 'Right, thanks for that. I'll ask around.'

Davids said, 'There you go, looks like we've found your man.'

'Let's hope.'

MOY RETURNED TO the station and crosschecked a database until he found the correct John Preston. He rang and got caught up in small talk before eventually asking, 'You had a fella named Alex Naismith working for you?'

'Yes...I remember him. Did some harvesting, drove the trucks.'

'Good worker, eh?'

'What's he been up to?'

Not a lot, Moy wanted to say, but remembered how this sort of throw-away line used to get him in trouble. 'Unfortunately, Mr Naismith is deceased.'

'Dead?'

'Yes.'

'Fuck. How'd that happen?'

'Well, it looks like...' He stopped himself. 'We're not meant to say but...you know, someone else was involved.'

'Someone's killed him?'

'That's what it looks like. I was wondering if you could tell me about him?'

'Fuck...dead. Always comes as a bit of a shock, eh?'

'Yes.'

'To be honest, I didn't know much about him. Just come, did his job, that was it.'

Moy was scared it might come to this. 'No friends, relatives?'

'Don't know. Sorry.'

'What about Naismith himself? What sort of person was he?'

There was a shrugging sound, as though Preston had never given his farmhand much thought. 'He got on with the job, didn't say much.'

'Easy to get along with?'

'Mostly. I remember a few times telling him, do it this way, and he'd…well, not argue, but disagree.'

'So you wouldn't describe him as violent?'

'Not that I saw.'

'And he never talked about what else he did with his time?'

'Not so I remember. Mainly just the farm, and what needed doing.'

Moy realised this was going nowhere. Preston would probably describe everyone he'd ever met in the same terms. He thanked him, left his number and rang off.

THEY RETURNED TO Gawler Street, and the last clean-out of the house before the agent came to inspect it. Moy swept and Patrick followed behind with a mop. When they were finished they sat on the front porch and opened a bottle of Coke. There were no cups so they took turns swigging. Patrick spilled it down his chin and his T-shirt and broke up laughing. Then he snorted and spat out the remains.

'You okay?' Moy asked.

'Went down the wrong way.'

Mrs Flamsteed walked from her yard and crossed the road, carrying a shopping bag with something heavy in it. She asked how they were, and how the move went. Then, 'Would you like me to keep up the meals?'

'No, thanks,' Moy said. 'I think I'll be okay now.'

And she looked happy, as though her duty was done, and she could move on. But then she was taken by another thought. 'I was wondering if you could look at this?'

'Of course,' Moy replied.

'We were having a plant sale. We, I mean the Country Women's. I have a friend who collected some plants from another…friend.' She shook her head, unsure. Looking at Patrick, she wondered whether it was an appropriate topic. Then she decided. She took a plant from the shopping bag and showed Moy. 'Doug reckons it's a…' She stopped, unable to say the word.

'It is,' Moy confirmed.

'Right.'

He waited, savouring the moment, wondering whether he should act out some sort of official concern.

'So?' she continued.

'They're a hardy plant,' he said. 'Stick it in the ground in full sun, plenty of water.'

She almost stepped back. 'In our garden?'

'Why not? One won't hurt anyone, and it's not like…' He smiled at her, waiting.

'But they're illegal.'

'No, you can keep three.'

'Is it marijuana?' Patrick asked.

'Dope, weed, ganja,' Moy said.

Mrs Flamsteed was unsure. 'Maybe I should just pop it in the bin? I thought you might want to investigate?'

'No,' Moy said. 'You keep it.'

She placed the plant back in the bag and said, 'Righto, well, maybe I'll return it.'

'You should sell it,' Patrick suggested.

'That would be illegal, wouldn't it, Bart?'

'You've only got one.'

210

Mrs Flamsteed smiled. 'Well, look after yerselves,' she said, turning, walking back across the road.

Patrick looked at Moy. 'Is it really legal?'

'Of course not but...she's getting on.'

There were birds, and a light breeze through a sheoak. 'Listen...' Moy said.

'What?' Patrick asked.

'No more grain trucks.'

'Have they finished?'

Moy stopped to count the days, weeks and months. He remembered their own harvest and how cold and wet it was when it was over. 'I think so.'

The Coke was nearly gone when Patrick said, 'I think we ran down this street.'

Moy looked at him. 'You and Tom? No, you wouldn't have passed anywhere near here.'

'Are you sure?' Patrick was studying the footpath and trees. 'We just kept running, and we thought we'd lost him.'

'You hadn't?'

'We turned a corner and saw his car, and he saw us. Then we were off. He did this big skid and turned and came after us.'

Moy handed him the bottle. 'But he didn't catch up?'

'We ran through the park and hid in the wheels of the train. He stopped in the car park and got out and looked. He saw us, but I was running and when I looked he'd got Tom and I just kept going...' He stopped, still wondering if he'd done the right thing. 'I went into town, into that laneway, and hid between the bins.' He looked at Moy. 'I suppose he told you that?'

'Who?'

'The man who came out of his shop.'

'Yes, that's what he said.'

'After he put me in the boot we drove for a minute...and Tom, he was just telling me to be quiet.'

'How long were you driving?'

'I don't know…maybe half an hour. It was dark and smelled like petrol. Then we got to the farm and he locked us in a shed.'

'What farm?' Moy asked.

'I think it was a farm. There were pigs. It was a couple of hours before Tom found a spot where I could get out.'

'Was there anyone else at the farm?'

'There was an old man. They were arguing because he was asking why the other guy had brought us there…why he'd hit Mum…and…And the one who brought us was saying he had to, that he thought he'd…'

'Did you see this other man?'

'No.'

'What else did he say?'

'That the guy who took us had to clean up his own mess, he wasn't going to help him. All he wanted was us gone from the house.'

'And you got out?'

'They went away arguing and Tom found a spot where I could just squeeze through, but he couldn't. He told me to run, to find a road, to tell someone.'

Moy waited, hoping for more.

'I made it to the dirt road, and then I went back to our house. I remember, standing, looking in the door, walking towards the house…and I saw Mum…So then I went back to the farm. Maybe…I thought…I wanted to ask Tom what to do next. I hid in the bush, then crawled back to the shed, but Tom was gone.'

He emptied the last few drops from the Coke bottle. 'See, they'd taken him,' he said.

Moy put his arm around him. 'Don't worry, we'll find him.'

'No.' In the pause Patrick's face was ghastly. 'No, you won't.'

212

35

THE NEXT DAY Moy sat at his desk, looked at the clock, listened for the sounds of school recess. Nothing. Why? New bell times? Oval out of bounds? *Ah, holidays!* Obvious, he thought, especially to someone paid to solve problems.

Gary came in with a few forms that needed signing.

'I'll get them back to you,' Moy said.

Gary wasn't happy with this. 'Y'just gotta sign them.' He waited, and watched just to make sure. 'Oh, and Monaghan called earlier. Said they've assigned someone to that arson.'

'Creek Street?'

'Yeah. Said next week, perhaps.'

'You're kidding. How long's it been?'

Gary reclaimed the forms. 'You know how it is. If yer gonna get murdered, do it in town.' Then he was gone.

Moy knew he was running on empty. He searched his mind for anything, no matter how slight. Remembered the address. He grabbed his keys and set off, past Gary, to his car, and west, to Percy Street. A row of six flats that ran the length of a narrow block, separated from a neighbour's yard by a picket fence. There was a hedge along the same boundary but it was mostly dead, filled with chip packets and faded brochures.

He pulled into the driveway to flat four, got out and studied a small patch of ground that might have been a garden. A puddle, wet from an irrigation system that hadn't watered anything but weeds in years. A bird bath, with half its bowl missing. Six or seven copies of the *Argus*, still wrapped in plastic. He walked up a path and knocked on the door. 'Hello,' he said, looking through the window.

'You looking for Alex?'

He looked around to see an oldish woman—late fifties, but aged by weight, a cheap parachute of a dress and a liver-spotted face.

'Yes. Alex Naismith.' He showed his identification. 'Detective Sergeant Bart Moy.'

'Right.' She looked at him suspiciously. 'What's he been up to?'

He studied the woman's face. 'Well…his body has turned up on a beach.'

'No!'

'Sorry to say.'

'Dead?'

He thought of an appropriate reply. Resisted the temptation. 'Yes.'

'How?'

'The coroner's investigating. You don't know much about him?'

'Not really. He's…was a bit of a mystery, I suppose. He'd be around, then you wouldn't see him for weeks at a time.'

'You're a neighbour?'

'Second flat down.' She pointed.

Moy felt his way around the situation—the cracked path, the woman's strong body odour, a corpse with a shovel fracture to the back of the head. 'He kept to himself?'

'Very much so. No girlfriend, no mates much.'

'Quiet?'

'Yes. He bought this flat a couple of years back.'

'Nothing else you think might be relevant?'

She tried, but couldn't come up with anything. 'Sorry. I think his parents died years ago. I'm not even sure if there's a brother or sister.'

'I was hoping to get inside.' He turned and looked in the window again. 'But that doesn't seem likely.'

'Well...not that I've been watching or anything...' She walked over to a pot plant, reached underneath, produced a key and handed it to Moy. 'I won't get in trouble?'

'No.'

'I know they think I'm a nosy neighbour, but I do notice things.'

And she was gone.

He stepped into a neat, sparsely furnished flat. The lounge-dining area was simply set out: a recliner, a table, two chairs, a fridge and a gas stove. Everything was put away. Benches were bare. The fridge contained solidified milk, a furry chop and half a block of chocolate. There were no newspapers or magazines, DVDs, bills, papers, books or personal items. No photos, nothing even hanging on the walls, although there were hooks. Nine or ten lonely magnets on the fridge. The scent of a life that had been cleaned up, censored, partly or mostly removed.

The house of a murderer? Who the hell knew?

THE AFTERNOON WAS cool. He didn't want to go home so he headed out of town to the footy club, the place, he believed, that most defined Guilderton. The clubrooms were a favourite for wedding receptions and wakes. In the years between the kids could run around, play an old Space Invaders machine, drink a stray beer and daily strengthen the bonds that would get them through their wheatbelt lives. On the oval there were school sports days and fairs, footy training and Sunday morning dog obedience. The wives in tight circles, planning holidays and fundraisers. The men showing the under-twelves the perfect punt. As though if all of this were

215

protected they could preserve the simple balance that sustained them.

It was the start of the cricket season now, but the players would be the same. He'd known them at high school, these farmers' sons, with their open mouths and home-shaved heads. And here they were now, catching practice under three of the four functional lights around the oval. A mist rose from the gardens and grass, settling over a few mums in the 'Nigger' Johnson Grandstand.

He walked across the car park and stood at the oval fence. Each of the players cast a triple shadow. They motioned and shouted to each other but he couldn't work out what they were saying. There were younger boys kicking footballs through the goals. Perhaps, he thought, some kind of sport would be good for Patrick. A band of brothers that would take him, for a while at least, away from his memories.

'How are yer?' an old man asked, from further along the fence.

'Good. And you?'

'Yeah.'

A full minute passed before the stooped figure said, 'That fuckin' harvest is gonna finish my son.'

'How's that?'

'Hundred and sixty grand to put in a crop this year. All over in a fortnight.'

'What, too dry?'

'Not enough to cover his costs. Fourth year straight. What's the use? May as well get a job at the IGA. What about you?'

Moy shrugged. 'I'm a copper.'

'So, no worries with low yields, eh?' He moved closer. 'You lookin' for someone?'

'Yes.'

But the old man just turned and looked back at the younger boys. 'That one out there,' he said, indicating, 'that's my grandson, Michael.' They watched him fumble a catch. 'And over there, my

216

son, Todd.' They watched Todd, but he was just standing there, guarding his shadow and his few inches of threadbare turf.

'Who you lookin' for?' the old man asked.

'I rang earlier and spoke to the secretary.'

'Who?'

'The secretary?'

'No, yer fuckin'…missing person?'

'Have you heard of Alex Naismith?'

The old man watched his son lurch after the ball. 'Played Div Four, two or three years ago.'

'Know much about him?'

'He stopped, didn't see out the season. That's the last we saw of him.' Then he looked back at his grandson. 'He's too smart, anyway.'

'Who?'

'Michael. Clever little bastard. Good at maths. He'd be better off studying engineering, medicine. Steada throwing good money after bad.'

'Things might get better.'

There was a siren. Moy had no idea what it meant.

'You're not gonna tell us what it's all about?' the old man said.

'Well, Alex, he washed up at Mangrove Point.'

'What, dead?'

No, bodysurfing. 'We reckon.'

'Fuck.'

'So, you know, I suppose things could always be worse.'

The old fella shook his head and turned back towards the oval. 'Not at eight dollars a tonne.'

MOY PULLED OUT, back onto the road to town. As he picked up speed he noticed a deserted farmhouse. Nearby paddocks had been reclaimed by scrub. There was a windmill, still turning, although the axle and gears were hanging loose. It occurred to him that there were many places like this—forgotten, cheaper to ignore than demolish. He supposed they could be made livable if someone was determined. They would make decent places to live. Away from neighbours and prying eyes.

He wondered about the house on Creek Street. What if Helen had brought her two sons to get away from someone? What if she'd had to flee the city and remembered this place from some childhood holiday, or something someone had mentioned?

And what if Alex Naismith, whoever he was, and however he was connected, had found her?

As his open window sucked in cool air he tried to imagine Helen Barnes, and Alex Naismith, together. He could see Helen popping out to a crowded coffee shop when Austen was at work. She would be smiling, and saying, hi, Alex, offering her hand. They would be huddling together, their faces almost touching. She would be telling him how she was ready to leave Austen and the kids.

So then, he imagined, fast-forwarding through the highlights, Helen running off with him, him tiring of her, leaving her, Helen telling his wife or vandalising his car…

He drifted into a low valley, accelerated up a steep hill and became airborne on the crest, settling back onto the road with a gentle *hmph*.

Maybe an unpaid debt. Austen's. Maybe Alex had killed the husband and she'd fled with the kids.

Silly stuff, he told himself.

Or maybe it wasn't, as Patrick thought, Austen leaving the family. Maybe Helen had just got sick of her husband and left, some hot afternoon when she'd had time to think and realise how much she hated her life. Or maybe Patrick was right. Maybe Dad had just up and disappeared, and maybe they'd gone looking for him, returning to some accommodation they'd once shared.

That didn't explain the furniture, clothes and toys in the house.

Or maybe Naismith had nothing to do with the Barnes family? Maybe he was just there to welcome them, to warn them, to tell them to move on…Maybe things just got out of hand.

36

THE GREEN AT the Guilderton Bowls Club was freshly shaved, so precisely clipped it looked artificial in the morning light. There were a few patches but they'd been packed with loam, whacked flat and watered in anticipation of new growth. There were waiting bays with seats bolted to concrete slabs. Each one had a sign: *Have You Marked Your Score?*

Moy sat in one of these shelters with Patrick and watched George open his felt-lined bowls case. George took out one of a matching pair, wrapped it in a rag and handed it to the boy. 'A good five minutes.'

Patrick started polishing the bowl the way George had shown him. 'How's this help?' he asked.

'Makes it smoother.'

As Patrick worked on the bowl, George walked to the other end of the pitch and set out his jack. He stepped back, surveyed it from three or four different angles, shrugged and headed back.

'Let's have yer,' he called to the boy, turning up the collar on his club shirt and hitching his pants. He took his own bowl and found his position. 'No one'll bother us until at least ten.'

'Does everyone dress in white?' Patrick asked.

'Yes.'

'Why?'

'It's a tradition.'

'Why?'

George stared at him. '*Why why why?* You can't just keep using that word.'

Patrick looked at him.

'Otherwise you'd have people in T-shirts, sandshoes, work boots. What would that look like?' He looked pointedly at Moy's T-shirt. 'You're playing?'

'No, I'm happy just sitting here…watching…passing judgment.' Moy looked at Patrick and smiled.

'Right now Paddy,' George said, demonstrating his swing. 'See, like that. Follow through with your arm, nice and slow.'

Patrick stepped forward, grasped his bowl and copied George's swing.

'Good, but bend over,' the old man said, taking Patrick's shoulders and forcing them down. 'That's the idea. Just soft…you've gotta learn to judge…like so.' The bowl shot off, curved, arced back to the jack but stopped a few feet short. 'For now it's better to undershoot.'

Patrick assumed his stance, drew a mental line over the grass and bowled. The bowl started slow and went straight; it headed for the jack, connected and knocked it a few inches to the right. He turned and looked at George and Moy.

Moy applauded. 'Nice work, Clarry.'

'I hit it.' He was beaming. 'Can we try again?'

'Of course. You grab the bowls.'

Patrick sprinted down the pitch and George called out, 'Walk!'

The boy replaced the jack, gathered the bowls and returned. 'Do any kids play?' he asked George.

'It's an old person's sport,' Moy said. George glared at him.

'So I can't join the club?'

'You can if you like. It's good you're thinking about the future.'

He turned and tilted his head. 'Why?'

'Gotta have somewhere to stay, everybody does.' He looked at his son. 'Be good if you stayed here with us, wouldn't it, Bart?'

'Would you like that?' Moy asked.

It seemed to strike Patrick as a novel idea. 'Maybe,' he said.

'Unless your dad claims you.'

Patrick took a moment. 'He won't.'

'Why not?'

Patrick shrugged. He looked at George and asked, 'Did you ever come here with your dad?'

'God, no.' George almost laughed. 'We were always too busy on the farm. Hardly ever came to town. Certainly not to play bowls. My dad wouldn't have dreamed of doing something like this.'

'Was he grumpy?'

'No, practical. That's how it was in those days.'

'What was his name? Your dad?'

George smiled at him. 'You haven't worked it out yet?'

'I think…'

'His name was William, William Moy.'

Patrick turned to face him. 'William…the photographer's son?'

'That's him.'

'So…' He stopped to think about how it might have happened. 'He never came back for him?'

'Well, thing is, I never knew until I was about your age. Dad never told me.' George shrugged at Patrick's expression of disbelief. 'Mighta thought I wouldn't be interested.'

Moy was half-sitting, half-lying back in the shelter, listening to the fugue of old and young voice, the harmony, the poetry. The sky was a half-cloudy, indecisive blue, the breeze not cold, not warm.

'What happened?' Patrick asked George.

'Some time in the late forties, maybe? After the war anyway, one time I was looking through the photo albums and Dad says to me, you know, my father died in Sydney.' He cleared his throat. 'Course, I knew very well my grandfather Daniel'd died right there on the farm, so then the whole story comes out.'

There were only two photos of his father, Bill had said, probably it was always like that with photographers. He told George he could remember the sound of his father's raspy pipe-smoker's voice and his floppy bowtie, the hair that grew out of his ears and nose.

'He was looking for his wife in Sydney,' George told Patrick.

'What was his name?'

'Harrison…Harry. Apparently he got in a fight and ended up with a knife between his ribs.'

'What about Daniel?' Patrick asked.

'Well, after losing Elizabeth, he agreed to look after Dad. That's the sort of man he was…help anyone out.'

'William stayed with him?'

'Yes, the day after the photo was taken—the death photo.' George recalled the *memento mori*. 'Harry kissed Dad on the head and said, I'll be back soon, son, behave yourself, do exactly what Mr Moy says.'

Young William, with blood still dried on his throat.

'Dad told me he cried for a whole day,' George said. 'Harry got back in his cart and drove off and Dad never saw him again.'

Patrick, looking at the grass, seemed to be remembering.

'Anyway,' George said, 'Dad settled in. Elizabeth was buried, a cross was made. Life went on. He learned how to plough and seed and deliver lambs. And that was that.'

Patrick studied George's face.

'Until one day,' George said, 'this letter came saying what happened in Sydney. Then there were lots of waterworks. Daniel said, we don't know if this is true, son. But Dad knew. And then the months and years went by. He knew. Something had happened to his father. Maybe his mum had run off with someone, and Harry was after them. Maybe he was the fella that stabbed Harry.'

Patrick stared at George. 'So what happened then?'

'Well, Daniel was always a practical man. He said, how about we make this all legal? And Dad said, fine, and then they went to town to see a lawyer, to fill in the adoption papers.' George was enjoying the story. 'When I first heard all this I was shocked. Still, it explained a lot of things. Missing photos…different hair colour…' He squeezed Patrick's knee. 'See, that's Bart's grandad. A stranger. Someone that somebody met by accident.'

'And all in one day?' Patrick asked, seeing both photos—William and Daniel, Elizabeth, Daniel and Helen—but wondering, clearly. 'And what was his surname?'

'Who?'

'Your other grandad. Harry.'

'William never said.'

'Why?'

'Maybe he never thought to.'

'Why?'

'*Why why?*'

'Why?' Patrick persisted.

'Maybe he just wanted to move on.'

And Patrick stared at the jack, thinking, as the first of the bowlers came outside.

37

MOY SAT IN his room and stared into his monitor. Forensic evidence: a bumper bar; a bike that had nothing to do with anything but was photographed anyway; the soccer ball; even his keys, and a beer bottle they'd found in the back of his car.

Megan had asked when he'd drunk it. She'd claimed she could smell it on his breath, which was rubbish. It had been days since he'd had a drink. He could remember her screaming at him. 'If you've been drinking...'

Him yelling back that it was an *accident* and accidents, by definition, weren't something you anticipated. How he needed her support now, and she was being a complete and utter bitch. As if it was something he'd meant to do.

'If it goes to court, don't rely on me,' she was saying.

'What do you think happened?' He could see her face, set hard, and her arms crossed.

He went into his room to pack a few clothes and she followed him.

'So?' she asked.

'Tomorrow morning I'm going to split the savings and put half in my credit union account, and then I'm going to check into a motel.'

'You need both signatures.'

He'd stopped. 'Wrong. Check.'

He sat back in his chair now, staring at the soccer ball, remembering his wife standing at the door as he took his keys, wallet and pistol, and left.

His phone rang. 'Yes?'

It was Superintendent Graves wanting more information. The days and weeks are passing, he explained.

'Sir.' Thinking, *pompous old timeserver.* Irritated by the drone, the formal clunk of words. 'I've read the reports, and I've followed everything up. I've talked to everyone on Creek Street but no one seems to remember them. The house itself is a long way out.' He wanted to tell the superintendent not to bother him in his own space, his own time. Brave words and sentences were forming in his head. *I'm solving it in my own way, and if you don't like that…*

'So, it's probably time to get this boy seen to,' Graves said. 'There's probably a psychologist, or someone?'

Seen to. 'Yes sir. I don't think that's going to achieve anything.' *You complete fucking prick.*

'What about this brother?' Graves asked.

'I assume he's being…kept somewhere.'

There was a long silence from the other end. 'Why would someone want to keep him?'

'The boy's seen whoever it was attacked the mother. Maybe he's got away, too. Maybe he's hiding somewhere.'

'Lot of maybes, Bart.'

Moy noticed Patrick standing in the doorway. 'Well, Superintendent, I've done my best with limited means. I don't think—'

'Detective Sergeant, the normal—'

'I need to call you back…tomorrow perhaps. I have to go.' He hung up, placing the phone on his desk. 'Patrick?'

Patrick opened the door and stepped inside the room, pulling his T-shirt down over his underpants.

'What's up?' Moy asked.

The boy shrugged.

'Were you listening?'

'You were talking about Tom?'

'Tom, and Mum, and the fire. They think I'm taking too long.'

No response.

'They're saying it's about time someone else had a go. I said no.' He waited. 'Do you think I'm taking too long?'

Patrick shrugged.

Moy made no attempt to make the boy feel comfortable. 'If I agree, they'll send three major crime investigators. They'll start from scratch. Evidence. Witnesses. They'll get you to tell them exactly what happened. From the beginning. Would you like that?'

Patrick shrugged again.

'They might find things I've missed. What do you think?'

'You're doing fine.'

'You think so?'

'Yes.'

'Maybe I should've found Tom already?'

Patrick was trembling. 'If you don't want to…'

Moy sat up. 'Shall I tell you what I think?'

No reply.

'I think you think I've missed something.'

'No.'

'And that you'd like these other detectives, but you're too nice to say.'

'No.'

'You think if I was fair, I'd step away from the case.'

Patrick looked at him with red eyes. 'No, I want you.'

'You don't.'

'Please, Bart.'

Moy could see the boy's hands shaking. He wondered whether he should put his arm around him. He wanted to; knew he couldn't. It was his own fault that things had dragged, that Tom was still lost. A man who spent his waking hours indulging his own grief. 'You can say it, Patrick.'

'What?'

'That I've fucked up.'

AT ONE A.M. Moy was standing outside, hitting golf balls. He'd strung up a bed-sheet between two old trees. He'd got up and started smashing Q Stars with his five-iron. They pouched the sheet, but never tore it.

He looked up and Patrick was watching him, his head low above his window.

George called from his room. 'Shut up!'

So Moy kept swinging.

38

MOY WOKE UP, opened his eyes, sat up. His digital clock was glowing: 2.43 a.m. He wondered if he'd heard a woman's voice.

'Bartholomew...it's George.'

He stood up and walked a few paces, listening. 'Hello?'

'It's me, Mrs Miller, from next door.'

He ran from his room, to the door. Patrick was a few steps behind, rubbing his eyes.

'Mrs Miller?'

'Look.' She pointed.

He saw his father lying on the driveway.

'I was up doing my ironing,' she said. 'I heard someone calling... I looked out and saw him lying there.'

Moy jumped from the porch, followed by Thea and Patrick. He knelt beside George, gently shook him and said, 'Dad.'

The old man's eyes were closed, the lids covered with fine capillaries. His nose was flaring, chest rising and falling, fingers digging into the dirt beside the drive, clawing, gathering a fistful of soursobs.

'Righto,' Moy said, thinking. 'Airway.' He dropped his ear to his father's mouth. Then he looked up at them. 'He's breathing.'

'That's a good sign,' Thea replied.

'Circulation.' He placed two fingers on his father's carotid artery. 'Thank Christ,' he said, feeling a pulse. 'Everything seems in order.'

'He's unconscious,' Thea said.

'Yes. What is it?' He looked at her, imploring.

'A heart attack, or maybe a stroke? He might have just fainted.'

'What was he doing out here?'

'He often wanders in the garden at night, talking to himself.'

'So…' Moy tried to think what to do.

'I'll call an ambulance,' Thea said.

Moy looked at his father. 'No…I mean…' He looked up. 'Where does it come from?'

'They're volunteers. They have a pager.'

'Fuck.'

She flushed, but did not comment. 'They're pretty quick. They're used to getting to road accidents and—'

'Patrick, grab my keys from the buffet.'

Thea wasn't sure. 'I don't think you're meant to move them.'

'Go on,' Moy insisted, and Patrick ran inside.

'You might make things worse,' she said.

'Worse than dying?'

'No, I mean—'

'It's not likely to be a spinal injury, is it?' he asked, half-sarcastic. Then he realised what she'd done for him. 'You were ironing?'

'I can never sleep anymore.'

Patrick sprinted from the house, handed Moy the keys and asked, 'What should I do?'

Moy could see the terror in his face. 'Watch him while I get the car.'

As he went further up the drive, opened and started the car,

229

Patrick knelt beside George, holding his hand, wiping hair from his forehead. 'No,' he whispered. 'Please.'

'Don't worry,' Thea said, sensing his fear. 'He's still functioning.' As if George was an old mower that could still cut.

Patrick stared at the old man's face. 'Come on, George. You can hear me, can't you?' He squeezed his hand.

'He can hear you,' Thea said. 'But he won't be able to speak… give him a minute.' The old professional manner buoyed her voice. 'Come on, George. We're going to get you some help. Patrick… that's your name, isn't it?'

'Yes.'

'Patrick's going to make sure you're okay.'

Moy backed up, applied the handbrake and got out. There was exhaust, and red light on their faces. After opening the back door of his car he returned to his father and said, 'Don't worry, Dad, five minutes.' He took him under the arms, lifted and dragged him towards the car.

'Can I help?' Thea asked.

'I've got him.'

Moy sat on the back seat and dragged his father in. When most of his body was lying across the seat he got out the other side and closed the doors. 'Come on,' he said to Patrick. 'You're gonna have to watch him.'

Patrick got in the car. Moy turned to Thea. 'Thank you. I don't know how long he'd been there.'

'Not long, I'd have seen him.'

'I'll call you.'

'Yes.'

He got in the car and they backed out. Changing gears, they flew down Clyde Street. Thea stood watching them, her arms crossed, her eyes adjusting to the street lights.

Patrick strapped himself in, turned around and held George's hand.

'Can you feel a pulse?' Moy asked.

The boy did what he'd seen them do on telly. Surprisingly, it worked. 'Yes.'

Moy looked at the clock on the dash: 2.58 a.m. He wondered if there was an allotted time, and if he'd exceeded it. He pushed the accelerator to the floor. They became airborne and as he braked before a dip the car ground its bumper into the bitumen. He flipped on the warning lights. 'Dad, can you hear me?'

He spoke to Patrick. 'Keep checking.'

'I can still feel it.'

Moy flew down Ayr Street. One of the shops was open and a man was tiling the floor; he looked up, surprised, as they flew past, heading for the final winding road that led to the hospital.

Moy slowed. A mule-kick of memory. *Charlie*, he nearly said, nearly turning around, nearly looking. He could feel his heart racing and his own mouth drying. The body, he sensed, was on the back seat, and he was overcome with a feeling of despair.

I did nothing to cause this, he thought. Nothing. And yet here I am...'Patrick?'

'He's okay.'

He pulled into the hospital drive. Slowed; searched for signs of life. Came to a stop at a pair of sliding doors. Then he sounded his horn, switched on the siren, turned off the engine and got out.

Nothing. He hammered on the doors. 'Hello?'

'The intercom,' Patrick said.

Moy pressed a button. 'Hello?'

Eventually: 'Yes?'

'My father, I think he's had a heart attack.'

The line dropped out. A few moments later the doors opened and an orderly appeared with a gurney. He peered into the back seat. 'Your dad?'

'Yes.'

'Where am I?' George asked.

Moy almost smiled. 'Hospital.'

'Fuck.' George grimaced, and felt his chest. 'Bloody ticker, I suppose.'

Patrick looked at Moy; took his hand and squeezed it. Another orderly came out to help.

PATRICK WAITED OUTSIDE the room as they changed George into a gown; laid him on the bed like a frozen fillet left to thaw; connected a heart monitor and studied the trace, printing out a long strip of paper that said, somehow, the old man wouldn't die, today at least. As they inserted a drip (Heparin, 1000 units per hour GTN) into his arm and taped it down. As the ECG was watched, and adjusted, words like *infarct* muttered, shoulders shrugged, water sipped. All with the conclusion, 'I think he got off pretty lightly.'

Moy came out and sat beside Patrick. 'He's okay. It was a little heart attack.'

Patrick was unsure. 'And he'll get better?'

'Of course.'

Then the boy's head dropped, staring at well-worn carpet. There was a vending machine but he hadn't even bothered looking to see what it contained. And prints, all along the wall. Flowers sitting in pots the shapes of animals. It all seemed out of place. With the trolleys and wheelchairs, machines (all tubes and buttons) and little posters showing you how to wash your hands.

'We had fried chicken the other day,' Patrick said.

'It wasn't that.'

Moy was on a first-name basis with the bain-marie woman at Dempsey's Takeaway and any of the half-dozen people who worked at the pizza bar. But worse, there'd been a late-night adventure all the way to Port Louis for a feed of KFC, a couple of hours for the three of them to get there and back. On the way home Moy had said, 'You're not to mention this to anyone, understand? I could get in trouble for using the car.'

232

Patrick was nearly asleep in the hospital corridor.

'Come on,' Moy said. They went into George's room, Patrick looking shocked to see the sleeping figure with leads coming off his chest, feeding into a flashing box like the comms screen in the car. His face fatter, his hands larger, his fingers longer.

'Here,' Moy said, indicating a long couch.

Patrick took the few steps and lay down and Moy wedged a pillow beneath his head. He drifted off almost straight away, but not before he felt a rug settling over his body, before he saw Moy, sitting down in an armchair beside his father, taking and reading some notes, tilting his head, as if trying to understand something. But then leaning back, folding his arms and closing his eyes.

THE NIGHT WAS warm and the room hummed. Moy looked at a clock that marked every moment with clinical precision. It was just after five; enough time to salvage some sleep. He went next door and found a foam mattress and laid it on the floor beside his father; sheets, rugs, and two pillows that smelt of menthol. He rested, watching the vents rhythmically feeding them air. He closed then opened his eyes. Looked at his father, convinced that it might happen again at any moment. He was watching him shovel spilled grain into a wheelbarrow.

Can I help?

No.

Returning to his house, looking back at the angry figure working against the last bit of light. As he still was. The same neurons firing, cardiac muscle working.

He noticed Patrick peeling off his rug and sitting up. Heard his father saying, 'No, go back to sleep.'

The boy stood up and approached George. 'How are you feeling?'

'I'm fine. These things happen when you get old. No point making a big drama.'

233

He watched as Patrick touched George's arm. He noticed how he took a moment, feeling the rough skin.

'Were you worried?' George asked.

'Yes.'

'It's just like a cut, isn't it? You know it's gonna heal.'

'But it was a heart attack.'

'So?'

Silence. And a dog barking, again.

'It was so bloody stupid,' George said.

'What?'

He closed his eyes, remembering. 'I woke up, convinced I'd left the gate open.'

'What gate?'

'On the farm. I'd left the gate open, and the sheep would get out. I thought, Dad's gonna kill me. So I got up, and went out, and walked down the path towards the paddock.' He opened his eyes and looked at the boy. 'Only there wasn't any paddock, was there?'

'I guess not.'

Moy watched his father adjusting the leads coming off his chest. George was smiling at the boy. 'I won't be able to take you anywhere today. But if they let me out this arvo we can play bowls tomorrow morning.'

'Won't you have to stay here?'

'Better now. Best thing's to get on with it, eh?' He slowly sucked in a lungful of air.

'What is it?' Patrick asked.

'Dying for a pee.'

'Should I get the nurse?'

'No, over there.' He raised his hand, indicating.

Patrick moved around the bed and fetched the strangely shaped bottle. 'Is this to…?'

'That's it. Get back to sleep now.'

Moy watched Patrick return to his couch, lie down and close

his eyes. Hold them closed. George cursed and fought with the sheets and leads. '*That's it,*' as the stream gushed, and slowed. Then: 'Patrick! You awake? I can't reach the table.'

Patrick got up and took the full bottle. 'I'll take it out to the nurse.'

'Perhaps you better.'

Moy smiled and turned to the wall.

THE NEXT MORNING Moy felt like life had offered him a second chance. Unable to sleep, he'd risen at six, gone home and packed a bag for his father. Now, the sun through the window was warming the room. 'Right, I've got your pyjamas and your cross-word books.'

And George. 'Can't wear me pyjamas.'

'Rubbish, other people are. Listen, Thea came over as I was pulling in, askin' after you. I suppose I should get her some choco-lates or something.' He paused. 'She said she's seen you out before, wandering.'

'What? I'm not allowed to walk around in my own yard?'

'Said she hears you talking to someone.'

'Nosy old bitch.' George shook his head. 'No chocolates, right?'

'But she saved your life.'

'Bullshit. Wasn't dead, was I?'

'You might've died.'

'Bullshit.'

Moy noticed the boy, apparently asleep, smiling.

'You can't kill me that easily,' George said. 'Though I bet there's some'd like to.'

'*Naaah...*'

'You shut up.'

Patrick giggled, and Moy tickled him awake.

39

THEY SPENT THE day at the hospital and drove around to
Moy's old house at Gawler Street late in the afternoon, coffee and
doughnuts in hand. Moy parked on the street.

'Did you forget something?' Patrick asked.

'My car.'

'You never said you had your own car.'

Moy got out and tried the door of the garage. 'Shit.'

He walked around the back, Patrick following. Putting down
his coffee, he removed five glass louvres from a frame, stepped onto
a pile of old pavers and climbed in, falling and rolling.

'Get my coffee and go round the front,' he called to Patrick.

'You okay?'

'Yes.'

The sound of Moy fighting with the lock. Then, slowly, like the
grand unveiling of a game-show prize pack, the door lifted.

'Here it is,' Moy said.

There was a sheet over it, but Patrick could see the bottom
half—long, yellow—the tyres painted black.

Moy grabbed the sheet and pulled it off. 'See, a classic. Leyland P76.'

Patrick studied the car's racing stripes and chrome rims; blinds inside the back window; factory-fresh mud flaps and a front grille that looked like a pig's snout. 'It's old,' he said.

'Six cylinder. Targa Florio. Rare as hen's teeth—in this condition anyway.'

'Why don't you get a new car?'

'You're missing the point.' Moy got in and started the engine. There was a reluctant growl, then it roared to life. He gunned the accelerator, got out and stood looking at Patrick. 'Well?'

'It stinks.'

'It's meant to. A real car, eh?' He tapped the roof.

Five minutes later they were cruising around town. Moy had one arm out of the window, holding his coffee, occasionally steering with his knee as he ate his danish.

'I didn't know you had it,' Patrick said, sitting up in his bucket seat to see out of the window.

'I haven't needed it,' Moy replied, 'but I guess I might need it more from now on.'

'Why?'

'Have to give up the Commodore. When I throw it all in.'

Patrick stared at him. 'Throw what in?'

'Work. Time I stepped aside and let someone else have a go.'

Patrick looked forward. They turned down a side street.

'What do you think, comfortable ride?' Moy asked. 'The suspension's all new.'

'I told you, I want you to…'

'I've missed it, whatever it is. I don't know enough. I haven't been *told* enough.' He met the boy's eyes.

'You have.'

'No. I don't think so…' He shrugged. 'Frankly, it suits me better. I've got enough to worry about. George…and, you know, I had a wife and a son. You're not my only problem.'

Patrick looked over at the showgrounds, its rides and food vans set up ready for the show.

'That's not fair.'

'It's fair to me, and you. Everyone's a winner. You get Tom, I get simplicity.'

Patrick glared at him. 'You're doing this on purpose.'

'It's got a great stereo. Want to hear it?'

'No.' He crossed his arms.

'That's new too. In fact—'

'You didn't lose your brother,' Patrick said.

'No…my son.'

'Your mum.'

Moy came to a stop, turned and looked at him. 'It's a competition, is it?'

'No.'

'Well?' He drove on. 'I'm considering this…for your sake.'

Silence.

'I just don't have enough to go on.'

Patrick took a deep breath. 'I told you everything.'

'I hardly know who you are.'

'I told you.'

'No, you never have. Your name—that's it. How's that help?'

They passed the Australian Farmer, but neither was interested. Moy just kept driving. Ayr Street, the dirt road to the airport, three-point turn, back again.

Then Patrick said, 'We've never lived in a house for more than a few months.'

'We?'

'The four of us.'

Silence. The sound of rubber on bitumen.

'We were in this shack. At Port Louis.'

Moy took it slowly. 'In town?'

238

'No, on one of the beach roads. Me and Tom used to walk to the beach.'

'To swim?'

Patrick nodded. 'We found an old surfboard once. It came up in Tom's face and he cut his lip.'

Oxford Street, Cambridge, King Edward. Geraniums growing through fence wire.

'Anyway, Dad just left. I told you about that. Didn't even say goodbye.'

'Took all his stuff?'

'Yeah. Then after a bit...we ran out of money. Some bloke told Mum he knew this place in Guilderton. Said he used to live there.'

'Creek Street?'

'Yes. So we...Mum loaded everything in a taxi. The furniture in the house, that was already there.'

Taxis. Damn it, Moy thought. Why didn't I think? He started heading back towards Gawler Street. 'I don't understand why she didn't send you to school.'

Patrick shrugged. 'We thought she just hadn't got round to it. At Port Louis we went most days.'

Moy cursed himself again. 'And then?'

'You know the rest.' Patrick swallowed. 'The man came, he hit Mum, we ran away. We got to town, he found us and put us in his boot. He took us to this farm, there were pigs.' He looked at Moy. 'I told you about the pigs.'

'Yes.'

'And then I got out and ran away...'

But here, Moy was confused. 'You hid?'

'Yes.'

'But why...You could've found the police. You could've told someone. Isn't that what Tom was expecting you to do?'

Patrick's head dropped. He stared into his lap.

'So?'

'I was…' His white face spoke of fear and shame. 'I thought…'

'But Tom was in the shed.'

A whisper. 'I made a mistake.'

Moy waited.

Patrick sat up. 'That's all there is.'

'No, it's not.'

'No one tells everything.' He looked at Moy, challenging him, his eyes glowing.

'You want to know?' Moy asked.

No reply. Just his eyes, waiting.

'I was sitting in this seat. I was going to move the car, so Charlie could kick his ball in the driveway.' He paused, remembering. 'I was thinking of something else. I put the car in reverse, released the handbrake and put my foot on the accelerator. And then I ran over him.'

Patrick looked down.

'I stopped, I got out…and there he was, just sort of wriggling on the ground.'

He pulled over and stopped. The engine chugged, waiting.

'Then he was still…'

Patrick looked at him. 'I shouldn't have asked.'

'You're allowed to ask.'

'Do you miss him?'

Moy took a slow breath, and switched off the ignition. 'That's why,' he said.

Seconds.

'Nothing else matters…mattered.' He opened the door and got out of the car.

Patrick watched him struggle across an irrigation ditch, into the bush.

'Just takin' a pee,' he called, although Patrick could tell he was still looking for Charlie.

*

240

TEN MINUTES AND he was back, as if nothing had been said. He started the car, spun the wheels on gravel and turned onto the road back to Ayr Street.

Moy pulled up in front of Goldsworthy's Store and they both went in. Five minutes later they emerged, Patrick carrying a new bowl, wrapped in tissue paper, deposited in a zip-up plastic sleeve. As they drove towards the hospital, Patrick examined it, testing its weight, throwing it up a few times and catching it, studying its name (Taylor SR Redline Black) and even smelling it.

'You give it to him,' Moy said.

'Can I?'

'Tell him you bought it from your pocket money.'

They entered George's room and found him sitting up in bed, minus his wires. He was wearing his pyjamas, done up to the top button. Patrick gave him the bowl and he unwrapped it, rolling it in his hands, taken by the concentric circles painted on its side. 'This is what you get for having a heart attack?' he said.

'Patrick picked it out,' Moy explained.

'Really?'

'It wasn't so hard,' Patrick said. 'They only had two types.'

'Well, how about you use this one?'

'It's for you.'

'Go on.'

Patrick took the bowl, holding it in his cupped hands in his lap. He looked at Moy.

'Okay,' he agreed.

Moy left the room in search of a doctor. Along the corridor a nurse told him there was only one, and he was on an emergency callout. He walked back to George's room, but stopped short at the sound of voices. He stood outside the door, listening.

'Did you used to play bowls with Charlie?' he heard Patrick ask.

'No. He was too young,' George replied.

'What did you do with him?'

There was a long pause. Then Moy heard his father say, 'I never saw him really. Bart and Megan were living in town, and they hardly ever visited.'

Hardly ever? Moy thought. Once a month? No, every few months. Well, no. Not even that.

'How often?'

'Sometimes…if I was sick…or like the time I broke my hip. Slipped in the bathroom.'

'How did you get out?'

'Just dragged myself to the phone.'

Moy started to walk into the room, but Patrick was saying, 'And what happened, when Charlie died?'

'What do you mean, what happened?' George asked.

'Was Bart upset?'

'Of course he was upset. You would be, wouldn't you? A father and son…that's about the worst thing of all. He's still not the same, prob'ly never will be. Still, I shouldn't be telling you about that.'

'It's okay.'

'He'll find your brother, don't you worry about that.'

'He won't.'

There was a long pause. Moy wanted to go in. Stopped himself.

George said, 'You want to tell me something?'

'I suppose, if Bart works out who killed the man…'

'What man?'

'The man who burned our house…'

'Go on.'

'If he finds him, then they can put him in prison, and it will all be over. Bart can write his report, and his boss will be happy. And then…'

'What?'

'They'll find me somewhere to go.'

Moy waited, anxious.

'Well, what's wrong with stayin' with us?' the old man said.

'But that's just…until Bart finds out.'

'Not necessarily. You can be wherever…wherever you're happy.'

There was another long pause.

'Maybe they'll never find him,' Patrick said.

'Who?'

'Whoever killed the man. Bart still doesn't know.'

'No, they'll find him. Sometimes it takes months, years…but they, Bart, he'll find him.'

'Mr Moy?' He turned to find the doctor behind him. 'You were looking for me?'

'Is that you, Bart?' George called.

'Don't worry, Dad, it's all under control.' He looked at the doctor. 'I just wanted to have a talk about the…old fella.'

'I can hear you,' George called.

'Let's go in,' the doctor said. 'He's got a few good years yet.'

40

THEY DROVE TOWARDS the showgrounds. Toffee apples and gleaming axes, the screams of teenagers and the smell of coal smoke from the steam preservation society. As they slowed towards the car park Moy noticed Patrick watching a boy done up in a red and blue scarf. 'Do you know him?' he asked.

'No. Those are Lions colours.'

'Lions?'

'Port Louis Lions. Me and Tom used to play for them.'

'You any good?'

'Not really. I couldn't mark the ball.'

Moy smiled. 'That was my problem. Cricket. The ball's coming towards you but you just know...It always ended badly.'

Cars were queued along the road outside the showgrounds. They waited, and eventually parked in a paddock, then trudged through mud to the front gate. Stood in another line before handing money to a woman trapped in a booth with a couple of kids.

As they went in, Moy said, 'This used to be the highlight of my year.'

'*This?*' Patrick replied, looking at the food stands lined up behind the sideshows.

'Yes, as a matter of fact. When I was in high school I was in the cattle club. We'd come and exhibit. Led Steer. Hoof and Hook.'

'What was that?'

'You'd lead your steer around and they'd judge him. Then they'd whip him out back, cut his throat and display his carcass.'

'All in the same day?'

'Yep. All the girls would be in tears.'

They made their way to the main arena just in time for the tractor pull. Two yellow beasts: an International and a Massey Ferguson backed up to each other with a tethering chain attached. An old woman stood between them with a flag. There was an announcement on the PA: 'The event you've all been waiting for. Guilderton Tractors and Trailers presents…'

'Which one's going to win?' Patrick asked.

'The International.'

'Why?'

He indicated the smaller tractor's driver, a bulldog-faced man in overalls with the sleeves cut off to reveal a tattoo of a fire-breathing dragon clutching a terrified rabbit.

Both drivers climbed into their cabs and the woman waved her flag. There were two clouds of exhaust and the chain tightened. The tractors roared and their tyres ate into the soft grass. Forward, back, and again, the International's front wheels lifting a few inches off the ground.

'What do you think?' Patrick asked.

Moy considered it. 'The Massey's saving himself.'

An orange flag in the middle of the chain returned to a centre line. The crowd became vocal, pig farmers moving to the edge of their seats, children jumping up and down on the old boards of the grandstand. Moy was applauding, stopping himself, wondering why he cared about tractors.

Eventually the International shot forward, pulling the flag over the finishing line.

Twenty minutes later they were watching the sheep shearing. Smooth strokes of the comb, scraggy wool tossed off; a few teenagers gathering fleeces and throwing them on a grading table. Moy had bought Patrick a bag of hot chips.

'They're all I used to eat when I was hiding,' Patrick said.

Moy turned to face him. 'Where did you get the money?'

'You know the big plastic guide dog in front of the deli?'

'Yeah, I know it.'

'On the bottom there's a long split in the plastic. If you give it a bit of a kick…'

'Patrick.'

'I only ever took as much as I needed.'

A shearer finished and released an animal. It looked around then slipped down a ramp into a pen.

'So, you went to the fish shop?' Moy asked.

'Most days. I got three dollars worth of chips. Until one day the man said, you must just about live on chips. That was the last time I went there.'

They walked out, past dozens of sheep pens crammed with big-horned rams and ultra-fine Merinos and Corriedales, even goats, their shit trodden into the gaps between floorboards. They stopped to look at a lonely alpaca. 'I ran over one of these,' Moy said. 'It was standing on the road when I came around a corner.'

Patrick stared at the animal. 'Did it die straight away?'

'Not sure. I just kept going. Would've died eventually, I suppose.'

'You should've checked.'

'It shouldn't have been on the road.'

They passed through a doorway into an adjoining hall. There were dozens of pigs sitting and standing on concrete slabs. Monsters as big as small cars. Sows, their legs open, their battery of pink

246

nipples erect in the morning cold. 'All of this so I can have a bit of bacon,' Moy said.

'They put a bolt through their head, but they stun them first.'

Moy was lost in the little eyes, so ridiculously small compared to the rest of the body. 'Maybe I'll become a vegetarian.'

'She'll still get killed.'

'Let's go look at the scones.'

They moved to the next hall, and glass cabinets full of hand-made dolls and doilies. Then the baking. A bank of sultana cakes with the sultanas too close, too far apart, spaced just right. Pavlovas sitting white and perfect in their cabinets and, finally, scones: uncrumbly, undoughy, exactly two inches high and wide, topped with a tight perm of jam and cream.

They passed a lucky dip and Patrick looked at Moy.

'Five bucks? They're always crap. I'll buy you something decent when we get to the sideshows.'

But the promise of the big pink and blue boxes had captivated Patrick. Toys wrapped in six layers of newspaper. 'Please?'

Moy took out his wallet and handed an old woman five dollars. She smiled.

Yeah, he thought, looking at her. It's meant to be a country show. Better be something decent.

Patrick felt around in the blue box, produced the biggest parcel and started unwrapping it. One, two, three layers, revealing a small plastic racing car with one of its wheels already missing. 'Look,' he said, beaming.

'Great.' Moy smiled at the woman. Then he noticed they were outside the toilet. He looked at Patrick. 'I'll be two minutes.'

'I'm going to look at the paintings,' Patrick said, noticing a wall covered with water-colour gum trees and paddocks.

Moy stood at the urinal and unzipped. Waited. An old farmer came in and stood beside him.

'How are yer?'

247

Moy nodded. He waited.

'Havin' a bit of trouble?' the old man asked, directing his copious stream into a pre-existing puddle of piss and stepping back as it splashed his shoes.

'Yeah,' Moy replied, turning and walking into a cubicle.

When he emerged the old man had gone. He went into the hall. Paintings: water-colours, oils and acrylics, but no Patrick. Walking over to the Artists' Corner, he looked along the aisles formed by stands displaying art.

Nothing.

'Patrick?' he called, and then loud, as his heart started to race. 'Patrick...over here.' Surely he wouldn't have wandered off, he thought as he stood sweating. Surely.

He took a breath and forced himself to think. It was a big hall, set out for a casual stroll. He started against the far wall and walked up and down every aisle: art, craft, cooking; compositions and crayon portraits; ships in bottles, model tanks and planes. 'Patrick!'

He ran back to the toilet, elbowed the door and cannoned inside.

Nothing.

Fuck. Think, Moy, think.

Four, five, six long seconds. Light on the cracking wall, piss and lemon scent in his nostrils.

He took a deep breath.

No, what a stupid thing to think, you fuck.

And then, forcing himself again, he became the detective and not the parent. He thought how Patrick had run away before. How he'd hidden in a hole, stolen money, eaten chips and fried chicken for a week. How he'd lost his whole family in a matter of days. How he was a scared little boy.

But he could see his smiling face, his hand in the lucky dip.

He wasn't scared now.

He wouldn't run now.

The lucky dip. He ran back to the woman. 'Have you seen my boy?'

'Yes,' she said.

'Where?'

'The paintings.'

'How long ago?'

'A few minutes.'

'Was he with someone?'

'Not that I noticed. Has he wandered off?'

Moy didn't answer. He retraced his steps, stopping and asking a show society guide. She couldn't remember any boy. A middle-aged woman at a coffee stall. No, sorry. Half-a-dozen people admiring the crafts. Is he lost? And a woman who remembered them, together, looking at the scones.

He ran up and down every row, calling, 'Patrick, are you here?'

He'd gone. Or been taken.

A fragment caught in his mind. Someone beside them in the grandstand. A smile or lifted eyebrow. Asking the time. Sunglasses, a beard, looking up from a magazine.

But there was nothing, no one.

Was it the man with the shovel? Naismith's murderer? Or Patrick's father, come to reclaim a clue? The longing for his son too strong?

He ran outside. There were hundreds of faces—mums and dads, kids, some as tall as Patrick, with his hair, even his blue wind-cheater. 'Patrick!'

He wouldn't go any further than this, he thought. He's too smart, too careful.

He felt sick. Wiped his forehead with the back of his wrist. 'Patrick!' More faces; similar; passing; curious. Back to the cattle shed, the pigs, the sheep. And out the other end, minus the boy he was meant to be looking after, caring for.

Fuck fuck fuck.

He stood on a high ramp and studied every face. 'Go,' he said to himself, and ran back to the Arts and Crafts. Jumping up the steps, he ran up and down each of the aisles and, again, stopped at the lucky dip. 'My son, he's gone,' he said to the woman.

'You sure?'

'I've looked everywhere.'

She barely moved in her seat. 'I wouldn't think. Plenty of kids go missing. They meet a friend then they're on the sideshows or at the sample bags.'

'Not Patrick.'

'Just wait a while.'

Moy stared at her. 'Can we put a message out?'

She half-raised her eyebrows but Moy decided to let it go. Standing up, she looked across the hall and motioned to the guide. This woman, wearing a green dress and carrying a clipboard, approached them with a smile.

'This gentleman's lost his son,' the first woman said.

'That's quite common.'

'I've heard all that,' Moy replied.

'Give it twenty minutes, have a look around.'

'Listen,' Moy almost shouted, 'I'm a policeman.' Saying it slowly. 'A detective. The boy was under my care.'

'Your son?' the guide asked.

'Yes, no, look it doesn't matter. I want you to put out a call on the PA.'

'I don't think so, we generally only—'

'We're wasting time.'

'That's the secretary's decision.'

'Call him.'

She found a little walkie-talkie in the pocket of her dress and contacted the secretary, who was also unconcerned. Moy put it in simple terms. 'Tell him if he doesn't, he'll be charged with impeding an investigation.'

Impeding, he thought. *Impeding.* Turning the word over in his head.

'Tell him to do it now. Patrick Barnes. Four foot five. Nine years old. Brown hair. Tell him to return to the lucky dip.'

The secretary refused. Moy grabbed the walkie-talkie. 'If the boy's been taken you will be charged,' he said.

'You think I should do this ten times a day?'

'If it's needed.'

Silence.

And then the message, loud and tinny.

Moy waited, pacing the aisles as the two women watched him. He turned to a landscape painting and studied the hills and a blocky house with a curl of chimney smoke like Charlie used to draw.

Six minutes, seven. No Patrick. Moy decided he wasn't about to wander back in. There was only one conclusion. He'd been taken. Stepping outside, he called the station. 'Jason, it's Bart. Patrick's gone missing.' He scanned the faces again, still hoping for a simple solution. 'Who have we got?'

Jason told him it was just Andrew and Ossie, out on patrol (oh, and I think Ossie said they were gonna stop at his place for lunch).

'Okay,' Moy said. 'Call 'em, get 'em down here now. Ask 'em to check cars heading back to town. A man, a boy, Patrick. You remember what he looks like?'

He described him anyway.

'Then tell 'em to look around the showgrounds, the car park. What about Gary?'

'Three days off.'

'Ring him, tell him what's happened, see if you can get him down here.'

He rang off and looked at the woman. 'A fucking *broken* toy car,' he said.

But she just stared at him.

'If you see the boy, get your mate to put out another call.'

251

The guide seemed genuinely shocked. 'Is it a custody dispute?'

He shook his head. 'Don't move from this spot.'

GARY WRIGHT WAS still in his track pants, wearing his uniform jacket and carrying a radio. He kept checking with Andrew and Ossie who were combing two acres of agricultural machinery displays on the east side of the showgrounds. 'So what time was it, when you came out?' he said.

Moy studied his watch. 'Ten forty-five, fifty, I can't remember.'

'You okay?'

'I can't believe I left him alone.'

'You think someone might be after him?'

He held his head. 'I should've considered it.'

'I reckon it's the father.'

They walked along a dusty race between two rows of stalls. Dagwood dogs and hot chips from greasy caravans; a shooting gallery with rabbits strung up by their legs; open-mouthed clowns and wart-covered masks.

'You take that side,' Moy said.

They separated, stopping at each stand to ask about the missing boy.

The missing boy, he thought. *Missing boy.*

He'd hoped the horrors of the last few weeks were behind them. Helen Barnes, burnt beyond recognition, her son Tom, lost, murdered. But Patrick, precocious bowlsman and golfer? George's mate. He'd been saved from all this. He was protected, perhaps more than any child in Guilderton. No one could've got to him.

He felt too sick to go on. The sound of Patrick's voice, his hands, placing a seedling in its small hole. Moving into a gap between two tents, he closed his eyes and held his head. This won't have a happy ending, he convinced himself, aware that he was the detective that couldn't solve crimes. 'Charlie,' he whispered.

'You okay?' Gary asked, standing beside him.

He opened his eyes. 'Just getting my breath.'

'Should we get on?'

Moy worked his side of the alley. 'A boy, yes.' Again and again. 'This tall.' He tried to remember, to show them. 'Nine years old. Name's Patrick Barnes.' And that sounded worst of all: Patrick's transformation from survivor to victim. His face on a missing persons poster, the sort that were pinned up around the station. Almost none of the dates recent.

The sideshow attendants he spoke to weren't concerned. 'There's hundreds of kids by themselves,' one said, and Moy asked, 'A nine year old, with brown hair?'

'Who knows?'

'By himself? Looking lost? Maybe he was running?'

The attendant turned to a pair of fairy-winged teenagers.

'Are you listening?' Moy shouted.

The young man, with his cut lip and stubble, looked at him. 'What?'

'Don't *what* me. Listen.'

'Hey, simmer.'

But Gary was there. 'Come on, Detective.'

They moved into the crowd. 'You sure you haven't got a photo somewhere?' Gary asked.

Shit, Moy thought, have I taken a photo of him? Surely I have? Surely? 'Maybe at home. I could go look.'

Gary seemed to have taken over. 'I don't know. By the time you get back half of these people would've gone.'

'Let's keep going.'

41

IT WAS AFTER nine and Guilderton was drifting off to the sound of humming cold rooms and not-quite-tightened taps. Moy, cruising in his Commodore, heard a distant helicopter but knew it wasn't for Patrick. Where would it look anyway? Pig sheds? Under logs? Guilderton was no Simpson Desert, Patrick no little boy lost, wandering in scrub. This would be a search in sheds and creek beds, chook houses and seed bins. In places where no one would think to look.

Jason Laing sat beside him, scrolling through information on the comms screen. 'They've locked the showgrounds,' he said.

'Nothing?'

Moy knew there wouldn't be. He'd seen the State Emergency Service volunteers, done up in their orange overalls and black boots, prodding haystacks and climbing up to look in the hoppers of the big seeders. Spread out, crossing paddocks, calling, 'Patrick Barnes...can you hear us?' Waiting at the coffee caravan, leaning against fences.

'He might've tried walking back to town,' Laing suggested.

'Why?'

'Maybe he thought you'd gone home?'

'I was in the toilet.'

They passed up and down lanes that ran behind shops and homes. Moy would stop and Jason would get out, looking behind bins, over fences and in and under grain trucks.

'I shouldn't have left him,' Moy said, as they drove.

'It was only a minute,' Laing replied. 'When we were kids we'd be gone all day. Down the creek, up those trees in Civic Park.'

'No, he wouldn't have gone off.'

'He doesn't have a mate, someone who might've said—'

'He doesn't know anyone…that I know of.'

'What about his brother?'

Moy looked at him, thinking. 'How?'

'What if he wasn't missing? What if he'd been hiding too, and seen Patrick?'

He did a circuit of Civic Park. 'That wouldn't make sense. Patrick's been talking about him for weeks.'

'Maybe Patrick didn't know.'

'What was he hiding from?'

'The dad?'

Moy shook his head. 'Either way, it's not gonna help us find him, is it?'

They got out and looked around the old train, the playground, the wisteria arbour and the Rotary lunch shed. 'Patrick, it's Bart.'

Nothing.

They got back in and drove. 'This is fucking pointless,' Moy said.

'What else y'gonna do?'

There was something, or someone, missing, he guessed. The person who'd killed Alex Naismith. Who'd argued with him, knocked him on the head and driven him to the coast. Who'd dragged him from his car or ute and rolled him over rocks into the ocean.

His phone rang.

'Dad? You still awake?'

He could hear George dropping the phone, fumbling his sheets and picking it up. Followed by rustling paper and a glass being knocked. 'Someone here reckons a boy went missing?'

'Yes.'

There was an uneasy silence.

'Well? Who was it?'

'Patrick.'

There was another pause, and George saying, 'Fuck.'

Moy told him. From their time at the lucky dip, the three-wheeled car, the scones and water-colours. 'I just left him for a moment...there were people everywhere.'

'And no one saw anything?'

'No.'

There was another long pause, but Moy could see his father shaking his head, whispering curses. 'They said a nine-year-old boy but I didn't think...'

'Don't worry, we'll find him.'

'He's been taken, hasn't he?'

'Maybe.'

'It's the same fella, isn't it?'

'Dad—'

'Right, I'm dressed. Come and get me now.'

Moy took a deep breath. 'What good'll that do?'

'I'll help you look.'

'We've got patrols, CFS, the SES are looking on the outskirts of town.'

'I had no idea there was any sort of threat,' George said.

'There are other options. He might've found his dad or his brother.'

'And just gone off without telling you?'

'Perhaps. Or they made him.'

256

'Or someone else made him,' George said. 'Listen, I'm not gonna lose Paddy, right?'

'There's no point picking you up, he might come to you.'

Silence.

'You've gotta find him, Bart.'

'I know, Dad.'

'You *have* to.'

Moy could hear his father's breathing. 'I will.' He looked at the empty street and wondered if Guilderton would ever yield any of its secrets.

'I will,' he said, and hung up.

Laing was looking through the pile of notes clipped into Moy's folder. 'Your old man still tellin' you what to do?'

'Yes.'

'Same as mine. Never any fuckin' help, but lots of advice.'

'They've grown close,' he said. He saw Patrick's face, confused, staring up at him. 'He's a good kid.'

'I know. Funny, always thinkin'.'

Moy could see Patrick's red cheeks, tanned by the wheatbelt sun. His neck, with one big freckle beside his carotid artery.

'We'll find him,' Laing said.

'Dad takes him bowling.' He trailed off again. His head was full of faces, landscapes, snatches of news reports; headlines, photographs torn from newspapers. Long minutes filled with every comment, smile and lifted eyebrow he'd noticed since that morning in the alleyway. The key was there, he realised. But it was small, and it wouldn't look familiar.

And then he was back at Mango Meats, talking to Justin Davids and the apprentice, Ray Foster. He was listening to the young man's words: *worked around the place...*

'Shit,' he said.

'What is it?'

Moy made a U-turn and returned to the station. He went to his office, looked up the butcher's phone number. 'Justin? Have you got Ray Foster's number?'

'Yeah…somewhere in the mess.'

The phone dropped and Davids' wife asked if there was something wrong.

'It's that copper,' Davids replied. 'Something's up.'

A few moments later the butcher was back on the phone. 'Here it is.' The numbers careful on his lips, as though he sensed the importance of each digit. Moy wrote clearly, crossing a seven and looping a two.

He called the number. 'Ray? Sorry to disturb you; we've got an emergency.' He didn't stop to explain. 'Listen, when we were talking about Naismith, you said he'd worked around the place.'

'Yes.'

'You mentioned John Preston.'

'That's right.'

'Do you know of anyone else?'

There was a long pause. Then Foster said, 'There was a fella called White…has alpacas. And whatsisname…Humphris. Jo Humphris. Place out along Creek Street.'

Moy felt his heart racing. His mouth was dry. 'Humphris?'

'Yes.'

'End of Creek Street?'

'Yes.'

'Whole heap of pigs?'

'Yeah, think he's got pigs.'

And then Moy remembered. The small man, sitting on the tractor, watching.

42

IT WAS ALMOST ten-thirty when they turned down the dirt road, driving slowly, stopping to open and close two gates, crossing stock grates, following the track across the lip of a dam, through a small forest of old sheoaks and finally, to a sprawl of sheds and lean-tos, silos and the farmhouse.

They stopped and got out.

'Watch for dogs,' Moy warned, but all they could hear were pigs, sniffing, shifting about in their own shit.

'Hello, anybody home?' Jason Laing called.

Moy walked towards the house and a security light came on. A 1960s cream-brick box, complete with a terrazzo verandah and collapsing gutters. There was no driveway or paths, just dirt and gravel spread out around the house. He approached the front door, littered with a pile of muddy shoes and boots, and knocked. 'Mr Humphris…police.'

He knocked again. 'Hello?' Then he moved around to the front and side windows and looked in. He turned to Jason. 'Torches.' Laing returned to the car and fetched two torches. They spent a few minutes looking in windows. Drawn curtains. A few gaps. Shadows. Furniture.

Away from the house, in a shallow valley, there were six long pig sheds. They walked down and around them and Moy asked, 'Why would you build your house so close?'

Laing shrugged. 'Maybe he likes pigs.'

They looked around the tractor shed, up and over a near-new John Deere 7030, a spray unit and a seeder with long, languorous arms sprouting hydraulics and seed tubes. There was a hayshed, chooks, an old transportable work-room and two old silos. They were rusted, laid flat beside a collection of smaller scarifiers, ploughs and seeders. And behind all this, a sort of junkyard of things-that-might-come-in-handy. Rolls of wire, galvanised iron and piles of sand, gravel and lime.

Moy studied the sheets of iron. They were the only material not under- and overgrown with oats and weeds. He lifted a few sheets. 'What do you reckon?' he asked Laing.

'What?'

But then something else caught his eye. He quickly walked the ten or so metres towards a fence-line that separated the compound from an area of bush. He stopped and looked down. Laing came up beside him and asked, 'What is it?'

'You can see,' Moy replied, indicating.

A concrete slab, three by four metres, freshly cured. And nearby, a mixer, a bucket and a coiled hose.

'So?' Laing asked.

'Patrick said they were kept in a shed.' He knelt down, running his finger along the side of the slab.

'What is it?' Laing asked.

'Here,' Moy replied, and showed him. 'A depression, where there's been a wall, and maybe a post.' He used both hands to move soil.

Laing shone his torch on it. 'You think Patrick's here?'

Moy stood up. He turned in one complete orbit, taking in every detail of the compound. 'Patrick,' he called. And then waited, listening. 'Patrick?'

'Maybe there's another—'

'Ssh.'

Moy was listening. To everything, no matter how distant. A rusty hinge, miles away; Doug Flamsteed locking his car. 'Patrick?'

There were headlights. Through the bush, then on the drive. The gates. Stopping. Jo Humphris got out of a battered ute and stood looking at them. Moy recognised the small, flannelette body, the pot belly and short legs, the fat face and wild black hair.

'Detective Sergeant Bart Moy,' he said. 'This is Constable Laing.' They walked over to him.

'Yeah, I remember you,' Humphris said, attempting a smile, taking both men's hands and greeting them. 'You were looking into that fire, at that old squat?'

'Yes,' Moy replied.

'You catch your man?'

'We did, as a matter of fact. Alex Naismith. You know him, eh?'

'Yes.' He turned and headed towards his front door.

'He worked for you?'

'If you'd call it that.'

Moy and Laing followed him.

'And you know what happened to him, don't you?'

They reached the door and Humphris turned and looked at them. 'I took him on for a harvest, and he stayed on after that. But then he started turning up late…never finished nothin'. Then he started arguing. So I sacked him.'

'How long ago?'

'Last year.' He slipped off his boots. 'So that's what you're here about, eh?'

'Sort of,' Moy replied.

'At this time of night?'

'I just thought it was strange. Alex…that place…up the end of your drive?'

Humphris glared at him. 'He was probably screwin' her. That's one thing he was good at.'

'Yeah?' Moy paused. 'Screwed her…then killed her?'

Humphris tried his key in the door. 'I don't know what he got up to.'

The door opened and Humphris switched on the hall light. He looked at Moy. 'So that's what you wanted to know about, eh? Naismith?'

Moy stepped between the farmer and his front door. 'You been out?'

'Yeah.'

'Where?'

Humphris' face began to harden. 'What's it any business of yours?'

'*Where?*'

'The pub.'

'And before that?'

Humphris took his time. 'You got a warrant…to be on my place? In the middle of the night?'

'*Where?*' Moy almost shouted.

'Home,' Humphris replied, calmly. 'All day.'

'By yourself?'

He smiled. 'I'm a bachelor.'

'*All day?*'

'Yes. Watched the midday movie. James Stewart.'

Silence.

'Why? What am I meant to have done?' Humphris asked.

'You never met a boy? Patrick Barnes? Or his brother, Tom?'

Humphris shrugged. 'Don't know 'em.'

'They used to live just down that road.' He indicated.

'Nup.'

'And you didn't go to the show today?'

Humphris took a moment. He looked at both men. 'Yeah, sorry, popped in for half an hour. Got a price on some new equipment.'

'Was that before or after James Stewart?'

Humphris glared at him and almost took a step forward. 'Bit of a smart arse, are you?'

'What time?'

'After lunch. One, perhaps. It was only thirty minutes.'

'And you didn't see the boy, or talk to him?'

'What fuckin' boy?'

'Patrick Barnes.'

'Told ya, I don't know any boy.' And he stepped forward.

'I noticed you've poured a fresh slab of concrete over there,' Moy said, indicating the yard of shadows and dark objects.

'So?'

'New shed?'

'It will be.'

Moy took his time. 'Well, you know, thought maybe he'd wandered up this way.'

Humphris glared at him.

'These questions, they're all standard. We're not accusing you of anything, Mr Humphris.' He studied the farmer's face, his red cheeks, his hard chin. 'You wouldn't mind if we came in, for a chat?'

'Christ!' Humphris growled. 'It's late. I'm tired. What's there to *chat* about? I know you've got a problem, but I'm telling you, I can't help you.'

Moy stepped back and smiled. 'We'll let you get to bed then.'

43

MOY DROPPED LAING at the kindy teacher's house. The porch light was on and he could see eyes peering out between curtains. 'She expecting you?'

'I think she cooked tea.'

He drove along the dark streets, thinking of what Megan would say. *Fucked that up too, then?* Her arms crossed, her head tilted. Then he'd say something like, At least I tried to help him, and she'd say *tried*, staring into his eyes, lifting her eyebrows.

He kept looking up driveways, down laneways. Got out and walked the bike track on Gawler Street. Twenty minutes later he was back in Clyde Street. He sat in the car. Unwilling, or unable, to go in. It was as though by opening the front door he was admitting defeat; by putting on the kettle, giving up on Patrick. As though life was about to return to the drab days before the boy's arrival. He thought about starting the car again, backing out, continuing his search, but it was after two and the events of the previous day had already begun to settle.

He got out and walked up the drive. Noticed the seedlings and a book Patrick had borrowed and sat reading on the porch. Looked down the side of the house. 'Patrick?'

And there was Thea Miller, standing in her nightie and dressing gown, looking over the untrimmed box hedge. 'No word?'

'You heard?'

'Everyone's heard.' She waited. 'You okay, Bart?'

'Yeah. He can't be far.' He updated her on the search.

'Anything I can do?' she asked, finally.

'No. Thanks. He's just wandered off.'

'Of course.' She paused, and smiled. 'He's such a lovely little fella, isn't he?'

'Yes.'

'Well-mannered, which always says a lot.'

Moy looked at the light glowing inside her living room.

'Ironing,' she said. 'It's this damn insomnia.'

Moy shrugged, but there was no point discussing anything.

He let himself into the house and stood in the dark hallway. 'Patrick?'

As his eyes adjusted he noticed clothes, piles of shoes, their mud dried, crumbling, forming a pile of dirt on the boards. He moved into the lounge-room. 'Patrick?' There was a shape on the couch; small, cramped, irregular. He touched it. It was just a blanket, twisted around the other rugs George nested in as he watched American crime shows. Asking questions like, 'They'd need a warrant to do that, wouldn't they?'

Think...think. What would I do with a boy? With Paddy? Probably the same thing I'd done with Tom.

He sat down and tried to imagine both of them. Track pants and T-shirts, tied up with heavy ropes, blindfolded, gagged. He had to feel the power, in his stomach, his chest and neck, his head. To know what it was like to enter a darkened room, to kneel beside them, to have the power of life and death. To work out what *he* would do next.

Silence.

He sat forward, his elbows on his knees. 'Patrick,' he whispered. He stood up, went to the boy's room, switched on the light and stood thinking.

He looked in the wardrobe. Pants, shirts, more jackets; empty pockets, apart from lolly wrappers and lint. *Robinson Crusoe*, borrowed from the library with a gleaming new card.

His phone rang. He fumbled it, studied it, answered it. 'Yes?'

'It's me.'

'Dad.'

'I'm waitin'.'

'What?'

There was a pause. 'I've packed my gear and I've signed myself out.'

'In the middle of the night?'

'They won't let me walk home.'

'I was just about to go somewhere.'

'Come and get me, will yer?'

'Now?'

'I'm all ready to go. This nurse isn't gonna let me be.'

'Okay. I'll bring you home, then I gotta go out.'

'It's Patrick? No point wastin' any time. I'll come with yer.'

'No.'

'I'm not sittin' around on my arse. Not when he's lost. Not like I'm gonna have another heart attack, is it?'

Moy stopped to think.

'Hurry up. God knows where the poor little kid's hidin'.'

Moy slammed the front door, jumped from the porch and was in his car in three strides. He shot back onto the road and selected drive. Then he saw Mrs Miller, running across her yard towards him. 'Have they found him?'

He wound down his window. 'Very soon, Thea...I'll let you know.'

266

He drove along every road at full speed, braking hard. A few minutes later he was parked in front of the hospital's glazed doors. George was standing in the foyer wearing slippers, track pants and a jumper with his old suitcase and a hard-faced nurse behind him.

'Ready?'

George was already putting his case in the back seat.

'Thank you,' Moy called to the nurse, standing watching them from the foyer. She smiled grimly and walked off.

'Old dragon,' George muttered, as he settled into the passenger seat.

'Seatbelt,' Moy said, slipping in beside him.

He followed a familiar route back towards Creek Street. He felt like he'd spent years trawling this town, cruising the same roads in fractured grids that always came back on themselves. Like he knew every front yard, every rosemary bush, every frangipani. Knew the people who lived in these little boxes, too, the colour of their cardigans, their dressing gowns. But the more you knew people, he guessed, the less you really understood them. What they did in their sheds, their spare rooms.

'So what's up?' George asked.

'Jo Humphris.'

'Humphris?'

'Farmer, on Creek Street. All that land behind the burnt house. Alex Naismith used to work for him.'

George shifted in his seat. 'Naismith…that fella that took the boys?'

Moy explained.

'So, I'm thinking…that's where they must have been taken.'

'Why didn't Paddy tell us?'

Moy shrugged. 'Too scared.' He braked, and turned down the dirt road to the Humphris farm.

George was staring at him. 'So, what's this fella done to Paddy?'

'That's what I want to find out.'

267

'I'll kill the bastard.'

'There's nothing that even looks like proof.'

'So?'

'Patience.' He looked at his dad, and saw some old, forgotten determination.

'You just drop me at his front door.'

'Dad.'

'Don't worry. It'll all be down to me. That's how things used to get done. And it worked.'

'Sometimes.'

Moy slowed and pulled into an overgrown clearing that ran off the track to the Humphris farm. 'This'll do.' He killed the lights, and engine, and they managed to climb out, scraping the doors, their skin and face on wild blackberry. 'You wait here.'

'No.'

'*Dad.*'

'I can help.'

Moy placed his face an inch from his father's. 'That's just what I need. You flat on the ground with another heart attack.'

George crossed his arms. 'What you gonna do then?'

'Wait here.'

Moy walked up the road until he could see the house. Then he moved onto a verge of soft sand and continued slowly. He could feel his breath and the sweat on his neck and chest. When he was on the edge of the compound he surveyed the area. The ute was still there, and he approached it. He looked in the back: wire and a long-handled spade. There was sand, and oil stains, and blood smeared on the tray and splattered on the sides. But there was also a pile of ear tags with hair, skin and bits of ear attached.

Then he stood back and looked at the ute. He saw something on the ground, bent over and studied it. A fifty-cent coin. He moved it with his finger and picked it up. Something else, further underneath. He reached for it. Felt it. Small, light, plastic. The toy car

268

from the lucky dip, its fourth wheel still missing.

He started moving down towards the pig sheds. Stopped when his feet crunched gravel, jumped onto a small patch of grass. Walking around each of the sheds, he looked inside. And cursed himself for not bringing a torch. 'Patrick,' he whispered.

All he could see were small stalls, sows and their grunting, wriggling litters. Rows and rows of pigs. The smell of shit and stale feed. He turned a corner and there was a dark figure staring at him. 'Jesus, Dad, what are you…'

'I checked the others…just pigs,' George said.

'Christ,' Moy hissed. 'You promised you'd stay put.'

'Yeah, well,' the old man muttered, 'reckon you need all the help you can get.'

Moy just stared at him. 'Go back to the car.'

'No.'

Then shook his head. 'Come on.'

They left the compound and moved into scrub and freshly ploughed paddocks. As they walked along an irrigation ditch they looked in pipes and under culverts, prodded weeds and reeds, searched under trees for any signs of disturbance. 'Where do you reckon he is?' George asked.

'*Ssh.*'

'You checked all those sheds?'

'Yes.'

'Should we check again?'

Moy had seen a track. Several. They ran off the compound and between each of the paddocks on this side of the farm. Disappeared into valleys and over hills. 'Where do you reckon they go?'

George shrugged. 'Far as the farm goes.'

Moy set off along one of the tracks. He walked quickly, then ran. George struggled to keep up. When he reached the top of a low hill, four hundred metres or so from the house, he stopped. He squinted, searching the paddocks, the bush.

George eventually came up behind him. 'Where you going?'

'What's that?' Moy said, making out a group of what looked like sheds, surrounded by a ring of pine trees, another hundred metres along the road.

'Pigs…chooks?' George attempted.

'Stay here,' Moy said, and he was off, running at full speed towards the dark shapes. When he arrived he looked around the empty sheds, full of more junk, wire, tractor parts. 'Patrick!' he called, a whisper-shout, but there was no reply.

He came out behind the sheds and there was a car. It still wasn't light but he could see it was a dark-coloured Falcon, boxy, beaten-up, and rusted. He could read the words on the peeling sticker on the back window. *Karringa Cars*. A back mud flap hung from a single screw. Opening the door, he looked inside. There were a few chip packets and cans, a map book that had fallen apart. The glove box was hanging open but was empty apart from a few lollies and fuses. He popped the boot and went back to look. A spare tyre, a petrol can. He smelled it. Diesel. Gauged the space; saw where a small body might have squeezed in. Dents in the panels like someone had kicked it from the inside.

He sat in the driver's seat, looking back towards the sheds. Of course, he thought. Of course. There could have been a thousand cars in Guilderton that fitted the butcher's description. Until you found the one that did.

He stood up and sprinted back towards the crest of the hill, and his father. 'Let's go.'

'We haven't finished.'

'*Let's go.*'

They walked back to the fence that surrounded the compound. Moy lifted a wire and George squeezed through. His pants caught and tore on a barb. 'Shit.'

'*Ssh*,' Moy repeated, following.

They moved around the edge of the compound, past the tractor shed and the silos. George tripped on a length of metal, fell and then sat up. 'Christ,' he said, loudly, forgetting.

'*Ssh.*'

A light went on in the house.

'Quick,' Moy said. He helped his father up, took him by the top and dragged him towards the back of the shed. They hid behind the double wheels of the big John Deere and waited.

'What's the time?' George asked.

Moy checked. 'Quarter past five.'

'Maybe he's feeding the pigs?'

'Maybe you woke him up.'

The front door opened and Humphris emerged from the house. He was in shadow. He straightened his back, coughed, and looked around the compound.

'What's he doing?' George asked, looking across the twenty or so metres between them.

'Not a word,' Moy whispered in his ear.

They waited. Humphris went back into the house and re-emerged with a lit torch. He slipped his feet into a pair of boots and started walking towards them. Moy pushed his father's head below the tyre. '*Ssh.*'

Humphris stopped in front of the shed. Moy watched the white beam working its way through the dark: a wall lined with hessian bags, halters and chains hanging from rusty hooks, the green and gold reflection from the machinery.

Father and son almost stopped breathing. They heard the torch click off, footsteps, then on again. Humphris was searching the other sheds, his scrap yard, the mid-distance of sheep pens and a small cattle yard with a broken crush. Footsteps. Light. Shallow breathing.

'Be light soon,' George whispered.

'Ssh.'

'You got your gun?'

Humphris returned to his house. He took off his boots and went inside. The outside light stayed on.

'Should we go?' George asked.

'Wait.'

'It'll get light.'

'Wait.'

Twenty minutes later Moy was ready. They moved around the compound, staying hard up against the sheds. They walked quietly, without talking, the first whiff of sun on their skin. When they were back on the road Moy said, 'That wouldn't have happened if you'd done as I said.'

George just shrugged. 'Y'never get anywhere by listening to common sense.'

44

THEY ARRIVED BACK at the car and Moy said, 'Right, get in.' He held the door open for his father.

George climbed into the passenger side and Moy went around, and sat beside him. 'I've gotta deal with all this, and then the thought of you, lying on the ground.'

'Stop fussing. Get on with it.'

Moy called the station and waited while the radio hissed.

Eventually Gary came on. 'You heard anything?'

'You couldn't do me a favour?'

'Go on.'

'Anyone you can get a hold of, call 'em, ask them to get to the station as soon as possible. Then, can you get down here? Watch this place while I get a warrant.'

'What do you need a warrant for?' George asked.

Moy glared at him. 'Dad, let's just dot the bloody i's, eh?'

Half an hour later, Gary arrived.

'I'm pretty sure he's got Patrick inside,' Moy said. 'Just stay here, wait, watch, while I drop Dad home, and go see Sutton.'

George didn't look happy. 'I'm not going anywhere.'

'You are,' Moy replied. 'And this time I'm not arguing.'

At six-thirty, after dropping his father home, Moy knocked on the door of 18 Dunlop Terrace, offering his hand to Andrew Sutton, JP. 'Bart Moy,' he said. 'Guilderton police. We have a missing child.'

'I heard.' Sutton massaged his unshaved chin. He appeared determined to make the most of what might be his only big moment.

'I think I know where he is.'

'Come in.'

For thirty minutes, as Mrs Sutton made tea and toast, Moy explained the last few hours and days, concluding, 'So, the chances are he'll act soon. I have a car parked in his drive, watching.'

Sutton reached for his briefcase. 'I'll just arrange the paperwork.'

Moy returned to the station to muster the other officers. They strapped pistols over T-shirts and Moy found the biggest of the door rams. Then he gathered them in the lunch room and explained. 'If I'm wrong, I'm gonna look pretty bloody stupid.' But he knew he was past the point of inaction. He *felt* he was right. Knew, somehow, Patrick was inside the house.

They set off in two marked cars: Moy and Jason in the first; Andrew, Bryce and Ossie in the second. They sped towards the farm, slowing onto the dirt road.

'It's gonna be warm,' Jason said.

Moy ignored him. 'Bolt cutters?'

'Got 'em.'

The scrub was three metres thick on each side of the track, dense melaleuca and ti-tree growing around gums, themselves over-grown with mistletoe and blackberry. Moy could see that it might be a good hiding place.

'Early summer,' Laing said.

Moy looked at him. 'What?'

'Early summer...might even get a sweat up today.'

274

But Moy didn't know what he meant. A sweat? Searching? He just didn't get Laing. 'You should be careful. One day she's just gonna walk in on you.'

'That would simplify things.'

He looked at him. 'I should have called for an ambulance first.'

Laing stared ahead, at the house in the distance, on the hill. 'Wait.'

When the two marked cars arrived back at the side-track, Gary was missing. They got out and looked around before making their way towards the house. When they were just short, Moy saw Gary kneeling in the bush, using the dawn light to study the compound. He knelt beside him. 'Anything?'

Gary kept his eyes on the house. 'Bit a' movement. Curtains. No one's come out.'

Moy turned towards the others, who had gathered, their revolvers drawn, behind him. 'Right, follow me,' he said. He ran from the bush, supporting his pistol wrist, looking back, telling them to spread out.

A few moments later he was at the front door. He knocked. 'Patrick, you there?'

No answer. He waited, and for a moment, imagined the scene inside.

'Patrick?'

'Bart?' he heard from inside.

He shook the door. 'It's me. Open up.'

Patrick threw the door open. He stood, making sure, half-smiling, half-crying. 'I'm okay,' he said, before taking a single step forward.

Moy took him, and pulled him close as Laing and Gary brushed past, guns drawn, shouting for Humphris to show himself. Moy buried his face in the boy's dirty hair. He could feel him crying, struggling for breath, finally consumed by the horror and relief that washed over him.

Patrick put his arms around Moy's waist, locked his fingers together and said, 'I'm sorry.'

'Why?'

'I shouldn't have left the hall, but he said if I came with him he'd take me to Tom.'

'It's okay, Patrick.'

'I couldn't bring you here, I couldn't.'

'I know.'

The sounds from the rest of the house had tailed off. Laing and Gary came back out, holstering their weapons and shrugging.

Moy gave the boy a squeeze and let him go. 'Watch him for a minute, will yer, Gary?'

With his gun still drawn, Moy moved into the house. It was clean, neat, smelling of lemon. He went into the lounge room and the television was blinking with Xbox hockey. He stopped and looked at a pile of games sitting on a coffee table: racing, golf, football. Scooby Doo, different episodes from the ones he'd bought. He walked into the kitchen. The dishes had been washed, stacked to dry. There were Frosties and unopened Coco Pops and a bottle of Coke left open on the bench. Then he went into the farmer's bedroom, his single bed, the cover tucked tightly, the smell of an old body, and powder.

Laing came into the room. 'Patrick's in the car.'

'I'm coming. One minute.'

Laing went out and Moy sat on the bed. He opened a drawer, found a pile of papers and leafed through them. Bills, manuals, a holy card. Standing up, he approached a window that looked over a fence, across paddocks, towards a distant horizon. Peaceful and ordinary. Quite still.

No; there was a movement. He squinted. A squat figure, running, stumbling, correcting himself, stopping for breath and looking back. Moy opened the window and thought of calling, but realised the little man was too far away. Still running.

276

He ran from the room, out through the laundry, into what passed as a backyard. Grass, a few spent flowers, freshly turned soil, stubble. A moment to find his feet and stride, and he was sprinting, although he knew he couldn't do it for long. He studied the humpty-dumpty man, and could make out his flannelette shirt and the shotgun in his left hand. Faster, moving through the air, barely touching the ground. He felt his heart pounding. Called, '*Humphris.*'

Jo Humphris stopped for a moment and looked back, then continued. Stopped, put the gun to his shoulder, thought better of it, turned and went on again.

There were only a few more strides. Moy launched himself, took Humphris around the waist and dragged him down into what was left of the crop. Looked up, spat dirt from his mouth, saw the gun, moved and extended his body and kicked it away. He watched Humphris to see what he'd do, but the man had no intention of resisting.

Moy fought for breath. He looked back at the house but couldn't see anyone. He turned over, managed to get onto all fours, then sat back on his sore arse. Felt for his pistol, but it wasn't there. Looked around and saw it in the stubble in the distance. *Just my luck.* He looked back at the shotgun. Humphris could make for it, but wouldn't.

He was done, Moy could tell just by looking at him.

He studied the farmer's fat cheeks, and the little capillaries on his nose.

Humphris said, 'Why couldn't you a left me alone?'

Moy didn't respond.

'It woulda …' He stopped and met Moy's eyes. As if that might do as an explanation.

Procedure, Moy thought. He crawled towards the shotgun, picked it up and opened it. Removed the cartridges; placed them carefully in the stubble. Closed the breech and rested the gun on his knee, pointing it at Humphris.

'Go on,' Humphris said. 'Two more minutes, I woulda done it.'

Yes, he would have, thought Moy. He watched Humphris, the way he fought for breath, clawed at the dirt, the delicate finger trails on the worked earth. He wondered if the farmer was about to have his own heart attack. He said, 'Where's the other one?'

'The older kid? What, you don't know?' Not making anything of it. Humphris had arrived at some place where he didn't care anymore.

Moy stared. 'Tom. That was his name. And you've dumped him in a hole like a sack of shit, haven't you, and poured the slab for your new shed—'

'It wasn't me.' Old anguish, worked like chewing gum, stretched across the defeated grey face.

Moy looked back at the house. Still no one. But he could see figures in the tractor shed, searching.

'My stupid fuckin' nephew,' Humphris gasped. 'None of it was me.'

Moy placed the gun on the ground. Humphris studied it, his tongue moving over his lips.

'What did he do?' Moy asked.

'All I ever did was tell him to move 'em on. He fucked that up like he fucked everything up…next thing I got two kids in my shed. And I said, take 'em back.'

It rang true. Moy knew, he could see, Humphris had spent these last days and weeks looking for a way out of the mess Naismith had made.

'When the little one got away, he went and got the other one and…' Humphris looked down, ashamed of his own words, his voice, everything. 'I tried to stop him.' He dared to look up.

Moy could see his father's eyes. The hundred times George had manufactured his own disasters. The hundred times, like all farmers, all country people, he'd devised his own solutions.

'None of it!' Humphris said again.

Moy knew he was right.

'But I stopped him, before he got the other one...he was gonna. I stopped him, Detective.'

Moy sensed Humphris had worked out the easiest fix for the current disaster. You couldn't continue the killing. Or take people away from the ones they loved. Make them do as you wanted, or even think as you did. Sometimes you just didn't get rain. All you could do was stand and watch your crop perish. He wanted to say something, offer some consolation. Something like, I know how you feel but you just gotta carry on, don't you? He knew this was the sort of phrase you taped on the back of the toilet door, not the sort of phrase you uttered to another human being. Instead, he said, 'They weren't hurtin' you, were they?'

Humphris didn't reply.

'They had nowhere else to go.'

Humphris bowed his head, and waited. Moy thought about the mess, and the shame. And the harm. Past a certain point, he thought, life was just clinging to the few things you'd got right. George had taught him this. And Charlie.

Moy stood up, looked at Humphris, and decided there was nothing to say. He turned and walked away. He was aware that this was stupid, but it was the only thing he could do. Waiting, as he moved closer to the house, for the sound of the gun-shot. It didn't come until he was in the laundry, and it didn't surprise him, or persuade him to turn and look back.

He walked through the house and back out to the compound. Patrick was sitting in the front of one of the cars.

'Was that a shotgun?' Gary asked.

Moy shook his head. 'Where did it come from?'

'Ossie went to look.'

Moy approached Patrick and knelt beside him. 'We can stop for dim sims on the way home.' And looked up at Gary. 'No...what time do they open?'

Gary checked his watch. "'Bout now. Don't know if they'd have the fryer goin' for a while yet.'

Moy took a deep breath. For the first time in a long time he felt that the life going on around him everywhere might somehow be relevant. He could even taste the stale oil. He looked at Gary and said, 'I'll take him home...to Dad. I'll be back later.'

BART MOY AND PATRICK BARNES drove into a morning that had barely begun, despite the fact that the sun was already high in the sky. There was a breeze, like the first wash of tide on dry sand. The smell of hot bread.

Moy guessed Jason was right. It would be a warm day.

As he drove he looked at the boy, wrapped in a blanket, and noticed his wrists, red, from the deepest of the indentations.

Patrick looked up and said, 'He told me to play the Xbox, and wait an hour, then call you. Then he said goodbye, he said he was sorry...and went out the back.'

'And you just played a game?'

'Hockey. I watched the clock. But then I heard the knocking...'

'It's all over, all done. *And*...' He waited. 'I promise, as long as I live, I'll never ask another question.'

'Never?' Patrick replied, smiling.

'Never.'

When Moy pulled into the drive George was waiting. As if he knew. He came out to the car, and without a word, took Patrick inside. Soon Mrs Miller would be there too, and Mrs Flamsteed, and half of Guilderton with the casseroles that would make things better.

Bart Moy stood in the driveway, waiting. He heard a child's voice off somewhere, and turned, but then looked back towards the house. He took a deep breath.

Patrick was standing at the door. 'Come on,' he said.

45

A WEEK LATER they drove to Port Louis. Trawled each of its sandy streets, searching for the shack Patrick had lived in. They stopped at a fish shop. A few minutes later they continued, George happy in the back picking vinegar chips from a torn bag, offering them around, steaming up the windows.

Patrick wasn't hungry. 'Right here,' he said, sitting forward. But it wasn't the shack. 'I thought this was it...no, left, left here.' And there it was: fibro, iron roof and a fishing net strung across the porch.

They left George in the back seat complaining about the scallops, still frozen in the middle, and approached the front door. They knocked, but no one was home. Walked around the back, through a mess of toys, bikes and fishing rods. Patrick said, 'Wait.'

He ran behind the shed, then called, 'Bart!'

Moy joined him. He was holding a surfboard. 'This is it.'

It was smashed up, but usable. The fin had snapped. Patrick said, 'It got Tom, just there.' He indicated a spot on his own forehead. 'Mum said he was lucky it didn't get an eye.'

Moy ran a hand over the surfboard, as though it might help him understand, or know Tom. 'Did he need stitches?'

'No. Just bled. Then he had a scar.' He stopped, looking into the weeds between shed and fence. 'But it healed okay, and Mum said...'

Moy took the surfboard from him and walked back to the car. Patrick followed. 'What are you doing?'

'It's yours. Come on.' He opened the back door and said to George, 'Put the window down, will yer?'

'You're not puttin' that thing in here.'

'Go on!'

George looked at Patrick and guessed he'd better. Once it was down, Moy adjusted the surfboard so it rested horizontally through the back windows. Then he looked at Patrick and said, 'Wipeout!'

They drove to the beach and got out. Patrick said, 'Should I?'

Moy smiled at him. He realised, somehow, this boy meant everything. Love, whatever. He had no idea what that was all about. There just wasn't anything he wouldn't do for him.

'Come on.' He grabbed the board and ran down to the breakers. Patrick came after him, and George sat on the bonnet, eating the last few chips, licking his fingers, watching them.

Moy and Patrick stood on the hard sand. They looked out at the Southern Ocean. They'd driven hours to get here, and Moy was determined to make the most of it.

Patrick said, 'It's a bit cold.'

Moy looked at him. 'Rubbish.'

So Patrick smiled, sat down, took off his shoes and socks and pants and took the surfboard. 'This is where we came,' he said.

Moy took a moment to think of the right words; he knew he was bad at finding them. 'You two must've had some...adventures.'

Adventures? No, not right, he thought. But he saw from Patrick's face, it didn't matter.

Patrick looked at him. 'I thought...if I waited...But I'm not gonna see him again, am I, Bart?'

Moy moved closer and took him around the shoulder. 'No.'

George watched as he tipped the last batter crumbs into his palms and knew what they were saying, and thinking: his son, and the boy, who reminded him of a younger Bart.

Patrick was crying, and Moy held his body tightly; felt ribs, and little lungs, gasping, and bony shoulders. 'If I could do anything to get him back for you…'

But Patrick said, 'You can't.'

There were no more words. But luckily the sea: singing in their ears.

George screwed up the paper and started thinking about what they'd have for tea.

Patrick wiped his eyes, but the spray made them wet. 'It's too cold,' he said.

'Bullshit.' Moy sat down, took off his shoes and socks, his pants, stood up and almost tore off his shirt.

Patrick looked at him and smiled. 'You first.'

Moy ran in. Patrick was right, it was way too cold, but he knew he had to keep going. He stopped and looked back. 'Come on!'

Patrick hitched the board and followed him. 'It's freezing.'

And they both laughed, and then Moy sank in the sand, over-balanced and fell and grabbed Patrick and took him with him. And cleared the long fringe from his face and said, 'What are we gonna do with a surfboard?'

But it didn't matter. It had drifted too far out for them to retrieve.

Acknowledgments

Thanks to all at Text, particularly Mandy Brett, Michael Heyward, Anne Beilby, Rachel Shepheard, Kirsty Wilson, Shalini Kunahlan, Chong Weng Ho and Michelle Calligaro.